Sipsey

by

Reed Blakeney

PublishAmerica

Baltimore

First printing

ISBN: 1-4137-1531-1
PUBLISHED BY PUBLISHAMERICA, LLLP
www.publishamerica.com
Baltimore

Printed in the United States of America

Dedication

To Thomas Blakeney, 1800-1896, and all the generations that descended from that pioneer planter in Fayette County, Alabama.

Acknowledgements

I have received kindness and support from many quarters. I especially thank the following people:

Dr. Rhodes Burns Holliman

Dr. A.L. Blakeney

Linda Wade

My late wife, Donna Blakeney

My present wife, Penelope Blakeney

Revis Blakeney, Pauline Blakeney, Montie Dye, Jim Dye, Laudice Williams, Doris Ellis

My daughters, Deborah Jones, Diana Bradford, Reida McCutchen, Rhonda Jordan

My grandchildren, Stefanie, Jessica, Kristen, Keri, Alana, Jillian, Jamye & Brian

And last, but certainly not least,

Ms. Betsy Bowman, who read and believed in Sipsey before any publisher ever saw the manuscript

Prologue

1796

The slave ship remained offshore during the night, pitching in gale-swept seas. Its decks were awash and the miserable human cargo, deprived of air beneath the hatches, choked from the stench of filth and excrement. They rattled the holding chains and groaned in their misery, but their cries went unheeded. At mid-morning the gale passed to the northeast and the slender brig, its raked masts flying English colors, moved under close sail into the port of Charleston, South Carolina.

A crowd gathered on this early spring morning, curious as always of foreign vessels, but no longer as wary of the English flag, billowing on the wind. The Revolutionary War was past history, but the memories remained of battles fierce and very personal. Loyalties had been mixed throughout the settlements and the price of revolution against the Crown had been very high. Neighbors plotted against neighbors, even brothers against brothers, and raids resulted in barn burnings and outright murder. After the war, lawless trappers and traders flooded the region. The ship rode easily now at anchor, and the crew opened the hatches. The crowd was repulsed by the odors, and moved back as sailors drove the blacks up the ladders to the deck.

"Lay yersevs for'ard," a burly sailor yelled, and he snapped a whip in the air, herding the lot of men, women, and children toward the head pumps. When each was freed of the leg irons, that person was stripped and doused with a heavy stream of cold salt water. The male slaves were handed sackcloth britches and the females were given plain smocks by the ship's agent.

After being led ashore, they were paraded one at a time before the slave traders. The traders pried open mouths, pinched muscle tissue in thighs and buttocks, made their choices and signed the papers. The slaves were then herded off to holding pens to await the public sale.

Captain John Barkley stood on the dock with the rest of the crowd, adjusting

7

his cloak against the stiff breeze. His gray-blue eyes took in the scene before him, eyes that had witnessed the struggle for independence in his state of South Carolina. He had not come to Charleston to buy slaves, but to meet with a political action group representing the Old Cheraws. He had made the choice to separate from the Crown, but the ties were not severed cleanly. There were unraveled ends… yearnings, for an estate in Ireland where he would never go, and for a lovely English village known as Barkley-By-The-Sea.

Captain John noticed a strongly built boy being led away to the pens. His eyes appeared glazed with shock and his mouth trembled from fear. The other slaves tended to stick in family groups, but it was obvious this boy had no family.

The captain returned to his lodging, but he couldn't get the boy out of his mind. He had some intuition that caused him to return for the afternoon sale. When the young boy was led up to the platform, he watched one of the buyers turn the boy roughly about and enter a bid. The captain outbid all competition. When the boy was released to his custody, he led him by a short rope leash toward the supply wagon. The boy cried as he shuffled his bare feet in the dust because he didn't know what fate awaited him. When they reached the wagon, the captain ordered the driver to feed the boy and give him something to drink.

The sight of the food basket was a new experience for the boy. He had subsisted on a meager diet of salt pork and hard biscuit for the entire voyage. Now there was fresh venison, baked bread, rice, and a sweet root baked in ashes that the driver called yams.

He ate with relish. With a full stomach, he turned in wonderment to the man who had purchased him. The tears had dried now into little salty trails down the blackness of his skin. The important man smiled at him… the first smile the boy had witnessed since he left his village. He attempted to smile back.

"Your name is George," the man said. The boy listened to the strange sound of the words. He struggled to understand. The man pointed his finger toward the boy's chest. *"You are George."*

"Yerwarjaja," the boy replied. The captain roared with laughter. The boy stepped back in alarm, but the captain did not appear to be angry with him. "George Barkley," the man said again. Before they had reached the Barkley plantation on Lynches River, the young black servant could smile at his master and utter two words of the English language, *"Jaw-ja Baw-ka-lay."*

He would serve the captain's son, William, as a personal servant. He would also serve the grandson, Thomas, who would migrate to the Indian lands in the state of Alabama, along a river called the Sipsey.

Chapter One

Georgia, 1838

The old Cherokee stood on a granite projection that offered a view of the valley and the Blue Ridge Mountains. His face was stolid as the granite, as scarred and impervious to change, but there was an anxiety in his eyes. There was no sign of the Georgia Militia, but a signal had come to him and he watched the night sky for further confirmation. He spoke softly to the night wind: *"I have heard the voice of the Raven Mocker."*

The words fell on the ears of a dusky-skinned maiden, their portent clouding the beauty of her sculpted bronze features. She trembled now as she considered the words. She dropped the stone pestle into the wooden bowl of crushed corn and turned toward the old man. "No, Grandfather, no... *no!"*

"I fear so, child. I saw a fiery trail in the sky last night. Someone is going to die—very soon I think."

"Please, Grandfather, let us pray the Little People to help us."

"We have displeased the Little People, daughter. They are angry with the Cherokee now. We have left the Nation to the white man, and they have no respect for the ways of the Little People."

The girl's face was streaked with tears and she lifted her outstretched palms to the sky. "What could we *do*, Grandfather? They came with soldiers and guns to force us away to the land of their choosing—"

"We could have died fighting them, daughter," the old man said. "Instead, our people have been taken like cattle, placed in pens, and driven along a foreign trail to the land across the Great River."

The girl's face turned defiant, her eyes flashing with anger. "I'm glad you would not go with them, Grandfather. I'm glad that we have come to the Blue Mountains to hide. They cannot find us here."

"Perhaps not," the old man said. "Perhaps it was only a shooting star that I saw. Perhaps the voice was not of the Raven Mocker. I am easily confused and worth very little."

The girl sat down beside him on the granite ledge and ran her slender fingers down the creased lines of his weathered face. "I will pray the Little People to forgive us," she said softly.

"That is a good thing to do, little Yellow Moon. It is good to pray, for we are but small creatures that inhabit the earth." The old man patted her tenderly. He leaned his head backward on the surface of granite behind him and searched the evening sky for the fiery trail that would reveal the presence of the witches. All Cherokees knew the Raven Mockers would steal the heart of a dying man and eat it, thus adding all his years of life to their own.

He reflected on the mythical *Little People* who inhabited caves and who were known to assist the Cherokees in times of trouble. Many times, lost and wandering members of the tribe had found markings that led them safely home, or a gift of food might greet a starving brave. He watched, but the sky revealed nothing more than the familiar placement of stars, and soon the girl discovered that he was asleep.

Two white men slept also down the trail by the mountain stream. They were members of a new breed to inhabit the Cherokee Nation. Jake Tanner and his partner, Abel Sprocket, had come to the Blue Ridge in search of gold.

The grubstake they brought consisted of corn meal, slab bacon, coffee, a pickax, shovel—and several jugs of white corn whiskey. Although gold mining was their announced intention, they did not avidly search for the mineral wealth. They were basically thieves and pillagers. They had found much to pillage in the remnants of the Cherokee possessions.

The weather was unseasonably warm for April, and perspiration ran in rivulets down their hairy, unwashed bodies, sweating away the torpor of a night of heavy drinking.

The Indian girl didn't see them when she brought her pail for water. The gold seekers' camp was downwind from the cave where she and her grandfather had spent the night.

Jake saw her first, nudging his companion ever so gently, bringing a finger upward across his mouth to signal silence. They watched her as she dipped her water pail into the clear fresh mountain stream, watched her search the shallow bottom for signs of rainbow trout, and while she was so absorbed, they quickly rose and sprinted in her direction.

Yellow Moon's screams cut through the silence of the forest. Then she threw the bucket of water toward the men, striking Abel Sprocket in his belly, dousing him with the cold water—which quickly brought him angrily alert.

She ran, and so did the gold seeker, running now as he would chase a rabbit. He sprang upon her, as he would have dived upon a rabbit. She kicked and struck at him in terror.

Her efforts were useless now. Abel held her down for Jake's gratification. Then Jake held her down for Abel, both of them prodding at her without mercy. Their dirty hands covered her mouth and nose so that she struggled to breathe. They gagged her with a dirty cloth, tied her hands and feet, and pulled her up by the cold ashes of the campfire.

"You think she got kin about?"

"Hell… course she got kin about. She ain't more'n sixteen, I'd say. She ain't tucked off up here by herself."

"Then we'd best git the hell on out of here. You don't know how many of them damn savages may be hid out up here."

"I say take her with us, by God," Jake said.

"You're crazy as hell. We do that and they'll never stop looking for us. I say kill her and hide the body. Grab that damn shovel and start digging a hole. She ain't gonna make much noise with her throat cut."

"Damn, I sure hate to give her up," Jake said.

"You ain't never had no common sense," Abel said. He drew his knife from his belt and walked toward the girl where she lay in the soot from the campfire.

He saw the terror in her coal-black eyes. He observed the large vein bulging in the slender throat. He squatted down beside her. With his knees on the ground, he studied her, running the edge of the knife along his thumb. "She reminds me of a damn scared rabbit," he said.

The arrow, when it struck Abel, traveled all the way through his chest and out the back of his shirt. Only the feathered butt remained at the front. Abel looked down at crimson feathers and then up toward the edge of the clearing. He saw the old Indian bend to place another arrow into the notch of his bow. He saw the long white hair as it fell upon his shoulders, and he saw in his eyes a dreadful vengeance. Then he toppled forward on his face.

"What in the hell… ?" The partner, Jake, wheeled frantically about so that another arrow missed a vital portion of his body, piercing his groin instead. He screamed, reaching for his pistol. He screamed as he aimed and fired it. He screamed as the old Indian staggered, yet managed to release the bowstring.

He saw the feathered shaft coming, and he screamed until the arrow severed his windpipe, turning his scream into a strangled, gurgling geyser of blood.

The old shaman crawled over the ground to his granddaughter, tears mingling now with the blood from his wound, and he removed the gag from her mouth, and the forest was awake again with her cries of anguish.

He untied her hands, and cradled her head in his arms, and rocked back and forth, crooning to her, running his fingers along her tear-stained cheeks. The old man whispered so softly that it was difficult for her to hear. *"Beware the Raven Mocker,"* he said.

Chapter Two

Yellow Moon hid his body in a large crevice in the granite. She sealed it up with stones so that the wild animals could not feed upon him, and so the Raven Mockers would not be able to take his heart and eat it. She fled then, with her meager possessions, away from the small camp they had established at the mouth of the cave. She had no sense of direction, no thought but to flee the place of destruction. The whites had found them, and she prayed to the Little People to aid her flight and protect her.

She lost track of the days, and of the weeks, keeping to the banks of the stream, following it downward now as it twisted and turned, the stream falling over sheer rock faces, which she was forced to spend hours in circling.

Her people had gone west, toward the setting sun, and toward a waterway they called "the Great River." There was no choice left but to follow in their wake. She hoped she might yet be reunited with her people before the threat of capture by white soldiers or the terrible abuse of other gold seekers. Tired and hungry, she drank from a small stream and then crawled under a large rhododendron and slept.

Fog swirled in patches through the trees, and the warmth of the afternoon was replaced by a chill that hung over the moss and lichens where Yellow Moon had made her bed. She came awake now, sensing change. Something moved along the evening breeze, an odor so overpowering that the girl almost fainted from its promise.

The smell was fried quail. The girl knew that she must have lost all touch with reality. She had not eaten for a long time and she rose without thinking. She moved toward the exquisite aroma. She felt her way through the branches, following the smell, then crawled on hands and knees as she neared the source, knowing instinctively she had made a mistake in judgment but feeling also the hunger gnawing at her insides.

In the clearing, she saw a man squatting over a campfire. He suddenly stiffened. She turned and ran now, knowing the flight was useless even as his body slammed her into the earth. They wrestled briefly. The slender girl was no match for the brawny man pinning her to the ground. She felt his hold on her loosen, then she was yanked roughly to her feet and dragged into the circle of light from the campfire.

"A squaw ye be, by God!"

"Please, I meant no harm.... Food! I have not eaten—" She stopped short as the campfire started to revolve very slowly in front of her, and then the ground came rushing up.

"Oh, and it's waking up ye are." His voice was gruff, but not unkind. "Ye'll need have no fear of Tim Malloy. Ease yourself down, and we'll share this quail and biscuits."

His manner was reassuring, and her hunger so powerful, that she did as she was bid. He spoke no more but refilled the tin plate he had extended to her and watched her devour it. "Ye were a bit famished, now, eh?"

The girl did not respond. Having the needs of her stomach met, she began to think again of the evil white men lying dead back there in the cove. Perhaps this man had come to revenge them or worse, yet...

"Don't be afraid, I mean ye no harm. Here, take this hot cup of coffee. It will restore ye."

She accepted it and drank slowly, studying the man across the fire. True, he was a white, but not in the same manner of the evil ones. His hair looked clean and was yellow in color. His skin, too, was clean and of a ruddy nature, and the eyes were a piercing blue like the sky in October.

"I'll be fair with ye," the man said. "I take ye for a runaway, and I'll be the last to blame ye. There's a strange cast to your features, though. I've trouble making ye out."

Yellow Moon felt reassured. His manner had been nothing but kind and the food had been a salvation. She relaxed a little. "My father was but part Cherokee. His own father married a white woman, but she died when my father was a small boy."

"So it's Indian and white ye've become."

"And black. My mother, who died of the yellow fever in the year of my birth, was a slave in my father's house."

"Good God! What a mixture ye are then."

He shook his head and stirred up the coals and then sat down again, legs crossed at the knees in the Indian fashion. "I've a bit of mixed blood of me own—Scotch, Irish, and French, if me recollection's right. In any case, like I

14

say, ye can stay if ye choose, for as long as ye choose. Trapping's me trade. I've got a wee cabin a day's walk from here. It keeps out the rain in summer and the snow in winter. But there's no need to decide now. Here... take this blanket and lie beside the fire there."

Yellow Moon began to shake with fear, despite the kind words.

"Now, now... don't worry. Tim Malloy will not abuse you. I promise that."

Somehow she reckoned his offer was sincere and there was no better option open to her. The warm fire and the full stomach and the exhaustion of the past few days combined to numb her senses, and she fell asleep. When she awoke once more, the man was already at work on the breakfast, the aroma of salted bacon rising from his frying pan.

"I've a barrel of salt pork back at me cabin, but this is the last of me provisions on this last trap run."

He strode back to a bundle of pelts hoisted up from the ground by a length of hemp, the other end of which was thrown over a limb. "This is the fruit of me efforts, a rare catch of otter, beaver, and fox. More than a man could carry almost... unless he had a bit of help?"

She realized the man was asking her to repay his kindness by assisting with the pelts. But was it a game, knowing that he held the high cards? Was there really any other alternative?

"I will help you," she said quietly.

"Aye and it's grateful that I am, Miss..."

"Yellow Moon."

"Well, Miss Yellow Moon, it's pleased that I am to make your acquaintance."

He bowed in mock high fashion, the blonde hair falling in front of his face and then throwing his head back, laughing, and she was startled at the sound of it, laughter having been absent so long in her life.

It was an easy relationship from the outset. The man had a unique ability to find humor in almost any situation. For the first time since she had fled the Nation, the girl began to relax and to enjoy living once more.

Tim Malloy, true to his word, made no physical demands on her. He slept under the lean-to shed, where the furs were stored, and since the weather had moderated into late spring, he was comfortable enough and close to his work, stretching and drying the furs from the trapping season.

For her part, Yellow Moon was finally at peace, no longer feeling the threat of capture, assured by Tim that no white soldiers would come for her while in his company.

Over the next few weeks the mound of furs, now cured and dried, was crowding Tim from his sleeping quarters. "I think it time, little one—(he rarely referred to her Indian name,)" "that we go southward to the market."

"I do not know that place."

"Ah, but ye should see it, little one! Ships come from the open sea to a port they call Mobile. They load the furs and take them across the ocean to England—"

"What is this England?"

"Well, it's on the other side of the world and of no interest to us."

"How could we make such a journey with all these furs to carry?"

"By raft, me little one, by raft!"

Yellow Moon frowned. "I am afraid of the boats."

Tim Malloy laughed his great laugh. "Ye'll *love* it, little one. We'll build the raft together—"

"I think I will wait for you."

"No, no. Ye kinna do that. The soldiers might come and you alone…"

He didn't need to say more. In the ensuing days they began work on the raft. Light poplar logs formed the bottom, and above them Tim constructed an elevated platform for the protection of the cargo, one end of which was raised higher to provide visibility. The steering would be accomplished by a long pole, placed in a fork at the rear of the raft, the water end of which was fitted into a long, flat section of white oak. On this structure he formed a crude, pole-supported roof, and lined the flooring in furs. He grinned at her and pointed to his finished work. "Even the King of England might envy a room lined in furs!"

Yellow Moon had no knowledge of kings, so Tim explained that he was the principal chief of the land, which was on the other side of the world, and which was of no interest to them.

Finally, it was finished and Tim began to stack the furs on the raft as Yellow Moon transported them from the shed. By midday the work was done. Furs and provisions were all loaded in place, and Tim pushed the raft away from the bank.

Yellow Moon sat fearfully on the elevated platform, sensing every movement, watching Tim maneuver the raft into the current. She relaxed a little as he faced her with his broad smile. She listened as he broke into a riverboat song.

The river curled and looped upon itself on the way to the sea. The raft proved to be a seaworthy craft. Their feet remained dry on the elevated portion. The long pole rudder kept them in the channel with minimal effort.

Heavy rains would propel them rapidly down the channel. At other times, the river would cut off one of its loops and leave them stranded on a sand bar.

Tim took it all in a day's work, and, with good humor, would jump over the side and push the raft back into the current. Yellow Moon became so confident in Tim's mastery of the waterway that she would even jump into the shallow water to help.

Now the richness of the land was apparent. As far as the eye could see, fields lay on either side of the river, flat and fertile with tree-lined borders separating property lines. Yellow Moon, accustomed to the mountain terrain in north Georgia, was amazed at the length of the cotton rows and the amount of blue sky visible above them.

Yellow Moon looked at the fields, the teams of oxen and mules pulling the plows, and the black field hands toiling under the sun. She thought of her own mother, and voiced her thoughts aloud. "*She was a slave, too*," she said.

"Your mother?"

"Yes, I never did know her. I wonder if she had any happiness with my father. He seemed to be a good man, but I was closer to my grandfather. My father was always at meetings. He was a friend of the chief, John Ross, whose name is also Cooweescoowee."

"And what would that name mean?"

"It means the large, white bird. Everyone knows him to be mostly of white blood, but his heart is Cherokee."

"I heard of him. Somebody told me he's only got a few drops of Indian blood. I hear Andrew Jackson hates his guts."

"The Great White Father?

"The President of the United States."

"My grandfather called him the Great White Traitor. He welcomed the Cherokee as an ally in war, but he hates the Indian."

"He ain't by himself there, I guess. What I can't understand is why the Cherokees would elect a white man as their principal chief?"

"My grandfather said any man with Cherokee blood is welcome in the tribes."

"Were you also welcomed in the tribe?"

"My father was a Cherokee—and so I am a Cherokee."

"But were you also his slave?"

"I was never a slave, *never...* " she drew herself up proudly. "I was the daughter of a chief! I would have fought the soldiers if I had known how to fire a gun."

Tim became serious as he listened and then he reached into a duffel bag and withdrew a small, percussion cap pistol. "This is called a Derringer," he said. "Have you ever seen such a gun?"

She admitted that she had not and she recoiled from it when he offered it to her.

"Nay, take it, little one. It might save your life someday. It is deadly up close. Keep it on your person and if anyone should try to harm ye, use it first and run later." He taught her to use the weapon, and as she became used to the noise of it, she felt comfortable having it in her coat pocket.

As the river's current took them farther south, fine whitewashed manor houses were visible through gray, hair-like strands of moss that hung in clumps from the branches of the water oaks.

"What is that?" Yellow Moon asked.

"You mean houses… ?"

"No—the gray beards hanging from the limbs."

He chuckled and winked at her. "You mean those? Why those aren't beards, little one—they're scalps!"

Her expression forced a quick retraction, and he properly identified the Spanish Moss.

The river widened and flattened now, and off to the left they saw the mouth of another waterway. Yellow Moon pointed and got his attention. "What are their names?"

"The rivers?"

"Yes. What do you call the rivers?"

"Well, little one, this here's the Tombigbee, and that one?" He nodded his head to the left. "Well, they call that one the Sipsey."

"The river of the poplar?"

"How's that?"

"That's an Indian word—*Sipsey*. It means the poplar tree."

Chapter Three

Barkley Crossing, South Carolina, 1838

Morning sunlight beamed through the window in the parlor, highlighting the muted colors in the faded tapestries, catching the red flecks in the long, auburn hair of the young man standing in the doorway. He was of medium height and robust build; his total bearing was one of strength and purpose. The handsome squared features were frozen now with the emotion that seized him.

"I never would have thought that you could do it!" Thomas Barkley exclaimed. "My mother—*my own mother*, for God's sake! You are robbing me of my birthright while my father's body is barely cold in the grave!"

The slender figure turned now from the window, face saddened, but resolute. She faced her son squarely, the gray eyes that matched his own never wavering from his face. "Your father's grave has held his body for more than three years now, Thomas. I think my son forgets that Barkley Hall was left to me." She kept her voice low and reasonable; however, the man was in no mood to be reasonable.

"Left to you, and to the descendants after you until you betrayed that inheritance."

"The fact is, Thomas, your father is dead, and I am still living. I have decided to marry again. It's that simple. Your brothers and your sister are married, as you are, and quite able to provide for themselves. Even so, it was never my intention to rob you of anything. You know perfectly well John May has always been a true friend of the family. He has offered an excellent price for Barkley Hall. Our lawyer and banker agree on that. The main issue here is my right to control my own destiny." She smoothed the white lace cover of the tea table and waited, but he did not reply.

She spoke again. "I have decided to accept John May's offer for the plantation, and also to accept his proposal of marriage. You, your brothers, and sister will receive your share of money."

Thomas' large hands grasped the edge of the table, his knuckles whitened.

"I never asked for money, Mother. It is the land I care about. The land, for God's sake! I could have made Barkley Hall one of the finest plantations in all of South Carolina! And there was land enough for all of us until…" his voice choking now.

"… Until I decided to live my own life," she answered for him.

"Aye, God, so be it then! I'll take my share, put it to good use. But hear me, Mother, and mark it well. I WILL have my own land, hundreds, thousands of acres, God willing. And as long as I live and breathe, NONE of it will ever be for sale!"

His mother watched him stride angrily across the yard toward the stables—like his father with that purposeful gait! Had she made a mistake after all? Was it right to deprive a son of his dreams in order to achieve some happiness for herself? Or should a fifty-six-year-old woman forget her womanhood and dry up in a corner of the study with her cat and her crochet needle?

Her spirit answered for her, and she walked away from the window. She had her rights also. She would allow no one, not even this strong-willed, eldest son, to take them away from her. It was her right to remain mistress of Barkley Hall, and it was her right to choose the new master.

The tavern on the dusty front street of Barkley Crossing was filled with farmers and townspeople on this Saturday afternoon in September. Thomas stood at the bar and ordered a bottle of the proprietor's finest Irish whiskey. Rough laughter and coarse language served as background to the voices of his neighbors. The talk turned to crops and cattle and the bad year of 1837, just past.

He was in no mood to hear it. He watched a stranger in a deerskin coat who had mounted one of the benches near the front door. The stranger's voice now rose over the din of tavern noise. "It's God's country, flatlands rich and fertile, hills full of mineral wealth, land for the taking, land to produce cotton such as we have not seen in fifty years, and water—river water, to float it to market."

Thomas pushed himself closer as the speaker raised his glass.

"The Creeks and the Cherokee no longer control these lands, my friends. Who among you would join our wagon train to the West?" The speaker turned now to the bartender. "Set a round for everybody who would join in a toast to the great state of Alabama!"

The response was immediate. Even those having no plans to migrate to the West were still united in drinking a toast with free whiskey.

But it wasn't the whiskey that beckoned Thomas to the speaker's side. Indeed, there was no opportunity for the stranger to socialize further because Thomas pelted him with questions regarding the new land, the anticipated duration of the journey, the availability of fresh water and game. There were questions about the Indians, of course. Were there remnants of Creek and Cherokee tribesmen in this wonderful new land of opportunity?

Assured the Indians were no longer a problem for the Alabama settlers, Thomas began to see a vision of his future. His future would, of course, include that of Sarah and the children, but that went without saying. An hour later, he vaulted onto the wide front porch at Barkley Hall and called his wife's name as he went.

He was touched, as always, by her beauty as she swept into the hall at the sound of his voice. Her movements were graceful. The long-lashed, blue eyes contrasted incredibly with the whiteness of her skin and the black hair that framed her face. Her head was slightly tilted to the side. A trace of anxiety clouded her delicate, porcelain features.

"Is something wrong, Thomas?"

His eyes flashed with the excitement bubbling within but his answer came in a hoarse whisper. "No, my dear Sarah, for the first time in many weeks, something is *right.* There are lands in Alabama, my dear Sarah. They're fertile and waiting to yield a harvest such as we have not seen in decades. Yes—let's create our own future in Alabama!"

"But… surely, you can't mean to abandon what we have here… to struggle in some *wilderness* for survival?"

"We have nothing here, Sarah. My mother has seen to that. I'll be damned in hell before I take orders from Master John May. I'll take his money, with pleasure. I'll own the land I homestead, more too, God willing."

"Couldn't we just purchase land near here and—"

The stubborn shake of his head discouraged further response. Thomas was not insensitive to the concerns voiced by his wife. He knew that she was a fragile woman, who was born to the privileged existence of the Southern manor, and who was accustomed to stylish clothing and fine tapestries. He knew there was little about frontier life that would meet her needs, and yet …

He had his needs, also. His success at farming the Barkley acres had confirmed his belief that he was created to promote the earth's bounty. He had planted and experimented with grain crops other than traditional corn and wheat. He had added substantially to the money crop of cotton. Now, it seemed all was to be taken from him, an action that he could only feel as betrayal on the part of his mother. He determined to make up for it. He would have land. He would have an abundance of it, God willing.

Thomas allowed the idea of migration to become an obsession. He could think of little else, and his enthusiasm became contagious, at least to his two brothers. Before the end of the month, they had succumbed to the excitement generated by their older brother.

The wives were another matter. While Sarah acquiesced for her love of Thomas, the wife of Hugh Barkley remained militantly opposed to the project. John's wife extracted a promise from her husband to return after the first year, if she had not accepted the change.

Chapter Four

There were reluctant goodbyes on the morning of their departure. The day dawned bright and crisp. By ten o'clock, the sun had dried the dew from the canvas wagon tops. The lead wagon moved into position.

Thomas stood stiffly in the background as his brothers and their families bade farewell to his mother. Then, it was his turn. "I may never see you again–" The words came starkly, awkwardly. He cleared his throat and tried again. "I mean, it's a far country… things can happen."

"There are no guarantees in this life, my son … except my love for you. That is guaranteed, and so is my promise…" She reached for a soft, leather bag that had rested with two others on the table beside her. She handed it across, using both hands because of its weight, and the clink of gold coins came from the bag. "Take care that no one knows."

"Never fear, Mother. I'll guard this share with my life."

"And guard your life more than you guard your gold," she whispered. She held out her arms, and he embraced her for an instant before turning toward the wagons.

Suddenly, a little girl with long, blonde hair falling in ringlets about her face and shoulders, ran from the crowd of well-wishers. She followed Thomas and Sarah into their position in the train.

"Oh, Thomas! It's little Katherine!" Sarah buried her face in her hands and sobbed at the sight of her baby sister's distress.

The little girl raised her arms in a pleading gesture. "Don't leave me, Sarah… don't leave…"

"I'll come back… believe me… I'll come back," Sarah called.

The dust swirled around the wagon wheels as their wagon took its place in line. Through this cloud she saw her father lead the child away.

The early days of the journey were uneventful, but they provided experience for the more difficult passage to come. The mild, autumn days were delightful and freshening breezes prevailed. The children walked alongside the wagons and sometimes lagged behind to gather fruit from muscadine vines or persimmon trees.

The wagons came at last alongside the clear waters of the Chattahoochee River. The ferry road looped and turned down to the water's edge. The wagon train slowly descended to the cable-operated ferry that would transport them to the Alabama Road.

Sarah looked now in her husband's direction, noting excitement in his eyes. She saw the broad smile that creased his face. She heard the squeals of their children—William, age five, and Elizabeth, age three—as the wagons rolled and skidded their way down to the ferry ramp. She knew they, too, had caught the sense of adventure that motivated their father. Until this time, she had hoped, even prayed, for some sort of divine intervention that might compel a change of heart. She knew now that it would never happen.

Fearing the steepness of the incline, the ox teams balked and the bullwhip in Thomas' right had whistled over their heads. The pop of its tail sounded like a rifle shot. The first wagon carried their bedding, cooking utensils, and a supply of dried fruits. There were bags of potatoes and flour, and sides of smoked pork. Hidden in the double bottom of the wagon was an iron pot holding a leather bag full of gold coins.

The second wagon was driven by the slave, George, who watched over the few items of fine furniture that Sarah had been able to bring. Sarah was most concerned about the china, which her grandmother had brought across the sea from Ireland. George had carefully packed the pieces in barrels filled with sawdust. George's wagon also carried Sarah's personal servant, Aunt Dicey. Her plump stature did not encourage walking. She rode, quite regally, in one of Sarah's prized wingback chairs, as she kept an eye towards the needs of her mistress at every stop.

The third and fourth Barkley wagons were laden with tools to tame the wilderness, such as axes and saws and iron plows to farm the soil. These wagons provided shelter for the slaves who slept beneath them.

The ferry moved out, sliding along its tether. The current caught, twisted, and tried to alter its course. The river surged against the sides of the boat. Poor Dicey cried out in fear.

"Don't worry, Dicey," Thomas called. "This river's just a creek… wait 'til we get to the Sipsey!"

"Wait 'til us gits to the Sipsey, he say!" Dicey shook her head in disapproval, muttering to herself as was her habit.

At last, the crossing was completed. Major James Coe, the old, retired soldier who commanded the wagon train, put the wagons into the approved circle for the night and posted his sentry.

The evenings were usually short-lived because of the next day's early start. Having completed the meal and socializing, the families retired to their wagons. The night sounds from the river soon lulled them to sleep. A bright and round moon came up before the cooking fires were extinguished. Its reflection sparkled in the river.

Thomas was not disposed toward sleep. His restless body yearned for the company of his wife. When Dicey led the children away to bed, he reached for Sarah's hand and walked with her toward the river.

"Is it safe to walk by ourselves?" she asked, the light now fading from the fires and only the moon to illuminate their path.

"Nay, sweet lady," he said. "I fear you are in dangerous company."

She turned to look up at him, seeing the mischievous grin that tugged at the corner of his mouth.

"You wouldn't dare," she whispered.

"I dare anyone to stop me."

"But there may be Indians lurking about—"

"No Indians. They've all gone west… well, not all of them. Some escaped the removal, but you can be sure they're not camped out by the Alabama Road!"

"Where, then, might they be?"

"In the mountains, hidden away in the coves and rocks."

"But what if wild animals—"

"What if you give me a kiss?"

He folded her into his arms and kissed her fiercely, feeling her respond in spite of her fear. Because he was afraid she might refuse, he hurriedly tore at his shirt and trousers.

"Thomas, we shouldn't…"

His hands moved, lifted the skirt and petticoat, and then pulled at the strings.

"No, wait—"

She helped him… breasts bare in the moonlight—then in shadow, as he buried his face between them. His passion awakened her. She shivered in the night wind.

He made a bed of pine straw and laid his shirt across it. Fearing still that she might change her mind, he hurriedly removed his clothing and reached for her, and they lay together in the moonlight.

"This… this is so… so primitive!"

"But it adds a bit of spice, don't you think?"

He felt the change in her, the unwitting acquiescence turning into passionate response and then an uninhibited shriek, quite foreign to her placid nature. They heard the sentry almost immediately, thrashing about in the direction of the outcry, his lantern making a dim circle of light which served only to identify his presence.

"You can get on back there, now," Thomas called. *"Mrs. Barkley just tripped on a root… it's all right."*

Sarah convulsed in laughter, and giggled like a schoolgirl.

Chapter Five

The rains came with a vengeance in mid-November, blown in on the prevailing winds from the west. The wagon wheels mired to the hubs in long sections of the Alabama Road which was, in fact, nothing more than an Indian trail within the former Cherokee Nation. In places, the road detoured around tall tree stumps, in others a corduroy bed of cut logs laid over marshes would rattle the trace chains on the wagons and shake and resettle every item of cargo.

Hugh Barkley approached Thomas on the morning of the fourteenth of November with a worried look on his face.

"Thomas... I'd have a word with you, if you don't mind."

"Well, what is it?"

"Betsy has some strong feelings now about this whole trip."

"And so, it's Betsy Bonner who's taken over in your household? I could have told you when you married her—she's just like her Ma! She led Old Man Bonner around with a ring in his nose!"

"Now, see here, Tom—"

"Well, it's true, nonetheless."

"I can't allow you to talk about my wife that way, Tom."

"I'll talk as I see fit—get on with what you have to say!"

"Well, I'll say it and be blunt about it. Betsy and me... well, we're leaving the train at the Black Warrior River."

"Damned if you are!"

"Damned if I'm not... John, too! We're going south... to Marengo County. There's a fellow named Cloud down there... got some new ideas on cotton production..."

"So where in blue blazes did you come up with this information?"

"Ben Sellers... he's been talking about it the whole trip, and John and me..."

"Are both a pair of blasted fools! You'll spend every dollar you've got in some wild scheme!"

"Now, Tom... you don't hold any patent rights on what John and me can decide to do."

"No, and it's a good thing… I don't want the responsibility! I had it in mind that the three of us would homestead together… make a name for ourselves—"

"That's the trouble, Tom… YOU had in mind. This whole trip was your idea, and you just expected John and me to fall in line. Well—our wives don't see it that way."

"I think it's pretty damned commendable that I've tried my best to look out for your interests!"

"Tom… you just won't learn! You're hardheaded and domineering… and that's what riles Betsy so. She says she's just not willing to spend the rest of our lives under your wing. The problem is nobody has asked you to look after our interests!"

"Go on! You do what Betsy tells you to do! Let Betsy tell John what to do, as well! I'm glad you found someone as all-wise and powerful as Betsy Bonner! Just like…"

"Shut your mouth, Thomas!"

It was fortunate for the sake of family relations that a bolt of lightning struck one of the pine trees close by, and they both ran for the cover of the wagons.

A soggy, mud-splattered, wilted group reached the outskirts of Tuscaloosa the third week in November. As they set up camp beside the Black Warrior River, they completed their chores as quickly as possible and huddled under canvas to cook their meals. Then they retired to the wagons for as much warmth as they could get from the bedding.

Major Coe called a council the next morning. "I am proposing that we rest the teams and wait out the rain for a few days. The river is too swollen to attempt safe passage on the ferry. I realize some would say we are running short on time and the winter will be on us, but we're within a week of Newton's Landing. I'll not come this far to risk our safety on a flooded crossing."

"But…"

"We'll not move until the river goes down," the Major stated firmly.

"Well, I won't stay here in camp and watch Betsy Bonner smirking around for a damn week," Thomas announced.

"Why, Thomas! I can't imagine you becoming so hostile toward your own sister-in-law!"

"She's no sister of mine," he snorted. He instructed George to look after their property, and he bundled Sarah and the children into the lead wagon and headed down Greensboro Avenue toward the Warrior Hotel.

The aroma of steaming hot coffee and a kitchen that boasted smoked turkey, baked ham, and boiled cabbage worked miracles for the mood of the family. They obtained clean and comfortable rooms for Dicey and the children, with an adjoining room for Thomas and Sarah.

Sarah collapsed into the feathery folds of the mattress and sighed with relief. The children explored the hotel with boundless energy, with Dicey in futile pursuit. Thomas relaxed in the taproom with a box of good cigars. The stage was set for a decision that would please Sarah as nothing else could possibly do.

"I'm going to take William and the wagons on to Newton's Landing," Thomas said. "You and Elizabeth and Dicey can stay here at the hotel until we throw up some temporary cabins for the winter. Luck holding, we'll be back for you by Christmas, with a warm cabin waiting."

Sarah was so grateful that she kissed him right in front of the guests in the lobby. The children were delighted in different ways. William wanted to get on to the new country, and Elizabeth was interested in sightseeing with her mother. She wanted to see more of the stately, whitewashed homes they had passed on Greensboro Avenue and especially the State Capitol and the University.

With the sun brightening the sky and the water down to a safe level, the wagons crossed on the ferry and headed west once more. The wagons of Hugh and John Barkley turned off the trail when they crossed the river, heading south to Marengo County. They waved and called goodbye to William, but neither of the brothers acknowledged Thomas' baleful glare.

Thomas and William got their first glimpse of the Sipsey River at Buhl's Crossing. A large, hand-lettered sign announcing the "Sipsey River Navigation Company" greeted them as they pulled up to the docks. A steam-powered riverboat offered passenger service between the Crossing and the port at Newton's Landing. Thomas bought passage for himself and for William, as he instructed George to take the wagons on to Newton's Landing.

The captain of the riverboat touched his hat as they came aboard. His hands and face were grimy with soot. He politely wiped them with the tail of his coat before extending his hand. "Fog'll be setting in soon," he predicted gloomily. "Best we git a' going. Could be we'll reach Newton's afore dark… then again, maybe not." There was, admittedly, some question about the journey's successful completion, but Thomas decided to make the best of it.

The steam whistle blasted the air and the buckets of the paddle wheel made great splashing noises as the engine built steam. A plume of black smoke belched from the stack and the boat began moving away from the dock.

Thomas and William stood by the railing at the bow, and the young boy's eyes were aglow with excitement. "Oh Pa," he shouted above the noise of the engine. "We're just like the Pilgrims, aren't we?"

"Aye, son, that we are, and with a *steam engine* to boot!"

The Sipsey River, wild and primitive, stretched before them now. It flowed beneath a vaulted canopy of bare branches in the brooding winter's light. It cut a channel 50 to 100 feet in width, and its shallows reached out to sloping banks lined with poplar, elm, hickory, oak, bay, and cedar. Mistletoe hung in clusters from the hardwoods, and the luminous white berries attracted scores of small birds. A flock of wood ducks took to the air ahead of them. A stately white heron watched serenely as they passed.

"Look there, William... over to the left, there... no, to your *left*, son..."

And then the boy saw them—a flock of wild turkeys, visible through the branches, strolling with heads high and alert but obviously unafraid. They passed turtles resting on partially submerged logs, and water snakes moving rapidly away from the boat's wake. Large-mouth bass broke the water, rising into the air for a winged supper, and then splashing back into a myriad of watery circles. They saw deer, rabbit, beaver, and a large shadowy form that might have been a wolf.

The entity of the Sipsey enshrouded them. The seductive mists held the sharp, clean smell of the bay trees and the woodsy smoke of hunters' fire. The intoxicating aroma of fermenting vegetation entangled their senses. It would never set them free.

Chapter Six

The original homestead consisted of 450 acres and was covered in thick forest with the bottom land near the river. Unlike the Indian inhabitants before him, who were content to live with the shape of the land as they found it, Thomas Barkley set about to change the shape, to make the land conform to his own vision. The task was monumental. Thomas knew by the end of the first week that he would never complete the temporary living quarters by Christmas. And so the fires burned until late into the dusk, and the men toiled on, severing the trees at knee height, trimming away branches and rolling the logs onto huge bonfires that lit the sky with showers of sparks and cinders.

The stump pullers came behind, their teams of oxen surging and straining into the traces, the drivers chopping at roots and cursing the sting of the sudden blow from an embedded root, newly freed and released like a live bullwhip from the earth.

Thomas was awake by four o'clock each morning, boiling the coffee water, impatiently waiting enough light to get the teams back into the field. Both he and the boy slept in the wagon with the warmth of the bonfires chasing the frost from the encampment.

The boy was as impatient as the father to greet each new day, and he added his own weight to the project, trimming branches with the bow saw, chopping at the smaller ones with the single bladed axe his father taught him to use.

The logs to be utilized in construction were separated and graded for placement, the stub ends of the branches carefully cut away with the adze, and the notchers and pullers began the work of shaping them into buildings. The ground was covered with sawdust and wood chips and mounded in huge circular piles. The ashes and cinders from the fires accumulated, to be later scattered over the fields as fertilizer.

Christmas came and went as any other day for Thomas and the boy. They worked alongside the slaves and the hired men from the community, placing the white oak shingles on the roof poles of the cabins, fastening the doors with leather hinges, carefully handling the few glass panes that would become windows for the Barkley cabin.

Sarah, Elizabeth and Dicey spent the day in the comfort of the Warrior Hotel, admiring the huge cedar tree in the lobby, decorated with garlands of colored paper and sweet gum pods dipped in flour paste that turned them into snowballs.

They dined on baked chicken and dressing, dried apple pie and cold cider, and warmed by the fireplaces. They turned into bed as darkness settled over the city, and Sarah Barkley dwelt on thoughts of her husband and son. She had experienced enough of the rough life on the trail to know that Thomas and William were facing hardships beyond that experience. She longed to see them, and at the same time, dreaded the thought of the journey into the wilderness that would become her new home.

Thomas came for them at the end of January, riding with William and George in one of the wagons. He had George drive by the livery stable, and to the delight and admiration of the boy, he purchased a shiny new buggy and a spirited horse to propel it.

They did a practice run down Greensboro Avenue and Thomas tipped his hat politely to the townsfolk while William held the reins. They drove up to the hotel in grand style, and the groomsman bowed politely before taking the rig to the stables. They spent the next two days shopping for articles not available in Newton's Landing.

The children rode in the back of the buggy on the return trip, and Dicey and George rode in the wagon with the load of supplies. A light flurry of snowflakes dotted the brown landscape, like icing on gingerbread, and William and Elizabeth gleefully reached out to catch the flakes. Sarah snuggled under the lap robe, drawing warmth and strength from her husband's body.

The land was indeed a wilderness, so covered in huge pine trees that it was possible to travel for twenty miles on a solid carpet of pine needles. And then they passed through the small village of Newtonville and before Sarah had time to grasp its significance, the road ended.

Thomas grinned in boyish enthusiasm as they pulled into a huge, cleared area. "What do you think of it, my dear?"

With admirable determination, she smiled up at her husband. "It will do nicely," she answered.

Thomas pointed toward a hillside covered with a thick growth of tall oaks, mixed with cedar and magnolia. "We'll build the new house up there. We'll clear the bulk of the trees except for shade of course, and I guess you'll want to keep the magnolias."

It was his only indication that Sarah had a part in the overall planning and she nodded, unable to visualize the picture that Thomas was painting, seeing only the rawness and crudeness of this hostile environment, so removed from the lush gardens and groomed pathways of her home in South Carolina.

The cleared area was covered in pine needles, sawdust, and wood shavings. It was interspersed with a series of log cabins. Each of the cabins housed a slave family. There were storage sheds and a barn for the cattle, all constructed of unpeeled logs.

The Barkley quarters were hardly different, except for size and the glint of the glass in the windowpanes, reflecting the morning sun. They had the same unpeeled logs in the construction, the same white clay between the logs.

The work on the permanent house began as soon as lumber could be shaped and dried. Sarah watched in admiration as Thomas worked his miracle. He and his team of carpenters worked from early dawn until dark, in bitter cold of February and under blazing July sun, until at last, the permanent house was finished.

It was an imposing structure, if lacking in certain refinements of the carpentry trade. Huge oak trees formed columns for the wrap around porches and heart pine became the ceilings and paneling. The most impressive quality of the house was the view. It was situated on the crest of a hill, and the slopes had been cleared all the way to the river, except for the shaded oaks and the magnolias along the driveway.

The cleared areas along the banks of the Sipsey gave the beholder glimpses of sparkling water and feathered landings of blue heron and wood ducks. Thomas turned with justifiable elation, one arm sweeping the panorama. "Look at her now, would you Sarah, my dear? Have we not built ourselves a proper home?"

"It is *very* fine, Thomas. I'm proud of you."

"And so am I proud—of you, dear Sarah." He took her hands in his and his gray eyes showed his genuine appreciation. "You've been wonderful to put up with living in little more than a logging camp. Now everything will be more like you deserve—and plenty of room for the children to grow."

Sarah smiled back at him now, her blue eyes strangely secretive, her mouth trembling ever so slightly and she removed her hands from his and clasped them together. "I wanted to wait a bit longer to be sure, but really Thomas— I think we're going to need that extra room for the children to grow…"

"You mean—"

She nodded and Thomas grabbed her up in his arms and swinging her around and around he yelled happily for the children.

"No... Thomas... wait... we need to be sure—"

"Oh all right, but I don't like to keep secrets."

"As if I didn't know!"

All the cleared acreage was planted in corn and vegetables the first year, so that the food supply was assured, and the clearing continued with new earth exposed to the sun, rich and black from the years of decomposed vegetation.

The work crews attacked the earth with a vengeance, removing embedded stumps, driving the double-teamed oxen pulling the breaking plows, curving the earth over for the next year's planting.

The land was full of promise, but their first season was a dry one. Some of the settlers were now thinking of moving on to Mississippi and Arkansas. Stories came back of relatives in the delta lands growing crops on land that never suffered drought.

The bad season tested the mettle of the homesteaders, who stood helplessly looking upward and praying for rain while the golden silks on the corn turned brown and the tender kernels started to wrinkle under the shucks.

"The grass is always greener in some other place," Thomas grumbled, but he searched the sky with the rest of them. He was a farmer and farming was a gamble wherever it was practiced. He watched and held on, and if a neighbor wanted to sell out, he was there to make a bid and his acreage increased steadily. The attainment of land became a passion. Land came to represent his attachment to the earth, and he wanted the bond to be substantial.

And so, when the Hammonds got ready to move West, he bought their place. And then the Corder farm and the Blackmon place, and so on. Thomas was a farmer, and he was a believer. He was a man of the soil, and his prayer was the same as for all men who tilled the soil—a prayer for sun and a prayer for rain.

"We ain't stayin, Thomas." The neighbor was Ernest Linebarger, who waited by the split rail fence that separated his 280 acres from the Barkley holdings.

Thomas reined in his mount and stepped down to reassure his friend. "It'll get better, Ernest. We had droughts back in South Carolina, too."

"Not like this one, Thomas. I just can't risk another dry season when there's wet land all over the delta."

"And when you get there, may be you'll find it too wet to plow."

Ernest shook his head. "I tell you square, I'd swap my best horse just to step in a mud puddle somewhere."

"Sounds like you've got your mind made up."

The neighbor swept his arm in the direction of his boundaries. "What will you give me for her, Thomas?"

"What did you have in mind?"

"I'd let it go for a dollar an acre.'

"Then you just sold it." Thomas reached across to shake on the deal. "I'll meet you at your house in the morning and I'll bring the money." He turned the mare back toward the stables.

When the entire household was sleeping, Thomas walked out to the cedar bell post with a spade. He cautiously dug at the base until the point of the spade struck iron. Then he lifted the dirt away by hand and drew out the cast iron "money pot" that held Sarah's dowry and the inheritance money he had received for his share of his father's estate.

He counted out twenty-eight of the ten-dollar gold pieces and closed the iron lid. He smoothed the dirt back around the base of the post and scattered some dry leaves and pine needles to hide the freshened earth.

Three days later, the rain came, drenching the parched soil, bringing the fields back to life.

Chapter Seven

Sarah filled her days with flower plantings and with teaching and with all the myriad duties of the lady of the manor. One of her greatest concerns was the need to educate the children. She had realized before leaving South Carolina that schooling might not exist in the new land. She had packed copies of *Webster's Spelling Book*, *Smiley's Arithmetic*, *Murray's Grammar*, *McGuffie's Reader* and, of course, the *Holy Bible*.

She set up a school, with hours to begin immediately after breakfast of each day. Elizabeth accepted this regimen enthusiastically but William was fidgety by the dismissal time of ten-thirty in the morning.

It was William's practice to show up with his best and only friend, a slender, slave boy named Jonas Watkins. They were the same age and they found many wonderful and varied activities that were of far greater interest than schooling.

Sarah was adamant that William must attend each session, and so he brought Jonas with him to class—and Jonas obliged in order to be near his idol and companion. Sarah was pleased that the young slave boy seemed to acquire knowledge as readily as any other student.

"Thomas, I have decided that our people," she referred to the slaves in this manner, "have a right to religious instruction."

"Well, Sarah, I won't say that I have any objection to that, but really, what purpose can be achieved?"

"Are you saying that you don't believe the Negro has a soul?"

"Well, there is that opinion, in some quarters... I have always felt," he said with deliberation, "that all of God's creations have a purpose. That would include, I think, the Negro, and in that life after death, well I—of course—I'm led to believe that the slave will play a part in the perfection of God's universe."

"Splendid! We'll start next Sunday."

Thomas sat with his family, on the hard and newly planed surface of the church bench, and listened to the visiting preacher as he presented the scriptures, and his slaves sat in their places in the balcony at the rear. Rather, one could say, Thomas looked more than listened and studied the new construction of the church with pride and satisfaction.

The fresh smell of the oaken timbers filled the chapel and he noted the alignment in the roof trusses above him. The giant timbers met squarely and the joiners were pegged with iron bolts from Thomas Murphy's blacksmith shop. It was a solid structure, built to stand the test of time, and it merited Thomas' admiration.

He looked now at the preacher, noting the hair surrounding his head in a thin fringe. He watched the preacher's scrawny neck as it erupted through his collar, jerking with the momentum of his words. He noted his voice was harsh and the words came raspy from the strain on his vocal chords. And he listened to the rhythm, which emphasized every third or fourth word.

The voice of the preacher rose and fell, and he began to gasp between the sentences and to add an extra syllable to the words so that they came out with an "uh" at the end. "There was a MAN-uh... in the land of UZ-uh... whose name was JOB-uh!"

The cadence swept the audience into movement and they swayed back and forth calling out *Amens* and the Negroes in the back began to moan and shout as well.

The increased volume awakened William as he slept on the hard bench and he almost tumbled onto the floor as the preacher slapped the pulpit with the palm of his hand and implored his audience to get ready for the Glory Day.

At last the invitation came and the converts walked the aisles and the singing continued as the preacher worked on the sinners to repent. The faithful moved up and down the aisles searching out those on the brink of acceptance. An extra hug here—a silent prayer there—and they were escorted downward to the pulpit.

When the preacher finally called for one of the deacons to offer the benediction, Thomas leaned across and whispered to Sarah that this was the "best part of the service." Her reproachful glance allowed no further comment.

Thomas offered thanks at the evening meal and having requested a blessing on the food, he added. "Lord help us to worship you in song and in deed and not in loud or angry voices, knowing that he that *keepeth his mouth*, keepeth his life—but he that openeth wide his lips shall have destruction."

William snickered in spite of himself, and Thomas directed a stern glance in his direction while Sarah tried to recall any such admonition from her Bible text.

They walked the fields the next morning, the man and the boy. The morning air was pungent with the smell of growing corn; the dew was still hanging in droplets from the darkly rich blades. They caught the first rays of the sun, turning each into a miniature diamond of light.

All about, the fields were a lush green and the notes of the mockingbird vied with the raucous chatter of blue jays. Thomas turned to the boy and his face was suddenly quite serious. "Do you see what lies before you, son?"

William turned a puzzled look upward. "I see the fields and the sky and the trees... ."

Thomas' left hand closed firmly on the boy's shoulder, and reached with the other hand and turned the boy's face to meet his gaze. "Those are not just fields, son, not just trees—what you see before you is Barkley land. Say it son—*Barkley land!*"

"Barkley land," William repeated and waited to be released but the hands were firm on his face and shoulder.

"What you see before you is Barkley land and some day it will be yours. If your mother and I have no other sons, it is all yours. But regardless of that, you are my first-born son, and I must have a promise from you. You must promise me that this land will never be for sale. Do you hear me, William?"

The boy nodded and the hands stayed firm upon him.

"Repeat after me," the man said. "Barkley land is not for sale."

The boy repeated the phrase, and only then did the hands go slack and allow him to resume the walk.

They walked in silence for a time and then the boy looked up at the sky. It was a startling blue but on the horizon loomed towering peaks of white clouds, stacked one upon another with the sunlight coloring the upper tiers with streaks of orange and gold.

"Yesterday," the boy said, "that preacher talked about a Glory Day but I didn't catch what he meant by that."

"You didn't catch it," Thomas grinned," because you were damned well asleep. You better watch that old preacher, though. He'll rap you with that cane pole he keeps back of the pulpit if he catches you snoring." Thomas considered the matter for a while before speaking. "*Today, son,* today is a Glory Day."

"How do you know?" the boy asked.

Thomas smiled at the boy and placed a hand on his tousled head. "It's a day when the sun is shining and your work is all caught up… and you have the vision to see all of the goodness and greatness of God's universe." Thomas thought about what he had just said and he was pleased with it. "Yep, that's a Glory Day, boy."

William turned the explanation over and over in his mind, and he marveled at his father's sagacious answer.

Sarah refused to believe the pregnancy was going badly—but it did. The little girl was born prematurely, fully formed, but lifeless.

She was to have been the answer to the aching spot in Sarah's heart that harbored the memory of the little sister in South Carolina. Instead, the Barkley family was forced to bury the first of its members in the family plot that Sarah had selected. The ground was elevated and shaded by tall cedars at the corners. Thomas felt she was too exhausted to attend the ceremony but she insisted. She held her sorrow inside as the simple burial took place.

There were only the family members and the slaves in attendance. He tried to comfort her, but he understood that she must deal with her own grief. As she walked away, she began to sing in her clear soprano voice, the old hymn, *Rock of Ages*, as if no other person was in hearing distance.

She walked down the hill to one of the magnolia trees, and she plucked a white, velvety bouquet from the tree and then she went inside and placed a blossom in every vase. She continued this practice throughout the summer months and the flowers spread their sweet scent during the day and then at evening, closed their petals.

"Why do the flowers close up at night?" Elizabeth asked.

Sarah looked out of the window and softly replied. "They close because there is no one to see them… but they are not dead, only sleeping… like my darling baby up there in the cemetery."

She sang her hymns every day until the family worried about her sanity. She seemed all right in other ways, however. She supervised the house servants and assisted in time of illness, but her attitude was one of reserved detachment.

Thomas could find no way to comfort her. He tried, on more than one occasion, but she gently pushed him away, and he started to feel more like an older brother than a husband. He suspected that Sarah held him responsible. There had been nothing unusual about the births in South Carolina. What made things so different in Alabama?

Now, more than ever, he realized the error he had made in bringing her to this new land. It was too raw… too violent for her delicate constitution.

The weeks of summer moved into the fall and her daily regimen of placing flowers in vases stopped, as did the singing, but she still held a faraway look in her eyes. Thomas would often find her sitting by the window of their bedroom, looking out toward the cemetery.

And because he could not lie with her without a desire to touch her, and because she rejected his show of affection, he moved into the spare bedroom over the hall, and turned his frustration into the hard work of the fields.

Often he read his Bible in those lonely hours of the night. He was a believing man, and he used God's services on a daily basis, asking blessings on his food and family and calling for damnation of anything or anybody that got in his way.

Sometimes he folded the book and silently made his way from the study, carrying his shoes and outer clothing. He might dress in the darkness on the porch before making his way down to the river.

Chapter Eight

1839

In their search for the sea, the currents of the Tombigbee, Black Warrior, and Sipsey rivers come together for a short run to the Gulf of Mexico, and these merging currents bear the name of the Mobile River.

Eight miles upstream from the city of Mobile, Tim and Yellow Moon spent the last night of their river voyage moored to a great water oak, its branches reaching down and completely surrounding the raft. They sat comfortably on the fur cargo and watched a great yellow moon peek behind the strands of Spanish moss.

They were insulated from the world, safely at the end of a long journey. Whether it was this realization that drew them toward each other or Yellow Moon's great fear of the unknown, it was a time when the rivers of emotion joined the currents to the sea.

Yellow Moon recalled that Tim Malloy had been her friend and her protector and he had honored his promise not to abuse her. She was acquainted with abuse, but she had no experience with sensuality, and her feelings both troubled and excited her. She wanted to be close to this man who so obviously loved life and all of its mysteries. She sensed that he held a genuine affection for her. She leaned her head on his shoulder as they reclined on the furs and watched the moon climb the branches above them. "You have brought me to a new world," she said softly. "I do not know if I will like it."

"Like it? Of course ye'll like it, little one. There is much I can show ye—stores of silks and linen materials and fur coats made from pelts like these and food and drink. I'll teach ye... "

"Tim?"

"Yes, little one?"

"Teach me now," she said and she curled her arms around him, feeling his body tremble ever so slightly.

"Are ye sure? All these long weeks I've wanted to hold ye in me arms and love—"

"I am sure," she replied.

Chapter Nine

The sign on the front lawn had cherubic little figures floating in little clouds around its borders. The sign read, "DEVINE ROOMING HOUSE." A black maid opened one of the French doors and stood, in white apron and cap, without comment.

Tim shifted uncomfortably and then frowned at the woman. "We'd like to rent a room," he said. The maid kept her eyes at shoe level, and still without speaking, turned back into the house.

They waited for some few minutes and then an imposingly handsome woman appeared in the doorway. She wore a lovely silk dressing gown and her face was carefully made up. She appeared to be in her middle years and her smile made them feel more at ease.

Tim coughed politely behind his hand and then rendered his own infectious smile. "We're in need of living quarters," he said.

The woman nodded her head slowly up and down, looking directly at the girl, noting the faded homespun clothing and the careless tresses framing her face. She noted also the supple, curvaceous body. "And what might your name be, pretty one?"

Tim quickly answered for her. "My... uh... wife's name is Serina Malloy." The lie came easily from his lips.

"And you came here from..."

"The Tennessee River country."

"That's pretty big country." The woman nodded to the maid. "Show the lady and gentleman into my office and bring some coffee."

She was absent for several minutes while Tim juggled the thin, porcelain coffee cup and saucer on his knee, and Yellow Moon marveled at the beautiful carpeting and draperies at the wide bay window.

"We have a rather select clientele," the landlady stated, entering the room with a surprisingly light movement considering her size. "But I think we can accommodate you—providing you can improve your appearance."

"Now see here—" Tim got up as if to leave.

"No… you see here. We have certain standards in our choice of clientele. I don't mean to offend you, sir, but several weeks of travel can put wear and tear on the best of fabrics."

The maid entered again, this time with ladies' apparel on her arm, which she handed to the landlady. "I believe these will fit you, my dear." She smiled in Yellow Moon's direction.

"Show her into a dressing room," she instructed the maid, and when Tim started to interrupt, she smiled engagingly at him but shook her head to silence him. "Shush now—the clothing belonged to my niece, now away in Europe— and it might as well be worn."

Tim couldn't believe his eyes when Yellow Moon walked back into the room. A fashionable brocade in lavender accented the burnished copper of her skin. The maid had brushed and pulled her long, black tresses into a bun at the nape of her neck. Soft, patent leather shoes replaced the rough, buckskin moccasins.

"My God, ye're beautiful!"

Yellow Moon looked at her reflection in the wall length mirror—hesitant to recognize that it was her own image.

"Now you folks get settled," the landlady said. "My name's Della… Della Devine. You have come to the right place, my dears. I not only have a vacancy, but I can offer you assistance in many ways. Should you ever need a mid-wife, I am the best."

They had a bedroom and a sitting room and a small pantry-like room, complete with a cast iron tub that could be utilized for washing clothes or for bathing. The fireplace in the sitting room had hooks and a grate for cooking, if the tenant didn't wish to eat in the common dining room downstairs. All the furnishings were in place and the girl was overjoyed to be in a real house once again. Not since leaving the Cherokee Nation had she enjoyed the comforts afforded by their new quarters. She was both grateful and bewildered by the good fortune that had come her way.

The fur warehouse on the Mobile River had a long, elevated section that ran down through the center of the room. There were wood dividers to separate each trapper's cargo of pelts. The auctioneer for the fur sale escorted representatives from the British, French, and Dutch trading companies on a preliminary examination of the market offerings. The trappers stood to one side, jostling each other when they noticed nods of approval from the buyers.

The market opened with the auctioneer moving from one divider to the next, the cries of the auctioneer echoing in the cavernous interior of the warehouse.

The sale of the furs brought Tim more money than any season he had experienced. The auctioneer shrewdly played one fur company representative against the other and when the sale was over, they swept Tim along in a spirit of goodwill to the doors of the nearest tavern. He came back to their quarters, pockets bulging with money, and a belly full of Jamaican rum. He carried a large box under his right arm and a smaller, circular box under the left.

"Get yourself prettied up, now." He laid the packages on the bed and grabbed the startled girl around the waist. He spun her about in a tipsy dance that ended with both of them flat on the floor.

She was immediately alarmed and studied his face with grave concern. "Why are you behaving so?" she asked.

"Because I am rich!" Tim gave a lop-sided grin. "And because I am very well drunk!"

And so it went for several weeks running. They tried all the restaurants. Tim was anxious to taste the liquors that he had missed since the previous year. He also played poker—although he had promised himself not to, having lost his season's receipts on the last trip. Life was, and had always been, a game to Tim. The possibility of winning large stakes at a poker table was an irresistible and thrilling challenge.

Yellow Moon was bewildered. She could not understand what was happening to the good-natured man that she loved. More and more, Tim indulged in alcoholic binges until finally she put the matter squarely before him.

"We have stayed far too long in this place," she said. "City life is not good for you, and it is not good for me. We must go back now to the high country."

"Now what's so bad about this life, little one?" He grinned in his most persuasive way, but she had seen enough.

"It is all bad—all very bad. You are throwing our money away—"

"Ah, so 'tis *our* money now?" He raised an eyebrow in mock astonishment "*OUR* money did ye say, me darlin?"

"Yes, Tim. Our money, as you would readily acknowledge—if you were in your right mind for thinking—"

"Faith and I remember a wee lost soul, needing the comfort of me cabin and fire—"

"Would to God we had never left that cabin and cook fire!" She turned away from him. She had seen the strange behavior of her tribesmen who had tasted the white man's whiskey. It made them act crazily, so that she was afraid to be near them. She suddenly thought to leave the city, with or without Tim.

But there were changes in her body now that could affect those plans. She began to realize that the landlady's joking remark might be all too real. She was almost afraid to reveal the secret—and she debated whether to tell Tim. Hopefully, it might change his conduct. She accompanied him to the dining room and then, as usual, he wanted to make the rounds of the taverns. They walked out into the night and she pulled at his arm. The desperation in her eyes penetrated the fog of liquor clouding his brain.

"Whatever's the matter, little one?"

"The matter is—you are going to be a—a father!"

"Good God Almighty! A father did ye say, me love?"

"Yes, Tim, and please, please, listen to me. You must find work and—"

"Aye, that I must do," he said, and she felt tenderness return to her heart. She smiled at him warmly and they embraced without embarrassment on the open street.

"Tim... I... "

He cupped her chin in his hand, smiling down at her, and she was encouraged to continue.

"I wonder why you never use my name?"

"Well, little—"

"No—not little one, you never call me Yellow Moon—and back there—when the landlady asked—you said—Sereena?"

"Serina Malloy—me mother's name. Look, it's not me that means to offend ye, little one, but this name—Yellow Moon—it's well, a native name, uh... it might cause ye some problems. I think ye should call yeself Serina Malloy."

"I think we should be married first."

"Eh? What's that ye say, little one?"

"Married, Tim. Our child will need a proper name—only then will I call myself Seree—"

"Serina Malloy. Ah, little one. 'Tis a fact that ye've got me number."

They were married in a small white chapel near the waterfront. The rector asked for the bride's name and she answered firmly and proudly, "Serina. My name is Serina Malloy."

The clergyman raised an eyebrow and Tim quickly added, "Cousins—twice removed."

While Tim busied himself looking for work, Della Devine took Serina in hand, calling for her carriage, and escorting Serina to the best clothiers in the city.

"Oh no!" Serina protested when Della held up one dress after another. "We cannot afford to buy such expensive garments."

Della shushed her with a smile and a wink. "You will be able to pay for it later, my dear."

And so saying, she marched upon the sales clerk with an armload of outerwear and underwear. "See to it that I receive my customary discount, you 'ear?"

The clerk nodded understandingly, giving Serina an appraising eye in the process. "Our best pricing will apply of course!"

And so it went. Serina was baffled by the interest and generosity of her benefactress. She was also thrilled to stand in front of the mirror and pose in the imported fabrics. Even with her pregnant profile, the garments were so tailored as to render the condition unnoticeable.

Tim had no trouble locating work. The shipbuilding industry was in full swing, with two coastal steamers and a dozen river steamers under construction. His big frame and ready smile won him easy employment in the ship's carpentry shop. The pay was good and it was made on a daily basis. Tim was unaccustomed to such largesse, having waited from one season to the next to be compensated for trapping. To go home at the end of the day with money in his pockets was actually too great a temptation for him.

Life had always been a game to Tim—and now he discovered variations on the game that had never been available before. He began spending hours after work in the smoke-filled back rooms of the saloons where the flip of a card could make a man richer than his best dreams or poorer than his worst. There was always the lure of the big pot and Tim got lucky enough to hit it time after time. He was hooked to the gills by an addiction that had lain in wait for him.

Serina became depressed again with his absence in the evenings and Della was quick to notice the change.

"Your man has a problem with money, does he not?"

"He is not used to it. Money is not a good thing for him."

"It is not a good thing to be without it, my dear. I fear that your man is wasting his opportunities. A day of reckoning must always come, however."

Serina was confused and miserable. The time was drawing near for her confinement and the future looked very bleak indeed. Tim's personality was changing from the exuberant, backwoods character that she had come to love. More often than not, he was now quarrelsome and slovenly.

"So it's you who's been out on the town again, eh?" Tim greeted her, reeking with a stale smell of cigar smoke and alcohol-burdened breath. "Seems Miss Della Devine's got her hooks into ye pretty good, my little one."

"Miss Della's been very kind to me. I don't know how I would have passed the time—with you never home…"

"Don't be handing me any high and mighty talk." Tim grabbed her by the arm and twisted her to him. She tried to pull away but he held her, leering drunkenly.

"Think I don't know what ye're up to, me pretty?"

"I don't know what you mean."

He laughed, mimicking her tone. "Don't know what you mean—" He slammed her against the wall. "What I mean is—your Miss Della Devine is a woman of many talents." He glared at her as she stood silently now. "Many talents… hotel keeper, midwife, and WHOREHOUSE madam!"

"You lie!"

"Nay—my dear. It's common knowledge among the townsfolk. She's grooming ye for one of her girls once ye drop that babe."

Serina stood stricken and disbelieving. She had been unable to account for the landlady's generosity—was it possibly this? No, it could not be. "You are shifting blame from your own bad habits." She fled the sitting room and closed the door to the bedroom, confused and hurting.

Tim began to avoid work a day or so each week, struggling with hangovers and despair. Finally, he stopped showing up at all as the cards kept falling and he kept losing, and his need to recoup his losses grew greater. The result was inevitable. Tim tried one last desperate measure to stay in the game. He turned to Serina.

"It's all gone." His eyes were bloodshot and his face had lost its healthy color. He sat on the edge of the bed and he was pleading now.

"Gone—all our money's gone?"

"Please help me—you've got connections now—the landlady—she's got more money than she can spend…"

Serina couldn't believe it had come to this. "Tim—you promised me—promised me—in good faith—"

"Aye—that I did, and it's sorrowful I am to have deceived ye. I only needed

47

one good pot, just one good pot—to recoup me losses. That's why I kept after it—I wanted to make up for what I'd done—otherwise I could have just caught a boat and left—"

"You would have left me—with the baby coming?"

"Nay—dammit, that's not what I'm saying—some coulda done it, but not old Tim. It's me that loves ye truly—"

"How can you say that, after what you've done to us?"

He began to cry, the tears running into his hollowed cheeks, his shoulders sagging. He swayed back and forth on the edge of the bed, in no way resembling the happy-go-lucky Tim that she had married.

"Just one more time, little one. I know I can make it all up—no way I can replace the money working by the day... I've just got to have one more run at the cards—don't you see, Serina? It's our only chance! Please ask her—the landlady—just one time!"

She looked at the broken man and her spirit went out to him. He was a good man in his heart. She knew this, but she also knew he was lost.

"I can make it all up, little one," he pleaded. "I promise you, by all that's holy—you get this loan for me and I'll recoup my losses and I'll never sit at a gaming table again!"

"Do you mean that, Tim? Do you really mean that?"

He shook his head vigorously. "By all that's holy!"

"I'll ask her, Tim."

He grabbed her to him, sobbing like a child, but Serina felt as if a chill wind had blown into the room. She shuddered and closed the window.

The woman, Della, stood before her with a small, half-smile curling her mouth, one eyebrow raised above the penetrating stare. "It has come to this, now?"

"He promised me. One last game to replace his losses, and he'll never gamble again!"

"That's what they all say, my dear. That's what they all say. I'll give you the loan, but you must understand the loan is to you—not to that wasteful derelict you call a husband!"

The contraction came as she walked to the toilet. She rang the bell by Della's door and the big woman knew instantly that the time had come. She brought her inside and placed her on a cot in a little room adjoining the kitchen. "I'm going to brew some hot tea for you now, Serina. You just relax between the pains and let me handle things. I know what I'm doing."

And somehow Serina knew that she did. She allowed herself to be bathed and lubricated and she welcomed the hot sheets brought from the maid's ironing board.

Della elevated her head and started to massage her body. "We're going to help you now and there's no reason for you to be afraid."

The little girl was born just before the noon hour. Her head was covered with a soft halo of dark hair and the small healthy body was exquisitely formed.

"What name have you picked for this beautiful child?"

"I have not picked a name... I thought Tim—"

"Your man Tim is not around, my dear. Why don't we call her Peggy? That's a good Irish name. I always wanted a daughter named Peggy but I never got one. Besides, it's a name your husband should like."

"I no longer care what my husband would like," the new mother responded.

At a saloon aptly named "The Scupper," as the dregs of the port city washed in and out of it, Tim Malloy sat in trance-like concentration. He was unaware of the wife now in labor at the rooming house down the street. He had one thing in mind—to beat the man across the table in one final game of poker... one final hand to replenish the many pots this man had taken from him.

The man was Alonzo Hogg, who appeared to be completely relaxed, his derby hat pushed back on his head, a silk scarf knotted about his neck, an unfired cigar clenched in his teeth. Day after day, and night after night, the man was incredibly lucky and Tim was always the loser. Occasionally, he would pick up a small pot at just the moment he was ready to leave the table and he would promptly be back in the game.

The noisy saloon had quieted down, the customers now surrounding the table, knowing the stakes were high and sensing the tension at the table. Even the sailors from the Dutch ship had ceased to argue with the English at the bar. The smoke from a dozen cigars blanketed the room and the smell of sweat and tar hung on the air. Alonzo threw the winning card onto the table, and Tim realized he had palmed it, knew he had been duped all the long nights by this professional card cheat. All the desperation and lost hope of the past few weeks resolved itself into a rage that burned throughout his body.

Tim stood erect, his huge fists before him, shaking uncontrollably. "You dirty, double dealing son-of-a-bitch!" he screamed. He reached out and lunged across the table, scattering the chips and money onto the floor.

Alonzo Hogg quickly drew his pistol and fired at point-blank range into Tim's chest. Still, Tim struggled forward and Hogg fired once more. The room became totally silent and Tim's dead body lay across the table. Alonzo Hogg pushed Tim's body onto the floor and casually raked the pot into his hat.

The voice of the proprietor boomed in the hush that had fallen over the saloon. He stood over the fallen Tim, shotgun at the ready, and looked around the room. "We want no trouble with the law here. This was a fair fight and a clear case of self-defense—but it ain't good for business—so I don't reckon any of you folks saw anything you need to report—am I right?"

There was a general murmur of assent. The proprietor nodded to the bartender and the man came out and dragged Tim's body into the storage room out back. The proprietor offered a round of drinks on the house.

The gambler adjusted his red suspenders, set the derby hat squarely on his head and looked around the room. "I believe I'll be getting on down to Miss Della's."

A short time later a teamster's wagon pulled up from the alley and took the body, wrapped in a tarp, and rolled it onto the wagon bed. The teamster drove down the alley and took the back road to the Pinto Island roadway. When he reached the river, he stopped the wagon and slid his cargo to the ground. He removed the tarp and laid some heavy rocks alongside the body. He wrapped it back again and tied the tarp at both ends. He loaded it back into the wagon, drove out onto the pier, and rolled the body into the water. It immediately sank from sight.

Chapter Ten

1844

The frail health that Sarah Barkley had experienced during her last pregnancy was not evident this time. The fact was, she was pregnant again and radiantly so. She wanted another little girl and she wanted the child to look like the little sister she had left behind. The memory was framed like a picture in her mind. She could see the angelic face, the golden ringlets of hair and the heavenly blue of her eyes. How often she had wished for some such likeness in her own family!

Sarah felt a compelling need to see her sister again. She could imagine how she must look in her young womanhood. She had talked with Thomas about her wish to name the baby after Katherine, if her intuition proved correct. She sat now, composing another letter to her sister in South Carolina.

"I have Thomas' agreement," she wrote, "to make a return visit home as soon as the baby is old enough for the trip. My days are filled with anticipation. I truly believe that the baby will be a girl, and I'm hoping she will be cast in your image. It will be enough reward in my lifetime to have it so, and to know that it is now only a matter of months until I can clasp you to my bosom once more.

"William and Elizabeth send their love and Thomas asked me to mention his sister as well in my letter, so I will ask you to inform her of our impending visit. Thomas has so much regretted that he could not be there for his mother's funeral. The circumstances of parting were disturbing, and he blames himself terribly for losing contact with the family there."

She paused in her writing and looked about her home with the knowledge that it had been worthwhile. The pattern of accomplishment was evident. The early rawness was softened now by flowerbeds and boxwoods and graveled pathways. The air was heavy with the odor of jasmine and honeysuckle intermingled on the trellis that shaded the porch.

She closed the letter and picked a handful of flowers and was arranging them into bouquets when Dicey came out with a cold glass of buttermilk. She sat in the shade of the trellis and watched as the field workers came up for the midday meal.

She saw Elizabeth coming from the direction of the orchard and she acknowledged with pleasure the changes taking place in this lovely child. She was a willing worker and she was becoming a proper young lady. She had excelled in all of the courses taught by Sarah and was now enrolled in Mr. James Boutwell's Shepherd Church School. Sarah hoped to send her to college when she was older. These days, Elizabeth skipped about the grounds, alternately playing with her dolls or reading from the poems of Phillip Pendleton Cooke and James Legare.

Thomas rode into the yard and dismounted, giving the reins to George while he washed himself at the watering trough. He came up on the porch then and leaning over Sarah's chair, kissed her lightly on the cheek. "Anything happening yet?" he asked.

"You will be the first to know when it does," she answered with a smile and accompanied him to the dining room.

She went to her bedroom after lunch and prepared to take a nap. She removed her outer garments and laid them over the walnut chiffonier that her mother had given her on her wedding day. She ran her fingers over the polished carvings on the doors and thought of her mother, long buried now. She had inherited the mother's love of beauty and her respect for all of God's creation. She felt relaxed and welcomed the cessation of thought and feeling for a little while.

When she awoke it was mid-afternoon and she slipped from the bed and dressed once more. Dicey came in to check on her and finding her comfortably situated, went to her own cabin to do the family ironing.

Sarah sat for a while reading from her Bible, and then a restlessness came upon her. She put the book aside and went once more to the porch. There was stillness now and the afternoon heat enshrouded her. George had gone to take drinking water to the field hands and Dicey was busy ironing in her cabin, not wanting to heat up the big house with her flat iron fire.

The first involuntary movement seized her body, catching her unawares and putting her into a momentary state of panic. She composed herself, knowing that the signal had been given. The time had come now for rational thinking and she moved to the edge of the porch. "It's time, Dicey!" she called.

"What time, Missy?"

"Time for the baby, Dicey, the baby!"

"The baby—oh Lawd—the baby?"

"I think so, Dicey. Please run to the field and get Mr. Thomas. I'll be all right for a little while."

"Ya'll sho, ma'am?"

"I'm sure, just *you* be sure to hurry!"

"I'll bring him fast as I kin fly!"

The thought of Dicey's bulk flying under any circumstance, brought momentary mirth, but then she was in the throes of the next contraction. She made her way into the house as the water broke within her.

Thomas was not in the first cotton field. Dicey looked frantically about and spotted young William, in a group of pickers, near the end of the rows. She gasped out her message—"Mist Will… yo Ma! She be taken bad! Got to find yo Pa!"

"What *is* it, Dicey… What's *wrong?*"

"Her *time* done come—dat's what!"

William dropped the cotton sack and sped over the rows, leaping terraces and kicking up puffs of dust as his feet flew over the hot ground.

He saw his father in the distance checking scales at the weighing station. He began calling his name before he got within range of hearing and by the time Thomas heard him, the boy's voice was hoarse from the effort and the anxiety.

"*It's Ma! It's Ma!*" He got no further. Thomas ran for the mare and William jumped up behind him, hanging on for dear life as the mare jumped the fence line and headed up the lane to the house. The boy waited in the hall while his father talked with the women in the bedroom. A sudden scream of pain caused his stomach to knot and he dug his fists into his eyes.

His father was at the door now, face drawn and sallow under the leathery tan. "Will," his voice was low and serious. "You've got a man's job to do."

"What is it Pa?"

"You've got to ride for Dr. Brandon. Take my mare—there's none faster here. Please find him son—and fast—I can't leave your Ma right now."

He rode, and later he couldn't remember how long it had taken to find the doctor. It seemed somehow very like a dream he had experienced… the need for flight was imminent, but his feet were glued to the ground.

He rode the mare to a lather and she was laboring for wind when they reached the post office building in Newtonville. The doctor's office was just overhead but a note fluttered on a nail in the door. With trembling hands he read that the doctor was in the Ridge community, making a house call to the Crowley family.

He got directions from Newton's Trading Post and borrowed a fresh mount from Carl Newton. He found the doctor's buggy parked in the yard and Dr.

Brandon just coming out of the house. William hastily explained why he had come.

The doctor followed him back to his office to pick up obstetrical instruments. William changed mounts again, retrieving the mare, and the doctor put a fresh horse to his buggy.

In the end, it made no difference. William knew, from the moment that he dismounted and caught the expression on Thomas' face, that all his efforts had been in vain. His father stood by the porch railing, features grimly set and his eyes staring into nothingness.

Inside the house there came a wailing sound that he recognized as Aunt Dicey, and then a new sound—a baby's new and angry cry.

"Pa, oh Pa… I tried as hard as I could."

Thomas held out his arms as the boy came up the steps and then he held him against his chest as the boy wept. "I know you did your best, son. Nothing could help, nothing but God Almighty could have helped," his voice turned bitter. "And he forgot us, son."

Eventually, the doctor came out, rolling his sleeves down, his face pale and sorrowful.

"Thomas?" The doctor looked anxiously into the face of his friend, bushy eyebrows raised in question.

Thomas made no reply and his face appeared to be carved from stone.

The doctor motioned inside with a nod. "We'd better get the little one over to Mrs. Steven's house. Her youngest is taking a little table food now and I expect she's got more than enough milk to suckle your baby." Thomas nodded and Dr. Brandon took the infant in his arm and went to the buggy. Dicey followed with a picnic basket, in which she had placed a baby blanket. "Oh Lawd God, Marse Thomas, what us gonna do now?" she wailed.

Thomas couldn't answer her. He walked to the river, unable to offer comfort to the children because he had no comfort for himself. He was unable to accept the lack of God's understanding, unable to love the infant child.

William stood with Dicey and Elizabeth and watched him walk away. "It won't never be the same," William sobbed. "I'll never forgive myself."

"You hush now, chile," Dicey smothered him to her bosom. "Yo Mama wuz gone befo you ever got to Newtonville."

Elizabeth turned her tear-stained face upward. "Is she in heaven this minute?"

"Sho she is, 'Lizbeth, sho she is… an' thet make heaven jes a little closer to us."

"… And we are only human," the preacher said over the freshened earth by the grave. "Only human—and it is understandable, if today we ask the question—why? We don't always know *why* things happen as they do… why this good wife and loving mother, this very fine example of a Christian woman, should be taken from us.

"We can ask why, and possibly never find the answer on this planet earth. Our only recourse is to accept God's word that all things will be revealed to us, in his own time. There will come a time, Beloved, when Sarah Barkley will be revealed again to us, to gather with us, and sing with us, in that greater life in heaven. One day, Beloved, there will be no more pain, no more suffering, no more asking… "

And Thomas thinking—*but this is today, God. I am in pain and suffering—what have you got for me today?*

"God so loved the world—that he gave his only begotten son, that all men might be saved, and have life everlasting."

But it's not… it's not everlasting. It's short and painful and thankless, and the sword of death hangs over every day of it—waiting to snuff it out at its most precious moment.

"I am the resurrection—the truth—and the life—I *will* come again, and receive you unto myself… that where I am, there ye may be also… and Beloved, we shall join Sarah Barkley, we shall gather at the river, in that sweet bye and bye. Praise God Almighty!"

The minister paused—and the weeping grew louder. In the back of the crowd, the slaves began to moan and then the preacher raised his arms aloft. They began to sing *Amazing Grace.*

The tears came then, salty and bitter, shriveling his soul and leaving him hollow. He buried Sarah in the gravesite she had selected, next to the infant she had lost. The grave was on the hillside west of the main house, overlooking the pastures and the roadway to Newtonville. It was to the left of the infant and under a large cedar that shaded the plot.

Thomas remained resolute throughout—inviting no sympathy. Grief to Thomas was a personal and private thing—nobody could help him and so his friends let him be. He came often to the grave in the following days. He selected a large slab of sandstone and with hammer and chisel he cut the words.

IN GOD'S HANDS
SARAH ROBERTS BARKLEY—1812-1844

He looked at the crude lettering, clenching the hammer and chisel. There was no refinement in the lettering and he realized with heavy heart—there was no refinement left in his world. He tried to pray but became angry, convinced that God was no longer listening.

Chapter Eleven

1844

Serina's concern about Della Devine's intentions was shortly resolved. The woman had befriended her when there was no one to help, certainly not the husband who had mysteriously disappeared after begging Serina to get a loan for him. The husband hadn't bothered to attend the birth of his daughter and had most likely headed back north.

It was difficult for Serina to believe that Tim could have been so heartless, but there was no other explanation. Della made discreet inquiries of the police officials who visited her establishment, but none of them had any word on the whereabouts of Tim Malloy.

There was no one who cared, no one to turn to—except Della. And Della laid it out for her in a straightforward manner. She would put Serina to work in her brothel. She would deduct the money loaned to Tim from her earnings. There would be a private living area for Serina and the baby. There would be free maid service and meals at the common table. There would be medical care available from the doctor who visited on a regular basis.

Serina considered the options and decided there really weren't any. She had no husband, no money, no job, no experience, and a child to feed. She made the choice that Della had expected her to make. She also made friends with Della's other girls; indeed, it was easy to do so because they were, generally speaking, likeable women. Most suffered the emotional scars of an abused childhood and in some cases, a woman had simply run away from poverty.

Such was the case of a young lady they nicknamed "Giggles." Perhaps nobody had less reason to giggle than she, but she earned her name by the most outgoing and lighthearted disposition. "Heck," she told Serina. "I ain't never had no better friend than Miss Della. She taken me in right off the street where I was dumped by a family going to Texas. I spent most of my early years going from one relative to the other, and none of 'em really wanted me.

"The last place I stayed—my cousin's husband took me off in a corncrib. Said he'd educate me on how to make a living for myself—and I guess he did at that, but he warn't payin and I decided I warn't stayin." She giggled at the unintentional verse.

"You know, this is the first real home I ever had. I got my own private room, got nice things to wear, and good friends like you—why it's just like a girl's school or something, only I don't have no talent for learning. Miss Della, she tried to make me refined like you, but it just didn't fit me, you know?" She giggled again and Serina laughed in spite of herself.

It was good to be in the company of one so unaffected by the vocation. Unlike Serina, she felt no shame about her surroundings—but also she didn't have a child to rear.

Serina determined that her little daughter would never know about this phase of her life and as the tip money accumulated, she looked forward to the day she might buy passage somewhere to the north.

Della Devine's bordello was located a scant two blocks from the boardinghouse where she made her own residence. The exterior revealed nothing of its purpose, conforming to the residential architecture surrounding it.

The interior was a different story. Red velvet drapes extended from the windows and gas lamps with tinted, leaded glass chimneys were placed on the walls in heavy brass sconces. Thick, Turkish carpeting covered the floors and perfumed vapors rose from incense in heated canisters.

Alonzo Hogg was a regular customer, as was a local judge, various members of the city government and the port authority, and of course, select members of law enforcement.

This day Alonzo came into the parlor, wearing his usual derby hat and red suspenders, silk scarf knotted about his neck. He smelled of whiskey and his woolen suit was stained with cigar ashes from the many hours at the poker table. He nodded to Irene, who was the hostess.

Irene was also a house mother to the girls and she kept the books for Della. She was totally accurate in her accounting. She moved in Alonzo's direction, smiling graciously and offering her hand, which he took in great pretense of politeness.

"How nice of you to visit us this evening, Mr. Hogg."

"I'm sure the pleasure will be all mine," Hogg replied, and he glanced around the room, smiling at the ladies, his gold front teeth contrasting with his swarthy skin. He seated himself on a sofa and one by one the girls came by, flirting, demurely fluttering fans, and he let them go by, nodding but not selecting, until his eye fell on a young woman with strikingly beautiful features. Her exotic skin coloring and long, flowing black hair set her apart from her associates. She made no move to flirt with him, but remained seated, and Irene hastened to apologize for the girl's lack of courtesy.

"Serina's just shy, Mr. Hogg, really a very sweet, young thing—"

He rose from his seat without waiting for her answer and strode across the room to Serina. He bowed and extended his hand to assist her from the chair.

Serina Malloy accepted his hand and walked with him to Irene's desk in the hallway. The hostess took his money and gave Serina a smile and a wink. "You have very good taste, Mr. Hogg."

"I'll be the judge of that," he said, and followed the young woman up the carpeted stairs.

Serina closed the door and turned the oil lamp down. There was no expression, other than a cool detachment, on her oval face.

Now the man watched hungrily as Serina performed the disrobing act that Irene had made her practice. He also undressed, but not in a graceful manner. He kicked his boots into the corner, left his pants on the floor, and grabbed for the woman, shirttail flapping.

She slipped through his grasp and stretched upon the bed without seeming to notice him. The man took her greedily, and expended himself quickly, and lay in frustration upon her body. She pushed him aside and pointed him to the washbasin.

"You could speak to me, Gawdamit!" the man said. "Tell me what it takes to get a little conversation out of you!"

"Money always talks," she said.

"Aye—and I've more than you've likely ever seen, my pretty!" He raised the shirttails to expose a money belt that encircled his waist. "How much would you like, if I should decide to give it?"

Serina had hoped for a tip of five to ten dollars and she was amazed to see him proffer a twenty-dollar bill.

"That will be fine, sir," the lady said, and she smiled ever so discreetly at him.

"Remember the name, girly—it's Alonzo Hogg. All the girls want my business and I don't blame 'em. I don't mind paying for good service. I went easy on you this time, but I'll be back." And he did come back, several times each month—and the lady of choice was always Serina Malloy. She did her routine, and he paid his money, and the tip box kept growing.

She personally found the man obnoxious; he had a mean streak that seemed to surface each time he made his visit. Something made him want to humiliate women and he was willing to pay for the experience. The lure of the tip money forced her to tolerate the situation, but she was always glad to see him go.

The months went by and on a bright day in the fall, Serina dressed and went to her private bedroom. All of the girls were afforded private rooms for their personal needs, and in Serina's case, there was also a babysitting service in the person of one of the maids. The little girl, Peggy Malloy, was sleeping soundly. Serina nodded to the maid and the black girl got up to leave. Serina went to a chest of drawers and removed a small metal box with a clasp lock. She put twenty dollars inside and marked the amount on the slip of paper she kept as her savings ledger. Della had taught her to write numbers and to read, and she had schooled her in the ways of polite society. The young woman no longer resembled in any way the backwoods girl who had ridden down river with Tim Malloy. It was Giggles who brought word to Serina that Della desired her company. "It looks to me like Miss Della—she got something up her sleeve. She sittin' in her office with Irene, going over the books. You ain't been working on the side have you?" She giggled, as was her custom. "Anyhow, Miss Della says for me to tell you that you should come right away—so that's what I told you!" She giggled once more.

"Come in, Serina." Della looked the proper business lady, carefully groomed and pleasant, but with a hard core of purpose evident in her manner. She sat behind the polished surface of her mahogany desk, spinning a letter opener with an ivory handle. "Do sit down, my dear, and join me in a cup of coffee." She poured from a porcelain pot, insulated with a white towel, and passed the steaming cup to Serina. She lifted her own cup and drank slowly, her eyes never leaving Serina's face. "Do you remember my once saying that there is always a time of reckoning?"

"It's not likely that I'd forget—given the circumstances—"

"Now let's not be bitter, dear. I wanted to inform you that you need no longer be bound to the arrangement we made."

Serina was taken aback by the words. She looked at Della, wondering if some hidden agenda was masked by the friendly demeanor.

"What I mean is—I have invested in you and your future, and the sum is now well over twelve hundred dollars."

"I had no idea. I know that I owe for Tim's loan of four hundred dollars... but..."

"But that is less than half of the monies I have expended for clothes, tutor, and rental fees that were never paid."

"But I told you that I couldn't afford those expensive clothes!"

"And I told you that you could pay for them later—and now that time has come."

"But how... what... I don't have that much money!" Serina became agitated, and Della hurried to calm her.

"Now, now, my dear. No need to be upset. I want you to think carefully about a proposition that I have for you. I say think carefully, because I'm not making this decision for you. I have strong feelings about it but I'll reserve those—"

She broke off as Irene knocked at the door, and motioned for the hostess to come in.

"Did you bring the ledger?"

"Yes, Miss Della, the accounting is up to date."

Della opened the book and flipped pages until she came to one titled *Serina Malloy*. She placed the opened ledger on the table and leaned back in her chair. "You have made a very strong impression on one of our gentlemen—I'm sure I don't have to tell you that Mr. Hogg has become quite attached—shall we say—to your company."

"He is no gentleman!"

"Perhaps not—but that's not the point of discussion."

"Then what are you—"

"Be patient, my dear, I'm getting to it. The fact is—Mr. Hogg would like to take care of your indebtedness—pay off your entire debt. It seems he is leaving the city for Boston very soon. Do you know where Boston is, my dear?"

"No, ma'am."

"I thought not. Suffice to say, it is a very long way from here. Mr. Hogg wants to pay your debt and then he wants you to accompany him to Boston."

"I don't understand..."

"Who understands men, my dear? He is—infatuated with you. You seem to fulfill a need..."

"But I detest him!"

"Then you may find it easy to make a decision. The fact is, you can remain here and pay your debt. You can continue to have maid service, free lodging, and medical care for you and your child..."

The mention of her daughter brought immediate concern over Serina's face. She had planned from the beginning to find a way out—to never reveal this secret life to Peggy, and now it seemed an opportunity was placed before her. But what a choice! The time of reckoning had indeed come. There was a steep price either way—but she decided in favor of the daughter's interest. "I'll go with Mr. Hogg," she said.

Della and Irene exchanged glances and Della shook her head in resignation. "I personally think you're making a mistake—but I said I'd reserve my opinion until you decided. In any case, Irene has balanced your account. Mr. Hogg will be responsible for the balance of your debt, and you will be gratified to know that you'll have a little nest egg to carry with you." She reached in her desk drawer and withdrew a small cloth bag and shoved it across the desk.

"I don't understand…"

"There you go again… what's to understand? I'm giving you a bag with money inside; a reserve account if you wish, to buy yourself some independence from men."

Della sighed, as if she were admonishing a child. "You may even find a way to free yourself from the clutches of Alonzo Hogg! Take stock of your assets, girl. You're not without them, you know. You couldn't read—much less write—when we first met. You've learned the manners of a society woman and you've got the clothes to match."

She smiled now, a genuine fondness for Serina evident in her outstretched hand. "I do wish you the best."

Serina, caught off-guard at the display of affection, mumbled a hurried "Thank you," and Della nodded in acknowledgement. Quite without meaning, tears gathered in her eyes and she quickly left the room

Della walked to the window and looked out upon the gathering dusk. Fog was rolling in from the bay and she felt a chill in the room. She turned to Irene, who still waited by the desk. "Please have Phoebe light the fire in here and have her bring my special brandy."

"Yes, Miss Della—would there be anything else?"

"No—that's all for now."

She went back to the window when Irene left the room. Her thoughts were far away. She didn't look up when the black maid lit the kindling under the fireplace logs, but she was waiting when the brandy came and she nodded to the maid to place it on the desk.

The liqueur had a greenish color. The French naval officer who had first presented it to her had pronounced it "ab-sant," and she had become increasingly fond of it, not knowing the wormwood and anise flavoring was endangering her nervous system.

She longed now for its numbing qualities. She had reached the point in life when there were no goals left. She had all the creature comforts that money could buy. She had her independence—and that was the greatest achievement.

She lived at her rooming house in order to be away from the babble and complaints, the minor bickerings of the communal society that she headed. The girl, Serina, had special qualities and Della knew she would miss her, just as she had missed others before her. She leaned back in her chair and sipped the green liqueur.

Once, she had been Odell McCullough, one of thirteen children sired by a farmer near St. Louis, Missouri. She was the eldest daughter, and she was kept busy as a nursemaid to the younger ones, and every year there seemed to be another.

She lay in her bed in the small, cramped dwelling and dreamed of a home with draperies and drawing room and servants, such as she read about in books lent her by the schoolmistress. She dreamed of this while she listened to the grunts and squeals of the drunken father, busy about the job of creating still another child for her mother to bear.

"A man is ruled by his passions," the mother explained. "You look for what makes a man tick, and it's right there between his legs. That's all he thinks about—all he cares about, it seems." She folded her thin hands over her swollen belly and spat a stream of snuff-stained saliva at the can by the hearth.

And one night, when she was in her teens, she awakened to the smell of the old man's whiskey breath by her pillow and a meaty hand groping under her blanket for the most private part of her, and she screamed in fear and rage and heard him curse as he kicked at the bedstead and stalked away into the night.

She ran away then—that next day. Just walked aboard a Mississippi steamer and told the First Officer that she wanted to work aboard the vessel. They gave her a job cleaning staterooms, and for the first time in her life, there were no crying babies for her to feed and change.

Della sipped the absinthe and thought about the years on the riverboat. She thought about her first paying customer, a clergyman, who asked her to clean his cabin. He feigned an attack of nausea, asking her to bathe his forehead with the damp cloth from his basin. Then, when she had done as he requested, he had suddenly grabbed her and pulled her down on the bed with him.

She finally slipped free of him, but threatened to tell the Captain of the incident. The preacher rewarded her with an astounding sum to hold her peace.

Della learned that men would pay for their sexual gratification. They would pay up front, or they would pay through extortion, but either way they would pay. The young girl discovered she possessed a valuable commodity in her shapely young body.

She opened her house in Mobile with the proceeds of several years' wages on the riverboats. Some of her former shipmates became regular customers when the boats came back to port, and word got around of the quality enterprise that she ran under the name of Della Devine.

More than anything, Della wanted the house to be grand and spacious, with draperies and staircases and wall sconces and tapestries and warmth and comfort. She had obtained all these things, just as she had dreams of doing back in the drafty, unpainted room of the farmhouse in Missouri.

Poor Mama, she thought, *spending all the good years of your life with a drunken lout of a husband and getting nothing for it but another mouth to feed and a curse for a greeting. I wish you could have done it my way, Mama. I wish you could have learned to avoid the babies and collect something for the use of your body. I suppose you would have taken me to task. You would think me a slut or worse—instead of blaming the men who helped create my environment. Well Mama, I did it my way—and believe me, it was one hell of a lot better.*

She closed her eyes, drifting on the numbing currents of the brandy, savoring its aromatic, bittersweet warmth. She no longer cared about sexual relationships with men. She knew now, late in her life, that real love for another human being could only be realized with a member of her own sex. She pulled the bell cord by her desk, and Phoebe emerged from the shadows of the hallway, barely discernible in the gloom. "Would you ask Irene to come in please?"

Irene entered silently, closing the door softly behind her. She walked over to the desk and smiled down at her employer, without the formality normally extended. She had felt that Della would be calling for her, and she was relieved that the woman, Serina, was out of the picture. She didn't know for sure, but she suspected that Della might have had more than a casual interest in the girl.

"Will you be staying over this evening, sweet Della?"

Della looked up into her eyes, the brandy softening her features, and a warm, mischievous smile spread across her face. "Would you like me to, my dear?"

"I would like it very much," Irene answered, bending over the chair and lightly brushing her lips across Della's cheek.

Della responded to Irene's long, sensuous, kneading fingers, so much nicer than the coarse and toughened hands of some horny male customer.

"I'm glad she's leaving," Irene whispered.

"What do you mean?"

"I was afraid you..."

"Oh don't be silly, Irene!"

Chapter Twelve

1845

The song of the cicada was harsh on the land, dry and brittle as the burrs on the cotton plants. The hooves of Thomas' mare kicked up little spurts of powdery dust as he rode through the ripened fields. The land lay dry in the heat and no threat of rain disturbed the blazing canopy of sky. The cotton hung from the bolls in loops of snowy lint, awaiting the nimble fingers of the pickers.

Thomas brought the mare to a halt at the crest of the tree line and looked pridefully down at the rich bottomlands along the banks of the Sipsey. When he had first viewed the river, the current had run swiftly from north to south from its origin at Nine Mile Creek. It had cut a deep channel, fifty to one hundred feet in width, on its way to the juncture with the Tombigbee River, a hundred miles downstream. Its sloping banks were covered with red oak, sweet gum, and poplar, and evergreens of cedar and pine.

The farms along the waterway had slowed its current and flattened its channel. The rains had come and flooded the fields, lifting freshly plowed topsoil and floating it down into the river. Thomas' belief in contour plowing and terracing, and the idea of crop rotation, had saved the Barkley land from much of the destruction. His view of the river was made through selected cuttings rather than a wholesale clearing of vegetation.

His gaze swung to the road and the large, white house situated on the rise above it, commanding a view of the road, the fields, and the river. The house was built like a fortress, the sills hand-hewn from eight-by-ten timbers. The window framing was made from cypress and the walls and ceilings of heart pine. Strong oak floors, planed and rubbed, were designed to outlast the occupants. The huge, oaken columns that supported the covered porches were circled with jasmine and wisteria. The large magnolias shaded the grounds and graveled walkways. The whitewashed exterior had faded, and Thomas reminded himself that there would be time for matters of maintenance when the harvest was in.

He had wrested the plantation from the wilderness, beginning with the 450 acres that constituted the original homestead. Now he owned over three thousand acres of fertile field and pastureland. And it was cotton, in the fields stretched before him, which had brought his dream to reality. It all came back to him as he sat with the sunlight streaming over the whiteness of the long rows. "You would have come to love it, Sarah," he spoke aloud. "You would have come to love it." He said it again but the sound of it came hollow and far away.

He watched the pickers straighten in the rows as the water boys held up long-handled gourds filled with fresh water from large, wooden buckets. Many of the pickers dribbled small quantities of water over their shirts or poured the balance in their gourds into the crowns of their hats. Their respite was short lived. The lead man whistled a signal to return to work and the rhythmic motion of picking began, only now it was carried on a musical chant. The bodies weaved to the sound and the fingers flew over the bolls in a delicate, cautious progress.

Thomas nudged the mare, letting the reins go slack, letting her choose her way to the river as she was accustomed. He heard the noise of laughter coming from the river and caught sight of William and Jonas, taking a break from their work. They were swimming in the current, racing each other for the sandy beach where the river made its big "S" curve. He watched as William allowed Jonas to pass him, yelling in mock fury as Jonas laughed with delight. He watched, and then moved silently away without intruding, sensing that nourishment of the spirit was in progress here. Somehow he felt lost in his own creation.

He had attempted to bury his grief over Sarah's passing beneath the layers of dust from the cotton fields about him. He had driven himself relentlessly, welcoming the fatigue that allowed him to drop off into sleep during the lonely nights. And God help him, he couldn't love the child, Katherine, as he knew he should. Her coming had signaled Sarah's departure, and he didn't feel it a fair exchange. He knew he was wrong, that God would not approve of him, but God did not appear to favor him very much, anyway.

The child was, in all fairness, a bright and chirpy little bird in an often somber cage. She was old enough now to eat from the table, and of course, Elizabeth and Dicey took care of her every need. She didn't need him anyway, he thought. Better that he devote himself to the plantation and the child's future. So saying, he could sleep; but the mornings came again, and in his pride for things accomplished, he mourned the fact that Sarah would never see the result of his labors.

A swirl of dust along the roadway announced a rider, and as Thomas was not expecting anyone, he waited with interest as the visitor drew near. Then he recognized young Drew Hall, from the neighboring plantation. The young man closely resembled his father, Nathan Hall, having the same freckled face and ready smile. He pulled up beside Thomas and swept his arm outward. "Ain't that a pretty sight, Mr. Barkley?"

Thomas nodded his head, watching the pickers moving down the rows, cleaning twenty rows at a time in an uneven progression to the scales. "This is the best year we've had, Drew. I think this is what old Major Coe had in mind when he drew up that wagon train from South Carolina."

"I think it's what my pa had in mind also—maybe he didn't know it would take so much hard work to get here."

"Probably not—I doubt that any of us figured the cost might be so high..." He broke off, recognizing they were thinking in different terms. He turned again to the young man. "What brings you to see me?"

"Well, sir, actually it's my Pa's idea—but I thought I'd mention it to you and see what you think..."

"Your pa's judgment is as good as mine," Thomas said.

"Oh yes, sir—I go along with Pa's thinking, but he was a little embarrassed to bring it up, seeing as how we're related to the folks in Mobile."

"I don't follow you, Drew."

"Well, it seems that Captain Sam Woodley..."

"You're related to Sam Woodley?"

"Oh no, sir! We're related to Hall & Sons..."

"Well, where's Sam Woodley fit in?"

"Cap'n Woodley, he thinks that we should ship our cotton direct to Mobile on his *Sipsey Queen*, and my uncle, Horace Hall..."

"The brokerage firm in Mobile?"

"That's the one. Uncle says if we ship on the *Queen* and we commit the entire cargo to Hall and Sons, we should be able to gain an extra 3 cents per pound on our cotton crop this year."

Thomas studied the young man before him, seeing the sincerity evident there. "This is pretty interesting—but where's the guarantee? I think we'd want something from Hall..."

Drew nodded his agreement. "Hall told my pa in a letter, he'd guarantee 2 cents over market price, if the entire cargo is handled through his firm. I think he has backed Woodley's riverboat company, and so the connection is pretty tight. Woodley is guaranteeing 1 cent per pound savings on the shipping cost."

"Three cents gain on the deal?"

"Yes, sir... the Captain says he'll guarantee it."

Thomas whistled slowly through his teeth. "I'd take the deal in a minute if I could bet on old Woodley getting down the Sipsey."

"What do you mean, Mr. Barkley?"

"Well, we've always dealt with Coker Brothers over in Tuscaloosa. They ship down the Black Warrior River and it seems a bit more reliable. The Sipsey's changed, son. It ain't the same as we navigated a decade ago. The bottom's treacherous now and sand bars shift from one season to the next."

"Well, Pa says Cap'n Woodley knows the Sipsey better'n any man alive."

"I expect your pa's right on that, too," Thomas said. "You hustle on now and tell your pa we made a deal."

The young man wheeled his mount and gave a jubilant wave of the hand as he headed back to the Hall plantation.

Thomas turned back to the pickers. They came down the rows, their long sacks trailing out behind them on the ground. Some dropped to their knees and crawled between the rows with scarred fingers still flying over the thorny burrs. Some wore pads of stained cloth about their knees for protection against the rocks in the hot, sandy soil.

The workers had done their part to bring this crop to harvest. It was now up to him to make the right market decisions, to make all the hard work, all the sacrifices worth something. And as always, he weighed the year's progress against the record years he had experienced at Barkley Hall.

Chapter Thirteen

A visit to Coe's cotton gin prior to the departure of Commodore Woodley's *Sipsey Queen* made a sudden change in the lives of the black and white residents on the Barkley Plantation. It happened purely by chance, or so it seemed. Thomas Barkley and Robert Coe were the only occupants of the office at the time the stranger walked inside the open door. Robert Coe nodded and the man introduced himself.

"Name's Smith," he stated, "John Smith, and I reckon that's a pretty common name hereabouts from what I hear. Myself, I come from over in South Carolina."

Thomas immediately looked up and the man nodded in his direction. "What part of South Carolina?" Thomas asked.

"Around Kingstree," the stranger replied. He reached inside a shirt pocket and handed Coe a sheet of paper. The handwriting was poor but Robert Coe could make out the words:

"You will find the man, John Smith, to be a likely person for driver of slaves. The amount of work produced during his employment with me was entirely satisfactory." It was signed by one Charles McEachern, owner, Timberland Plantation.

Coe looked at Thomas and handed the note over. A thought came into Thomas' mind and he looked keenly at the man. "And why did you leave this employer?" he asked.

"Mayhap for reasons not related to my working habits," the stranger answered pleasantly.

Thomas nodded and handed the note back across. He didn't address the man directly but looked at Robert Coe. "You know, Robert, if I was convinced I could find a reliable man for overseer, I might consider going along on the *Sipsey Queen* and handle the details myself."

The man, John Smith, was immediately ingratiating. "I didn't mean to give you no short answer, mister, regarding my leaving South Carolina. I had a falling out with my folks over there, and that's the simple truth. A family

70

squabble ain't to my liking and I just decided to leave. Believe me, mister, it ain't got nothing to do with my work habits, and ye'd have no need to worry. I know how to handle the job of overseer."

Perhaps Thomas wanted to believe him because he very much wanted to talk with the broker in Mobile on a face-to-face basis. In any case, he introduced himself and gave explicit directions to the plantation and a list of projects that would come under Smith's supervision.

William and Jonas rode in the lead wagon with Jonas' father driving the team. William felt possessed of a new sense of responsibility. He was, in fact, the ranking male figure on the plantation now that his father would be away— if one could overlook that new man, John Smith.

Newton's Landing was alive with sights and sounds of urgent activity. There were shouted instructions from the dock master and return shouts from the deck hands on the steamer.

Captain Sam Woodley, often referred to as the "Commodore" by the raffish river men, was supervising the loading of cotton bales to his vessel, the *Sipsey Queen.*

There was much cargo to load. Thomas' baled cotton was already stacked on the loading docks, but there were many bales ahead of his in the loading process. The cotton seed that had been removed from the lint would be loaded into the wagons and returned to the plantation. The baled cotton offered a vast improvement over the old method of stuffing the processed lint into huge cloth bags that rapidly filled all cargo space but accounted for light and unprofitable trips.

Before Sam Woodley's pioneering efforts at steamship navigation, the plantation owners had constructed barges and let the power of the current take the cotton south to the port city of Mobile. Having arrived, they would unload the cotton and break up the barges, selling the timber to the lumberyards. They made their way back home by stagecoach. Such trips were long and uncertain, and many a boatman lost his craft, if not his life, to the swirling, capricious current.

William and Jonas sat on the wagon tongue and watched the steam-powered jenny swing its boom from dock to boat. Each swing of the boom added another ten bales from its sling to the deck of the *Sipsey Queen.*

The boom operator was a wizened riverboat man, one eye missing from one of his several brawls. A long scar ran the length of his face to his neck where a bowie knife had laid it open. "Squint" Harper was a lowlife, drunken, riverboat bum, but his experience was in demand, and he worked with a will when his whiskey supply ran short.

On this particular morning, he had not fully sobered from the effects of a night's drinking and didn't notice that the sling line was parting near the hook. As the boom made its slow arc over the vessel, the sling let go and ten bales dropped like rocks onto the stacked cargo on the deck. The vessel rocked from side to side, and the towering cargo began to shift. Suddenly, bales were falling over the side amid the screams and curses of the deck crew as they scrambled to get out of the way.

Captain Sam Woodley surveyed the bobbing bales of cotton as they submerged and resurfaced on the water. In a cold fury he walked toward the careless boom operator. With one swift motion, he snatched him from the cab of the jenny and flung him to the ground, ripping his dirty shirt from his back in the process. When the man attempted to rise, the Captain gave him a swift kick in his rib cage and the man doubled over in pain, slobbering curses in his fluent and original style.

The job of retrieving the bales before they could reach the channel now required the attention of all hands. They would have to be returned to the gin for processing and drying, and the loss of the cargo was a loss to the Captain as well. Fortunately, Thomas' cargo was yet to be loaded.

At last it was finished and the tarps were tied in place over the cargo. The *Sipsey Queen* blasted the air with her steam whistle, and the pine pitch fuel blackened the sky and the passengers as well with thick smoke that smelled of turpentine.

William and Jonas waved to Thomas until the boat rounded the bend of the river. "One day I'm going to make that trip downriver, Jonas—all the way to the Gulf of Mexico."

"I guess you gon take me witchu, hunh Will?"

"'Course I will, Jonas, 'course I will."

The boys watched until even the smoke from the engine had disappeared, and then Jonas' father called them back to the wagon for the ride home.

Later in the day, Squint Harper came into Coe's Dry Goods store and obtained supplies for a trip downriver. He launched a canoe from the riverbank and paddled out into the channel. A full moon rose over the treetops and soon the shadow of the man and the boat fell across the water. He paddled with a slow, even cadence that measured each foot of the waterway. He was in no hurry.

Chapter Fourteen

The overseer, John Smith, took charge of the Barkley slaves in a no-nonsense manner. His first day on the job, following Thomas' departure to Mobile, was a portent of things to come.

He summoned the lead man and instructed him to have the entire body of field hands report to the barns immediately. He strode up and down before them, brandishing the ox whip that Thomas had never used, except as a motivation for the teams, and then only popping the tail above their backs to encourage a forward movement.

"Now I don't know about your work habits under Mr. Barkley's direction, but I can tell you that Mr. Barkley ain't here—and while he's gone, you're going to work the way I tell you—and I don't mind using this whip if I see you lagging about."

There was a muttering sound, and then the whip cut through the air and popped over their heads. "I also don't allow no backtalk from nobody, and the first one that tries it will learn a good lesson."

He gestured toward the woodpile at the side of the kitchen. "What I want from you in the next few days—is a stack of firewood that reaches right up to the roof of that kitchen. Now I know you want to keep warm this winter, and the only way to do that is to provide enough wood to keep them fireplaces going, night and day."

He looked over the group and swung around toward the big house. He saw William and Jonas standing on the rise in the background and yelled to William, "Send that little, skinny-ass nigger on down here with the rest."

Anger began to burn in William and his face flushed under the tan. Never in his experience had his father addressed their servants in this manner. William was not accustomed to defending himself or his playmate, but he intended to make the best of it.

"This here boy's name is Jonas," he called. "He ain't no little, skinny-assed nigger... and he ain't coming down there."

John Smith's face darkened, and he started up the hill in their direction.

"Don't you be coming up here, Mr. Smith. This boy belongs to me." This was an overstatement, but the only defense he could muster on short notice.

Smith paused, glowering, and then pointed to Jonas with the butt end of the whip.

"Well—you just keep yore nigger out of my sight because he ain't going to stand around shirking his duty in my presence." With that, he popped the whip once more and the crews set out for the woods.

The crosscut saws left mounds of sawdust piled on either side of the great tree trunks, and the leaves trembled as the teeth bit into their lifelines. Two men worked at each tree, backs bent over the saw handles, swaying in unison with the direction of the saw. Some of the smaller logs were cut into fence rails, and the balance went in shorter lengths for the fireplaces that heated the cabins and the big house.

William and Jonas watched as the two men nearest them cut into a large oak tree, stopping periodically to look upward at the top. Their saw had almost reached the notched section that would direct the line of fall.

John Smith strode into the clearing, oblivious to the boys and observing the slaves craning their necks upward, and shouted at them, "Get back to work and stop this lollygagging."

The men were still cautious, and they stopped the saw once more to gaze at the tree's inclination. The overseer was incensed at what he deemed to be an obvious flouting of his instructions and he popped his whip across the back of the nearest man. The startled black's eyes widened in shock and pain and he jerked the saw handle through the cut, pulling the other man into the trunk of the tree just as the top started to tremble.

The tree leaned momentarily in the direction of the notch, but then a strong gust of wind caught the uppermost branches, and the trunk broke loose from its stump, twisting and turning on its way to the ground.

The poor slave against the tree trunk had no chance to escape. He stared in horror as the base of the tree came crashing down upon him, driving him into the soft earth of the forest floor while the huge length of the trunk crashed through boughs and vines, breaking and taking the life from everything it touched.

The men stood with mouths agape, the forest silent now. The overseer cracked his whip and set the slaves in motion, cutting away the trunk from the man's body. They worked furiously at the task, driven by the rage they felt toward the overseer who had most likely cost the man his life. The overseer ordered the man's body placed in one of the empty wagons.

William walked across the broken limbs and ragged earth to follow the slaves carrying the body. The boy was almost equal to the overseer in height, but his slender frame was half the size. He made up for that by the cold steel in his purposeful stare. "Get off our land," he said softly.

"What do you mean, boy?" the overseer was astonished.

"Just what I said... get off our land."

"Why boy, you ain't got no right to be telling me what to do. Yore pa hired me to do a job and by God, I'll do it!"

William climbed aboard the wagon carrying the body. He motioned for Jonas to join him and picked up the reins without further comment. He had never been in a confrontation with an adult before, and the experience left him shaken, but determined. "You'll regret this day—Mister John Smith." He slapped the reins and the wagon moved forward.

"Oh, sweet Jesus God!"

The man's wife viewed the mangled body stretched out in the wagon bed. Her friends knelt about her as she fell to the earth and continued to beseech the Almighty. "Lawd God, what I gon do now?"

"We got to get him ready, Sue." Old Dicey put her arms around the widow. "We got to give him a good send-off to the place where he spends eternity."

The women helped to remove the bloodstained clothing and wash the man's body. "He were so manly... all the time I knowed him... and that old tree trunk done took him all away," the widow mourned.

William and Jonas helped old George build a plank coffin. George sawed the boards and William and Jonas were allowed to help with planing them. The old man then constructed them to form the tapered ends of the box and nailed them fast. He filled a large cotton sack with scrap lint and used it to cushion the inside.

Elizabeth felt the need to help in the awful time. She prepared a wreath of chrysanthemums and geraniums to lie on top of the casket. She also found one of Thomas' suits from the Carolina days and gave it to the widow for his burial dress.

The widow's eyes brimmed with tears. She grabbed the girl's arm and pressed it to her face. "He gon be so proud, Missy. Thank you... he gon look so good, nobody up there gon know he ever been a slave!"

"Where would you like to bury him?"

The widow wiped at her eyes, surprised to have a white person ask her what she would like. "Missy, my man… he always like the smell of that apple orchard when the blossoms come out in spring—and the good Lawd know he like to eat them apples when it come fall. If'n you don't mind—ma'am—I would like to see Joseph laid to rest on that high ground next to the apple orchard."

"Let me talk to William about it," Elizabeth said. She carried her wreath of flowers out to the woodshed where the boys and old George were putting the finishing touches to the casket. "Do you think Pa would object to burying Joseph above the orchard?"

"I don't know—that's kind of strange—burying someone in an orchard—"

"Not in the orchard, William. His wife would like to put him on that rise just above the orchard—but close enough to know he can smell the apples—in case God allows people do that when they die."

"I don't think he'd mind," William said. "It's just something we never talked about—but I know Pa would want us to do the right thing by him." And so the workers came up in the darkness, after the day's work, and they dug the grave deeply into the high ground by the light of pine knots stuck into the earth.

William took it upon himself to read from the Bible. He opened the book at the marker left in place by Sarah. It happened to be the Book of Ruth and actually had little to do with the business at hand, but he read it aloud, anyway. Having reached the sixth verse of the tenth chapter, and having heard the approving sounds from the slaves, he continued on to the end. By that time it was getting late. He closed the Bible and Elizabeth sang two choruses of *Take Up Thy Cross.*

William decided the affair had been handled responsibly. He avoided any further contact with the overseer, and it appeared to him that John Smith wanted it that way. He continued to direct the woodcutting, but for the most part kept to himself.

Some three weeks later, William took the bird dogs for a run. The day was sunny and he had spotted a covey of quail in the corner of the peanut field. The dogs were excited over the opportunity to exercise, and the spotted pointer found the covey almost immediately. They were near the edge of the field and close to a thicket of pine saplings. The dog held her point, waiting for William to catch up to her and flush the covey.

William approached the dog, and as he did so, a sharp sound of a whip cut the air. A terrified scream of pain sent him running in the direction of the thicket. He was appalled at the sight of poor Jonas tied to one of the pine saplings, his shirt torn off, and a thin, red line seeping across his dark back.

The overseer, John Smith, was in the act of delivering another blow when William rushed wildly through the undergrowth and plowed into his midsection with such force the man was knocked flat of his back.

"What in the hell do you think you're doin', you goddamned little whippersnapper?"

John Smith held up the butt of the whip as William lunged for him again and the hard handle opened a cut over his eye. William ignored the injury and flailed away at the man's face until the overseer had enough of him.

"You run at me again, you little bastard, and I'll open you with this!" He flipped a button on his knife and the long blade swung out with a click, the sun catching the wicked edge of it as Smith struggled to his feet. "You can all go to hell, all you damned Barkleys and your miserable, damned insolent black savages. Lucky I don't carve you up a bit as a parting gesture!"

William's face was ashen and his voice shook. "You touch me or any of our people again and I swear I'll kill you, so help me God!"

"I reckon you would at that, if you could sneak up on me to do it." The overseer brushed the pine needles off his shoulders and shook his finger in the boy's face. "I'll be back to collect my pay when your pa gets home, and I'll have a word or two for him in the bargain!"

"He'll have a word or two for you, Mr. John Smith," William replied. "I'd just send for the money, if I was you."

"Well you ain't—and I ain't skeered of your pa or any of you goddamned crazy Barkleys." He grabbed up his felt hat and stalked out of the thicket.

William untied the unfortunate Jonas with shaking fingers, and the boy blubbered his indignation.

"He… he was tryin to force hisself on Roscoe's daughter!"

"But how did you…"

"I seen him come slippin along behine her ez she wuz gathering pine straw to put in a hen house. Then, I hear her hollerin—and I jes run down and peeked through the bushes. He had her flat on the ground with his knees between her legs. His britches wuz open in front, and it wuz plain whut he have in mind.

"Well, I let out a screech lak a wildcat and he jump up an Miss Ceely, she jump up and run. Then that old overseer, he knock me upside the head with the butt uv that whip." Remembering, Jonas suddenly grinned and grabbed William's arm. "You shoulda seen that overseer's old dick shrivel up when I let out my wildcat screech."

He savored the moment and continued. "The next thing I know, I come to my senses an he have me tied up and say he gon teach me a lesson I won't never forget!"

William looked up the path the overseer had taken from the thicket. He brushed his own clothing free of pine straw and considered the likely consequences. "I think my pa will be teaching a lesson to Mr. Smith."

Jonas brightened at the thought. "I spec he will all right. Marsa Thomas, he gone kill him I guess, an that be a lesson HE won't forget!" The thought of it eased his discomfort, and he grinned as he gingerly placed the shirt back over his shoulders.

Chapter Fifteen

The voyage downriver was uneventful for the *Sipsey Queen* until they reached the little port town of Nanafalia, just below Demopolis. Recent rains had swollen the river at this point and undercut the banks, so that a large fallen tree had slipped into the river channel. The trunk was afloat, but just below the surface of the water. It was burdened down by the weight of its outstretched limbs.

The paddle wheel of the *Sipsey Queen* caught one of the limbs before the Captain could signal the engine room. There was a wrenching sound as one of the buckets was torn from its mount and the big wheel took on an awkward revolution.

"Damn it all to hell, anyway!" Captain Woodley berated the lookout in the bow and each man in the crew individually, before acknowledging they could not continue on to Mobile until repairs were accomplished. The passengers amused themselves with card games in the small salon or with walks along the riverbank until the crew repaired the bucket and secured it to its mount.

When the *Sipsey Queen* docked in Mobile, Thomas Barkley was immediately down the ramp. Everywhere he looked, the city of Mobile was a city of cotton. Cotton was stacked in bales on the wharves. It was piled as high as the ceiling in the warehouses along the quay, and the streets were full of wagons loaded with cotton.

Thomas made his way to the offices of Horace Hall, cotton factor. He was the relative that Drew Hall had mentioned, and Thomas had met him at the Hall plantation some years back. The cotton factor basically handled all the financial matters related to the marketing of cotton. He paid for river transport, the bill of lading, weighing, wharfage, river and fire insurance. He then calculated the factor's commission of 2.5% of the gross sales.

Factoring cotton had made Horace Hall a wealthy man. He was also a generous man, and clients found him willing to extend loans against the next year's crop. Many of them kept a running account, and the interest on these loans added to the coffers of the factor.

A male secretary ushered Thomas into a private reception room, tastefully done in dark oak paneling, polished brass lamps, and leather-covered chairs.

Horace Hall strode into the room at once, a well-tailored figure in gray wool trousers and checkered waistcoat. Large side whiskers adorned his lower jaw line and accentuated the baldness of his head. He extended a hand to Thomas and pumped vigorously. "Thomas Barkley? I'm Horace Hall, and delighted I am to see you again, sir!" He indicated a chair opposite the hand-carved, mahogany coffee table and waited for Thomas to be seated. "My brother's family has informed me of the untimely death of your wife. Please allow me to offer my condolences." Thomas nodded, and the cotton broker shifted to the matters of the day. "I understand that you've brought us a good crop—something over two hundred bales?"

"Two hundred and twenty-two bales to be exact."

"Well now, it's fertile soil you must enjoy in Fayette County!" He pursed his lips and nodded thoughtfully. "Yes, I'd say we're looking at ten thousand dollars—assuming all the bales are of standard weight." He brushed cigar ash from his bountiful midsection and turned a sober face toward his client.

"You are getting ten cents per pound for your cotton—at a time when it seems unlikely the market will go that high again—at least not in the foreseeable future."

"I believe the offer of ten cents per pound came from you, Mr. Hall."

"Ah, so it did, my good sir—but do call me Horace."

"Very well—but why is the market declining?"

"Production is just higher than demand. The European warehouses are getting filled up, and the northern mills are overstocked at this particular time."

Thomas studied the man across the table. "You may not see such large production a few years hence."

Horace lifted his glasses and peered at Thomas beneath the lower rims. "What did you say?"

"I say that cotton production is threatened if the planters continue to abuse the land unchecked. The problem is well apparent in Fayette County already. Many of the farmers are planting the same crop of cotton year after year until the fertility is sucked out of the soil, and then they simply pick up and move on to new grounds.

"I'm not a mover, Horace. I want to stay put, and I have invested profits from each year in additional acreage. One reason is—I want to have enough land so that the soil can rest between plantings. I want to plant different crops and rotate them—so that the fertility is replenished."

The factor removed his eyeglasses from their perch on the end of his rather florid nose. "Won't this reduce your cotton output... planting other crops where cotton should be?"

"The question, Horace, is whether to manage production with selected planting or wear the soil out for a paltry production."

"I follow your thinking, I believe, but I had no idea such results were already present in Fayette County."

Thomas reached into his coat pocket and pulled some papers. He laid a sheet on the table. "This is a survey map of some land adjoining my holdings. It is available at a price I consider to be fair, but at the same time, the purchase would run me close-hauled in cash."

"Appears to be a sizable tract."

"That it is. The land is suitable for corn or wheat or peas..."

Horace placed the eyeglasses back on his nose. "And this is going to help your old cotton factor?"

"Well, in the long view... the answer is yes. Cotton uses up the nutrients in the soil, but if the land can have a season of rest, if there is enough acreage to allow other crops to replenish the soil, then cotton production is assured."

"I'm afraid your ideas are new to me..."

Thomas folded the papers and placed them back in his pocket. He got up from the chair, and Horace made a protesting motion of his hand.

"No need to rush off now..."

"You are a busy man, Horace. I don't expect you to advance cash for a project you don't agree to be right."

Horace turned and smiled. "Go ahead then... just draw on us through the United States Bank of Mobile for such sums as you need."

Thomas shook his head and moved as if to leave. "The Barkleys don't accept charity."

"Now hold on, Thomas. H.G. Hall and Sons is not a charitable organization. We'll get our percentage, of course, but you are welcome to use our credit as you see fit."

Thomas smiled also and extended his hand. "It would amount to at least a thousand dollars, not counting the available proceeds from this year's crop."

"Done and done." The factor pumped Thomas's hand vigorously once again. "Come back to see us, Thomas, and tell my relatives to do so as well."

"That I'll do, and I appreciate your help."

Thomas discovered that Mobile had long since recovered from its disastrous fire of 1827. Now, large brick buildings lined the main thoroughfare called Government Street, which was free of mud, thanks to the use of oyster shell paving. It was one of two cities in the state to install gas lighting on its streets and as the evening progressed, Thomas was drawn like a rural firefly to the lights along the waterfront. The lights and their muted reflections in the water invited the visitor to stroll along the quay.

Unfortunately, the lighting was more attractive than the smells along the waterfront, and Thomas began to retrace his steps to Government Street. It was there, under one of the lampposts, that he became an inadvertent witness to a domestic dispute. There was a lady who appeared to be a foreigner, and not surprising, as foreigners made up a fifth of the city's population. She had long, black hair that hung straight except for a jeweled clip that brought it together at the back of her neck. Her features were quite exotic in the light from the streetlamp, and her upturned face revealed distress and anger.

Thomas caught the words "not a slave," from the woman and, louder, "bought and paid for," from the man. As Thomas drew abreast of them, the man drew back his cane as if to strike the woman.

"Here now, sir," Thomas intervened. "Let's have none of that. We don't strike ladies with canes where I come from."

"And who the hell might you be?" the man growled. "The goddamned Governor?"

He caught the steely glint in Thomas' eyes, even through an alcoholic haze, and decided to play the buffoon. He laughed loudly and doffed his hat. "Just excuse us by all means, your Governorship, and pass on your way!"

Thomas stood his ground and the man yanked at the woman's arm and headed toward a sidewalk café—but not before she turned and gave a warm smile to Thomas. He felt a small flutter inside and quickly dismissed it, walking briskly the remainder of the business district and returning down the other side of the street.

He decided to stop by one of the taverns for a nightcap before going to the hotel. Loud and passionate rhetoric greeted him as he made his way to the bar. The speaker was condemning the activities of the northern abolitionists and their campaign against slavery.

"The Negro, while in slavery down in the South, fares a damn sight better than the Negro at liberty in the North. Let the Yankee stick to his own affairs or learn to live without the raw materials of our Southland!"

"Here, here!" rang a dozen voices. Later, Thomas overheard the words "manifest destiny," which meant that the Southern states should annex both Cuba and Mexico. This would give the South control of the Senate, which was now split at a fifty-fifty ratio of free and slave states.

Another voice proclaimed advantage for the South's secession from the Union. Thomas found the talk disturbing. His father and his grandfather had fought for the Union against the British foe. The thought of breaking that union was not at all appealing to him.

He spent the next few days shopping for items not readily available back home. Topping the list was a barrel of good Irish whiskey and a selection of imported wines. He made good use of the alcohol both socially and in medical preparations. Whiskey was available in Fayette County, but the drinker was likely to suffer a temporary loss of taste, as well as memory, after sampling some of the local stock.

He purchased various items of clothing for the family, some fine Turkish tobacco for himself, and a carton of books that he requested the shopkeeper to select for a young lady. He knew Elizabeth would be delighted with them. He picked out a hunting knife with ivory handle for William. He had no ideas about the baby's needs, but a finely carved rocking horse caught his eye, and he bought it on the spot.

Thomas was an orderly man. Every day of his life was dedicated to some purposeful endeavor. Any quirk of fate that interrupted his planned activities could upset him, and now that his shopping was complete, he was pleased to learn that the *Sipsey Queen* would embark the next day for Demopolis and points north. He had all his packages stamped with his name and stored in the purser's cabin.

Chapter Sixteen

Black smoke curled along the wharf as the crew of the *Sipsey Queen* built steam for the return trip upriver. There was no cargo other than mill supplies and bolts of cloth. There was however, a full passenger roster.

Thomas Barkley stood by the rail, watching the passengers as they prepared to board. There was some friendly jostling, and a large amount of vocalizing as a tipsy group reached the boarding ramp. He noticed one couple, a swarthy man and a lady of remarkable beauty that appeared familiar to him. A sudden shift of wind whipped her long, black hair across her face and she raised her head to brush it aside.

Now he knew it was the couple he had encountered the previous evening. The woman caught his gaze and smiled at him. The man, following her gaze, also looked at Thomas. He didn't smile, but reached for the woman's elbow and jerked her into the salon. Thomas concluded their relationship had not improved overnight.

The steamer was plying the waters of the Tombigbee River en route to Demopolis before he saw the couple again. The dining room was stuffy, and Thomas was making his way through the crowded area feeling somewhat relieved at having finished his meal, when he caught sight of the couple seated at a table directly ahead of him. The woman glanced his way and smiled in recognition. Her companion turned around and saw the smile, and his face flushed red with anger.

Just as Thomas started to pass the table, the man made a sudden motion of his foot so that Thomas tripped over it and barely recovered his balance in time to avoid an embarrassing fall. Thomas abruptly stepped in front of the man's table. "I'll thank you to stand, sir!" he said softly.

"I beg your pardon?" the man's face was mottled with his own anger.

"You'll beg some more if I have any say," Thomas retorted.

The man began to stand erect, and Thomas was on the point of asking him outside when he saw the small pistol emerging under the waistcoat. Thomas slammed into the man with his big right fist, catching him just under the jaw and raising him a good two inches from the chair before he came crashing down to the floor.

Thomas kicked the pistol from his hand and pinioned the arm behind his back, holding him until the Captain made his appearance. Passengers on either side of the aisle confirmed that the man was a troublemaker who threatened Thomas with a pistol. That was enough proof for Captain Woodley. He ordered the man carried away in chains to the brig. "I'll let ye go at Demopolis," he stated. "But ye're not to come aboard my vessel again under any pretext!"

The woman, who had been witness to all of the commotion, rose from her seat then and dropped her napkin on the table. She murmured, "Excuse me, please," and quickly walked to the outer deck. Thomas encountered her at the rail, standing alone and subdued, and he approached out of a sense of consideration for her. "I am very sorry, ma'am… that I was forced to strike your companion."

The lady twisted her handkerchief and made no reply.

"Well," Thomas tried again. "Like I said, I'm sorry if I offended you."

"Oh, sir! You didn't offend me at all. The man deserved what he got and more!"

The light from the ship's lamp fell on her uplifted face and Thomas was again aware of the foreign appearance. She could be from one of the Caribbean islands or from the low country in Louisiana, perhaps a mixture of French and Indian. The dusky glow of her complexion was accentuated by full, sensuous lips and slender nose, slightly flared at the nostrils. Her eyes were unbelievably dark and mysterious.

Thomas realized that he had taken more time than was necessary to make his apology, and suddenly feeling awkward, he excused himself and headed for his cabin. He was more than a little surprised at the turn of events. The lady had referred to her companion as "the man" and not as her husband. So what was the relationship? And more importantly, what difference should it make to him anyway?

Some of the passengers debarked for a visit when the steamer reached Demopolis, glad to have a look at the bustling cotton town and thankful for a reprieve from the smell of turpentine and choking clouds of pitch smoke.

One of them, Alonzo Hogg, was released from ship's arrest and ordered to take his personal effects off the vessel. "I'll be back for you directly," he informed Serina. "I'm booking transportation on another vessel."

He did, in fact, make such arrangements, by way of the Black Warrior

River to Tuscaloosa. But he had another purpose in mind. He bitterly resented the outcome of the encounter with Thomas Barkley. He also was furious with the Captain of the *Sipsey Queen*. His rage at being chained and ordered off the vessel was an insult that would not go unpunished. The Captain would be sorry if he had his way about it.

He went to a nearby saloon as his first order of business. The interior was crowded with river men, and in his already irritable mood, Alonzo Hogg pushed his way up to the bar and demanded a whiskey.

He had the misfortune to push the wrong sailor, however, and the man followed him to the bar. The man was reeling drunk and looking for a fight. He reached for Alonzo's shoulder and spun him about. "You pushed me!" he declared indignantly.

"So what if I did?" Hogg responded. "Get your filthy hand off my shoulder!"

"Filthy is it? Then how'd you like it in your mouth?" The drunk threw a punch toward Hogg's jaw, which was still very sore from the punch Thomas had given him. The two of them fell to the floor, gouging and biting, Hogg trying to get at his pistol and the sailor clawing for his knife.

There was a blast from a whistle and a Demopolis constable placed the two of them under arrest. Handcuffed and belligerent, Alonzo Hogg was once more incarcerated, this time in the city jail.

Captain Sam Woodley shifted the large cud of tobacco from left cheek to right and spat an amber stream of juice that arced high in the air over the dock rail. The wind caught it and blew it into tiny droplets that fell like rain on the assorted flotsam of pine bark and chaff surrounding the bow of the *Sipsey Queen*.

The Captain's mood was as drab as the dreary morning mists wreathing the port city of Demopolis. The lopsided rotation of the paddle wheel on the last ten miles to Demopolis had convinced him that the repairs made on the way downriver had not prevented damage to the shaft and seal. He was now looking at the prospect of sitting out two or more weeks for the wheel to be dismantled and repaired and the shaft straightened.

The Captain turned to the crew, cursing them for lapses in performing their duties and vowing to berth the old *Sipsey Queen* permanently when they completed the return voyage to Newton's Landing. Having completed that duty, the Captain left the mate in charge and went ashore. He went immediately to the nearest tavern.

He found warmth and comfort near the tavern fireplace, consuming one round after another of the dark Jamaican rum served up by a rather surly barmaid. He turned now to the woman and in a mellower mood addressed her. "Ye're as sour as last week's clabber milk, me girl!"

"And it's none of your business if I be sweet or sour," she replied.

"Now, no need to get riled at a good payin customer, who's only engaged ye in the art of conversation."

"Cap'n, you ain't engaged me to no art whatever."

Captain Woodley laid some of the new bills received from his cargo transport along the center of the table and the barmaid stared in sudden interest. He pointed to his glass for a refill and, as she filled it, the Captain groped under her skirt and pressed her against his leg.

"Cap'n, I do suggest you ease up a bit on the rum—jist so you don't run aground afore you git to yore destination."

"I'll git to me destination all right," he said and grabbed her in a tight embrace.

She pushed him away, but good-naturedly. "Not here, me hearty sailor. Meet me in a half-hour at the Jefferson." She kissed him lightly on the cheek and expertly scooped the bills from his grasp. She gave him a gentle push out of the door and he made his way in the early light at a somewhat irregular gait toward the Jefferson Hotel.

He almost made it. A shadowy figure slipped from a corner of the alley and stealthily approached the Captain from behind. The sun had not yet burned away the fog and the Captain was a bit bleary. He took no notice of the man who was rapidly closing the distance between them..

The knife penetrated his jacket just below the right shoulder blade and as the Captain turned, the assailant plunged it once more into his side. Captain Woodley doubled over and fell to the sidewalk.

"Squint" Harper had followed the *Sipsey Queen* on its journey downriver and had waited patiently in Demopolis for its return. His broken ribs had mended sufficiently to permit his revenge on the Captain. He wiped the knife clean on a trouser leg and sheathed it.

The Captain's inert body was discovered later in the morning by the hotel's delivery man and a runner was sent to the Sheriff. A deputy found Captain Woodley to be unconscious but still breathing, and had him taken to the Stillwell Infirmary.

Now the Sheriff began a roundup of the passengers from the *Sipsey Queen*. One of them said that the Captain had made an enemy of one male passenger by placing him in irons on the way upriver. The Sheriff learned that this same passenger was the man he had just placed in the city jail.

Hogg's reputation for meanness was known to men in the tavern, and having no other suspect in mind, the Sheriff concluded that Hogg was most likely the villain who had stuck a knife in the unfortunate Captain. He had probably then headed to the saloon to stir up trouble and form an alibi.

No amount of protest could rescue Hogg from suspicion of being the Captain's murderer. There were even darkly hinted conversations in the jail that such a man was suitable only for the hangman's rope.

The Sheriff didn't discourage the talk. "Yore best bet is to confess to the crime and I'll see that you get a fair trial," he advised.

"You can all go to hell," Hogg replied. "I didn't have anything to do with it, not that I wouldn't have enjoyed the chance. I've got the best alibi in town—I've been sitting right here in this slophouse of a jail since last night."

"Yeah, they told me you would be the crafty one. You stuck pore old Captain Woodley and then went straight to the tavern and picked a fight. We got witnesses to that."

Hogg kicked the iron bars and cursed the Sheriff and the city of Demopolis and the witnesses to the fight. He was innocent, he argued, and no one had seen him stick a knife in Captain Woodley. His protests fell on deaf ears.

Thomas Barkley slept well and was unaware of any events of the past twelve hours. He had dined at a small restaurant on Walnut Street after leaving the *Sipsey Queen* and he found a small hotel nearby with an empty room and a huge feather bed. He slept through the night and when he wakened there was a thick fog surrounding the city and little reason to stir about. He had his breakfast at the lodging and went back to his room with a newspaper until mid-morning.

With the arrival of sunlight he made his way back to the riverboat. The only crew he found on board was the cook and two deck hands who seemed somewhat the worse for their evening in town, and no evidence of passengers. He walked the length of the vessel, approaching the stern section when he heard voices from one of the small cabins occupied by the female passengers. The voices ceased with the sound of his footsteps and then a door opened and a woman appeared in the doorway. He recognized her and started to move on, but she rushed out to greet him. "Oh sir! Have you heard the news of the Captain?"

"What news? I haven't seen the Captain today."

"Nor or you likely to—I fear. He was stabbed sometime during the night and the man—the man who was accompanying me… and… and… my child… has been arrested!"

Thomas was astounded. First the bad news of the Captain and then the fact the woman had a child. The time had come to straighten things. "What is this man to you?"

The woman's eyes were frightened and her hands were clenched at her side. "He is an acquaintance—of my employer in Mobile. He was supposed to accompany me and my child to Baltimore."

"But I saw you in an argument…"

"The man tried to force his attentions on me."

Thomas didn't doubt for a moment that she spoke the truth on that matter, but there was something missing. "How came you and your child to be in Mobile?"

"My child was born there. My husband was in the fur trade. We came to the city some years past to market his furs. He apparently met with foul play. I haven't seen him since my daughter was born."

"Mommee!"

The voice of the child caused the woman to move inside the stateroom. She reappeared with a little girl, dressed in a fashionable ensemble and holding one thumb firmly in her mouth. The child looked at Thomas with large, dark eyes.

"Peggy—say hello to Mr.… er…"

"Barkley—the name is Thomas Barkley."

Serina smiled now and some of the reserved manner seemed to ease. "I… my name is Serina Malloy, and this is my little daughter, Peggy. She has been confined to our cabin, due to motion distress, but is feeling fine now that the boat has docked."

Thomas removed his hat and smiled at the child and was rewarded with a grin. "Well, I'm very pleased to meet both of you."

The woman, remembering now, turned serious. "The Sheriff was looking for you this morning."

"Looking for me? Why the devil would he be looking for me?"

"He—asked about that fight—on the boat…"

"With your friend?"

"Not my friend—the man named Alonzo Hogg."

Thomas nodded, turning the hat in his hands. "So… they have Alonzo Hogg in custody and they want to see me also? Well, I'll accommodate them. I want some answers about Sam Woodley for myself."

The woman looked distressed and put a small hand on his arm. "Could I ask a favor before you go?"

"I'm at your service."

"My child and I haven't eaten today, what with the confusion, and I was hesitant to go ashore alone. Could you see us to a decent hotel on your way to the Sheriff's office?"

Thomas was glad to oblige and he escorted them to the little hotel where he had spent his quiet evening. "I'll come by here on my way back," he promised.

He was confused. The woman was obviously of good breeding, to judge by her speech and dress. That companion was another matter. He was annoyed at himself for wanting to know more of the particulars, aware that it was none of his affair and knowing he should leave it that way.

His first concern was the Captain's welfare and he got directions to the Sheriff's office. A deputy asked him to be seated on the hard bench in front of his desk and he left to find the Sheriff. He came back with a portly gentleman with walrus mustaches and piercing blue eyes. He looked at Thomas without greeting. "Say you want information about the Captain?"

Thomas nodded curtly. "If you have such to give me."

"Well, I'm still looking for more information myself." The Sheriff settled himself in a large chair and pushed another forward with his foot.

Thomas ignored the chair, remaining where he stood.

The Sheriff inspected a soup stain on his lapel and then came back to his visitor. "I need to know about an altercation between yourself and a man named Alonzo Hogg—at the moment held in one of my cells back there…" he motioned with his thumb.

"I smashed his jaw—if that's what you mean—and I'd do it again—"

The Sheriff chuckled and held up one meaty hand. "That's one way to get acquainted, but for my benefit, give your name and where you live."

"I'm Thomas Barkley of Fayette County, and a responsible citizen."

The Sheriff nodded. "Could you perhaps tell us if your responsibility includes a defense of the pretty lady who was with Mr. Hogg?"

Thomas jaw muscles tightened in anger. "Explain yourself, sir!"

"Well… was you fighting over the woman—and if so—since you apparently won the fight—did you win the woman, too?"

Thomas' fist crashed down on top of the desk and his hard, gray eyes let the Sheriff know he was not to be intimidated. "You are out of line, sir! I don't know who you think you're talking to, but I'll thank you to conduct yourself like a gentleman!"

Now the Sheriff leaned forward, pulling on his mustaches, a slight smile tugging at the corners of his mouth. "Would you by chance be related to one Hugh Barkley, of Marengo County?"

"He happens to be my brother."

"Thought he might be," the sheriff grinned broadly now. "Seems like a bit of temper runs in the family!"

"What do you mean… ?"

"Your brother's a very substantial citizen in this part of the country. I've supped at his table on occasion," the Sheriff grinned ruefully. "And we've had our differences on occasion, but I'd still be glad to pass along your respects if you like."

"Indeed you may," Thomas said.

The Sheriff stood now, extending his hand. "I think we can take your actions as being appropriate for the situation," he said. "Could I offer you anything further?"

"I'd like to see Sam Woodley."

"He's at the Stillwell Infirmary. Come on—I'll take you in my rig."

Thoracic surgery was needed but not available. Captain Woodley had been made comfortable as possible with large doses of laudanum. His wounds were bandaged but the wheeze and rattle of his breathing indicated a punctured lung.

Thomas found that a report of the stabbing had already been posted to Newtonville. There seemed nothing more to do and so the Sheriff drove him back to the little hotel. Thomas thanked the Sheriff for his courtesy and the Sheriff acknowledged it with a friendly wave and flicked the reins against the backside of the horse.

Serina and her daughter were waiting in the lobby. She stood as he entered the door and walked to meet him. "Could we talk privately?" she asked.

Thomas led the way to a corner table and she sat with her eyes averted. "I… I have to get out of this city at once!"

Thomas studied her face until she had to look at him. "I don't have much reason to hang about here myself, but I don't know when the next sailing—"

Serina opened her purse and read from a note. "A passenger from the *Sipsey Queen* was eating lunch across from us. I overheard him tell the manager he was leaving for Tus… Tusk… "

"Tuscaloosa."

"Yes… for Tuscaloosa—on the boat *Harriet*, by way of the Black Warrior River."

"Tuscaloosa would be just fine for me," Thomas nodded. "The distance to my home from there is only a day's drive. When is she sailing?"

"At noon tomorrow. I… I'm afraid Alonzo Hogg may be set free before that time… and I don't want to see him again."

"You needn't worry," Thomas said. "The Sheriff told me on the way back here he's the prime suspect in what will likely become a murder case. Old Woodley is on his deathbed."

A sigh of relief escaped her lips, but she recovered her composure. "I'm dreadfully sorry to hear about the Captain…"

"So am I—and more so because I feel a certain responsibility. If I hadn't gotten into that fracas with your companion…"

"Please don't use that word, 'companion'—to describe that—that creature!"

"Sorry, but you know what I mean—he was your escort, as it were."

"Not by my invitation. My employer…"

Thomas scuffed his boot across the floor and prepared to rise. "You never told me what employment you were engaged in?"

Serina clutched the back of a chair. A moment of panic almost drove her speechless. She recovered her composure, and returned Thomas' gaze with tearful eyes. "My employer owned a boarding house and restaurant. I… I was the hostess. I was in charge of housekeeping as well. Why do you ask?"

"I'm sure I don't know," Thomas replied, and he rose to leave.

Serina clutched at his sleeve, the dark eyes now focused upon his, the red mouth tremulous. "May we go with you to the steamboat?"

"If that is your wish."

The relationship ripened on the trip upriver to Tuscaloosa. They met for breakfast in the mornings and they dallied by the rail after the evening meals to watch the sunset. Thomas found the little girl to be well behaved and she readily took to her bed at her mother's bidding. More and more he found himself approving the good, motherly nature of the woman.

His mind played games when they were apart. The thought of her shapely body created an ache in him that he recognized as pure, unbridled lust. On the other hand, he tried very hard to convince himself that he really needed someone like this lady for housekeeping duties. She had mentioned that as her occupation.

A plan evolved in his mind that would permit him to remain in contact with this woman without compromising his principles. He knew he could not love her—could never really love another woman after Sarah, but…

"I'd like... I wonder... well, what I want to ask... are you already committed to a position in—where was it?"

"Baltimore—I have good references..."

"I'm sure that you do—but what I mean to say is—I'd like you to... to..."

Serina raised an eyebrow but her heart was beating overtime. "What do you have in mind?"

"The fact is—I've recently lost my wife..."

"I'm so sorry."

"Yes. I... she died in childbirth. My infant daughter is... well... there's old Dicey... but..."

Serina smiled sympathetically. "Would you like me to take charge of the household?"

Thomas privately cursed himself for being a babbling idiot but welcomed the question. "I would like that—very much."

There—it was out—and devil take the hindmost. He dared not look at her but stared at the dark water. He felt her hand on his arm, like the softness of a butterfly.

"I would consider it an honor, Thomas Barkley."

"So be it then," he said, and walked quickly away to his cabin.

He had been tempted to make a visit to see his brother, Hugh Barkley, when the Sheriff mentioned his name. Now he had frittered away that opportunity by allowing himself to be rushed away from Demopolis by this mysterious woman. He wondered if he was being influenced by a sense of responsibility to the woman and her child, or from the excitement he felt each time he found her in close proximity.

Chapter Seventeen

The knowing looks and whispers started the moment Thomas and his pretty lady reached the village of Newtonville. He had rented a buggy from the livery stable in Northport and it was piled high with the presents and supplies that he had purchased in Mobile. He stopped briefly at Coe's Cotton Gin to bring Robert Coe a bottle of his favorite bourbon. While he visited inside, curious town folk gathered in the vicinity of the buggy. They nodded to the lady and her daughter and quickly looked away.

Introductions were made when Robert and Thomas emerged from the gin office. Thomas informed his old friend that Serina was the new housekeeper. A member of the Ladies Worship Circle was heard to repeat that information—but she added, "Mr. Barkley is calling her a housekeeper—but a house mistress is the more likely case!"

The introductions at home were just as awkward. He tried as best he could to inform each of the children, and Dicey, of the position he had created for Serina. The explanation was met with sullenness from Dicey and a stony silence from William.

Only Elizabeth was cordial. She received Serina in ladylike fashion and showed her to the guest room at the top of the stairs that she would share with her daughter. George brought in the luggage and the household stood open-mouthed at the size of the wardrobe trunk.

At the first dinner, the atmosphere was strained and confined to "Pass the biscuits," or "More ham, please." Thomas ate his meal hurriedly, ignoring the imploring looks Serina turned in his direction. She too, finished the meal quickly and then sat silently until they all left the table. Serina began to help with clearing the table, but old Dicey grumbled, "I don't need no help!"

Elizabeth accompanied her to the room upstairs and helped Serina unpack her clothes. She was awed by the expensive, imported fabrics and the European styling. Serina was so relieved to hear a friendly voice that she insisted Elizabeth slip into one of the brocaded dressing gowns and stand before the mirror.

"You are absolutely beautiful, Elizabeth!" Serina said. "Please keep it. I could never bear to wear it now that I know it was made just for you!"

Elizabeth was overcome. The opportunity to go shopping had been denied her since her mother's death, and she had inherited her mother's love for beautiful creations. "Thank you so much! I... I do hope you will be comfortable here."

Serina smiled. "Because of you, I'm sure we will."

William was far more direct. He approached his father in the milking barn and his face was taut, hands clenched at his sides. "I can't see why you brought that woman here, Pa."

Thomas flushed in anger. What in hell was wrong with everybody, anyway? He hadn't touched the woman, for God's sake, and everybody from William to old Dicey was trying to make him feel like some criminal.

William took advantage of his father's silence to further press the issue. He had never in his short lifetime opposed his father in any way, but he was filled with resentment at the prospect of seeing his father with any woman other than his now deceased mother. "I think she's part nigger, Pa."

Thomas raised his fist before he realized it, and William turned pale but refused to give ground. Thomas was aghast at his own rage. "Will," he finally said, lowering his fist. "Don't you ever speak to me about this matter again. Do you understand?"

The boy turned and walked away, and Thomas saddled the mare and tore out to the swamp. Under the shelter of the water oaks he brought the mare to a halt and dismounted. He walked along the riverbank and kicked at the dead limbs in his path.

The boy had cut him deeply. He had not allowed the possibility of Serina having mixed blood to surface to his conscious mind. Now the thought was there—and he felt an unreasonable anger toward the boy for having stated the matter so boldly.

"I think she's part nigger," the boy had said.

A week went by and the changed conditions kept everyone on guard. Serina was still treated more as a guest than as one of the staff. Dicey was adamant that she would not accept any help in the kitchen, and Elizabeth wanted only to talk to the fascinating lady. There had been an absence of any learned conversation since Sarah's death. Elizabeth found the stranger to be well informed on matters of social graces and even discovered that they had read some of the same literature.

The news of the dead slave, Joseph, and the encounter between William and the overseer was relayed to Thomas from several sources. The lead man told him of the brutal treatment that had likely cost Joseph's life. Dicey told him of the man's coarse tongue. He listened in silence as William and Jonas related the story of the attempted rape and whipping. When Jonas mentioned that Smith had pulled a knife on William, a fierce expression settled on Thomas' face. He saddled the mare the next morning when the dew was still heavy on the grounds. He left before breakfast without telling anyone where he was headed.

There wasn't much activity at Robert Coe's gin at this time of year. Thomas found his old friend grading cottonseed for the new seasons planting and he asked casually of the whereabouts of John Smith.

Robert shook his head sadly and let the seeds drop into the hopper. "Sorry I recommended him to you, Thomas. It seems he spends most of his time at the bar down the street. Some folks just don't seem to measure up these days."

That's where Thomas found him. He was standing at the bar, one foot on the rail. A half empty bottle of whiskey rested behind his glass and it was yet early in the day. Thomas nodded toward the proprietor and turned to the man at the bar. "I've come to pay my debt!"

There was something in the way the words were spoken that got John Smith's attention. He moved his foot from the rail and turned quickly toward the newcomer. The proprietor glanced nervously from his stool behind the bar. "We don't want no trouble in here…"

"It doesn't have to be in here," Thomas said quietly.

John Smith's face lost some of its florid color, but then bolstered by the whiskey, he motioned to the polished surface of the bar near Thomas' left elbow. "Ye kin put the money on the counter there. Reckon ye'll be thinkin to deduct something for my early leave-taking, but that meddling boy of yours is responsible fer it!"

"Oh, no," Thomas said. "I intend to pay you exactly what is due." He counted the gold coins out and carefully laid them on the counter. He moved back from the bar then and motioned toward the door. "That's not all I owe you, Smith."

John Smith looked puzzled, and his eyes shifted from Thomas to the proprietor and back again. He moved from the bar. The knife that had been in his pocket was now suddenly in his right hand. "I'll cut ye, and I'll cut ye bad," he said. "Less'n ye see fit to git outa my way!"

He advanced down the side of the bar and Thomas moved aside to allow him room. Smith stopped in front of the coins and slid them into his pocket, keeping an eye on Thomas as he did so. Gaining confidence, he now grinned once more as he moved out into the street. "I reckon all the Barkleys know when to holler calf rope," he called back over his shoulder.

Thomas quickly stepped outside and the bullwhip that had remained coiled under his coat was now in his hand. It whistled through the air and John Smith's shirt was suddenly split in two sections in the back, and a red line showed on his bare skin.

The man screamed in pain and shock and rage. He drew the knife back to throw and the whip whistled again, gripping the wrist that held the knife in a leather vice. Thomas yanked hard and Smith stumbled forward, falling into the dirt of the street and losing the knife. Again the whip sounded, and this time its tail caught Smith's trousers at the rear.

"Air ye crazy?" the man screamed at Thomas. "I've done ye no harm!"

"Oh yes you have," Thomas replied. "You've done me and mine considerable harm."

The whip found Smith's behind once more and he scrambled to his feet, running madly down the street trying to keep his trousers from sliding down his legs. The whip found his naked buttocks again and again until the man rolled into a ball in the dirt of the street, sniveling and cursing in the dust.

There was a stunned silence now, the townsfolk staring at what had taken place. Thomas spoke to no one but remounted and rode calmly back toward the plantation.

Chapter Eighteen

1848

The warmth of the sun lay like a blanket upon the land, and Serina adapted easily to her new environs. She was reminded of the early days of her childhood, when she had the run of the woods and fields in the Cherokee Nation. The topography was much the same and she could believe she had been transported to her homeland. Even the duties of motherhood were shared with Elizabeth, who took every opportunity to entertain her baby sister, Katherine, as well as Serina's daughter, Peggy. They were all enjoying the first warm days of spring. Serina watched Peggy chase a butterfly. Elizabeth sat with the baby on a quilt in the sunshine.

Serina watched a rider come out of the tree line and take his familiar route to the river. The sight of him stirred her in a mysterious way. She had exchanged looks with Thomas. There was unquestionably a magnetic attraction between them. She knew the time would come, but she wanted to choose it carefully. She glanced about the grounds, noting old Dicey cleaning vegetables for the evening meal and apparently absorbed in the work. No one seemed to notice as she left.

She walked to the river, stopping to pick a wildflower and, on reaching the riverbank, paused to listen to a mockingbird in the hackberry bush. The face that she lifted to the sun was bronzed, the features sharp and clearly defined, the mouth full and sensuous. Her flashing black eyes were closed as she tilted her head backward with the long, black hair flowing like a dark river over her shoulders. Sensing that the man was watching her, she took her time unfastening the dress, in the provocative and practiced manner that had become familiar to her in Mobile.

She stood naked in the sunlight. Her body was still slender but reaching the fullness of maturity, her breasts barely pendulous, and her stomach rounded ever so slightly. She seemed to drink in the sun, twisting from side to side and oblivious to her surroundings.

At length she walked to the water's edge and eased into the river. She found the channel and dove beneath the surface. Thomas, who had watched transfixed, feared for her life. He sprang from the saddle and rushed to the water's edge.

And she suddenly appeared, spouting up from the water directly in front of him, a glistening volcano of flesh and dark foliage, splashing and laughing at the man's startled expression.

She walked out of the water then, straight and unashamed, and she reached her arms up to his neck and pressed her body against him, her mouth close to his ear.

"I will be your woman," she said softly.

Chapter Nineteen

Thomas couldn't get enough of her. It was as if his body, so long denied, demanded satisfaction at every conceivable opportunity. There was no liaison on the grounds of the plantation, but the wooded trysts were so numerous as to gain notice from the slaves, who gossiped daily around the evening cook fires.

"Up to no good is how I sees it," old Dicey complained. "She coming in here—big as you please—actin' like she be mistress of dis plantation! I don't know what she covering up, but I specs they be something she ain't telling. That boy, Jessie, he say down where he come from, they calls them Creoles. He say they kin make strange things happen—things they call voodoo. She a witch woman for sure."

It was poor Jonas, in the decaying heat of an August afternoon, whose curiosity overpowered caution. He decided to follow the master to his mysterious destination. He crept along a drainage ditch as the master rode along the fields, and he followed him up a hillock and through the cedars. He flitted from one tree to another and then stopped in his tracks. He caught a glimpse of petticoats as the woman rose from her place at the edge of the path.

Thomas stopped the mare and the woman smiled up at him. He reached down for her and she swung easily into the saddle behind him, the mare continuing now along a familiar trail. The woods gave way to a clearing, fronting on a dirt road.

A large, open-sided structure, consisting of a shingled roof supported by huge, hand-hewn timbers stood in the middle of the clearing. Heavy beams interconnected these timbers to the angled cross supports of the roof. The floor was covered with sawdust and row after row of hard benches separated the wide aisle. All around this structure were rows of small plank cabins. They had hinged window sections that would let down to capture any passing breeze and allow the campers to talk with their neighbors. Some of the cabins had cooking grates built over sand fire boxes and located just inside the open hallways. Even on rainy days, hot meals could be prepared. The box-like sleeping rooms on either side of the open hallways held built-in platforms that were covered with pine straw or shuck-filled mattresses. They were covered with tarp and rolled up and tied until the Methodist congregation held the next yearly "camp meeting."

Thomas pulled the mare around behind the last of the cabins and helped the woman to dismount. He tied the halter rope to the hitching post, and they looked up at the sky as thunder rolled in the background. The approach of the storm seemed to charge the air with electricity, matching the energy that now flowed in their veins. The storm broke in fury during their mating and was as quickly over. The steady rain that began to fall gentled their ardor and lulled them into sleep.

They didn't hear, nor were they aware of the presence of the slender black boy who watched them through a crack in the planking. The boy stood there for some time and regaining his senses, carefully moved from his observation post and fled into the woods.

Jonas kept the matter to himself for several days, though his burden of knowledge weighed heavily on him. He knew he couldn't trust such knowledge to the field hands, but he also knew that he couldn't keep it to himself much longer. Finally, he came up with the one person with great enough stature to share his secret. He waited, as patiently as he could, for the right moment to pass this information on to William. His relationship with William had always been one of loose formality, being one more of friendship than servitude. The boys had grown into their teens, and Jonas had begun to address his owner as Mister Will, or Mist Will. The time would come... he hoped he could wait for the right moment.

A Saturday afternoon fishing trip seemed to provide just the right setting. The boys set out with their bait cans full of red worms, dug from underneath the large stones in the barnyard. Their cane poles were carried over their shoulders; their straw hats shaded them from the hot sun.

Their laughter didn't disturb the cottonmouth moccasin, moving lazily along the bank, searching for a frog or its gelatinous mass of eggs. Their footsteps, however, caused it to react and it slithered underneath a fallen log at the edge of the water.

The boys baited hooks and threw their lines out, watching the cork floats bobbing on the surface. Immediately, William's cork plunged under. The fishing line grew taut as the fish began swimming away.

"You got a bite!" Jonas cried happily

"More than a bite… I've got a fish!"

"Hold on to 'em, Will, hold on to 'em now!" In his excitement, Jonas forgot his mother's admonishment to address his friend as Mister Will.

The line straightened as far as it would go and the cane pole bent to a dangerous degree as William sought to keep the fish out of the entangled brush.

"Hot damn!" Jonas called. "'At sucker mus weigh ten pounds!"

The battle continued until the fish finally tired. William could then risk pulling it in without breaking the line. He kept it low in the water, allowing the tail to drag on the surface. With Jonas' rendering advice and vocal encouragement, he pulled the huge catfish up onto the sandy bank.

The catfish grunted as they disengaged the hook. Jonas stood with his foot on the tail, and they carefully avoided the disguised dirks that the "cat" stuck out from its head. Jonas stuck his knife down through the bony head of the fish and into the fallen log. The knifepoint held the fish in place while William made a cut around the skin. He began to skin the cat, pulling the skin off like a stocking with the inside out, from head to tail. They now cut the head off and gutted the fish and hung it up to admire the great sides of white meat.

There was only one thing that could possibly top the monstrous catch, and Jonas knew the time had come. He put a fresh worm on his own hook and threw the line out as far as possible. He surveyed the ripples around the cork and then began to speak. "I seen em," Jonas confided to his fishing partner. "They was in the campgroun' cabin an they was doin it! I seen em!"

"You seen WHAT?"

"I seen yo pa, that's what—in the cabin with the witch woman… an… an they was doin' it."

"What in hell are you talking about, my pa and some witch woman?"

"That what they call Miz Serina in the quarters… a… a Creole—sumpin like that. Jessie say they do witchcraft."

"Oh he does, does he? Well, Jessie better keep his mouth shut if he knows what's good for him."

Jonas began to see now that he had made a big mistake. He began' scuffing his foot into the dirt under the log. He kept his eyes away from William and on the fishing cork.

"I'm telling you one time, Jonas, and one time only. Don't ever be spying on my father again and don't let me hear anything more about some witch woman."

Jonas's eyes clouded over. William had bantered with him before but not in this tone of voice. "I… I was jes repeatin what they say."

"What I'm telling you, Jonas, is for your own good. You can get into more trouble than you can imagine if my pa knew about this spying business. Now I'm going to just forget it, and you better forget it, too."

"Mist Will?"

"Yeah, Jonas?"

"Do we be frens lak befo?" his voice shook with emotion.

William put an arm around his shoulder and his words were very sincere. "You'll always be my friend, Jonas."

The slave boy smiled. He started to cross over the log. He wasn't looking when the cottonmouth decided to strike. The snake sank his fangs into the warm flesh of Jonas' right ankle, hanging on as the boy jerked backward. Jonas screamed in pain and horror at the sight of the loathsome serpent and kicked his right leg outward with all his strength.

The snake flew through the air and landed in the water with a big splash. William ran to him and caught him just before he collapsed from the shock. William took his knife and cut a cross over each of the puncture marks, deep enough to cause immediate bleeding. He squeezed on the leg forcing the blood to flow and then he put his mouth over the wounds and sucked blood mixed with venom and spat it out on the bank.

He tore his shirttail into a tourniquet, which he tied tightly above the cuts to force the blood out, and then he sucked again at the fang marks.

"Oh, God, Will, is I goin' to die?" The boy was alert now and shaking so hard that William had difficulty holding him down.

"From an old snake bite? Come on Jonas—you got better sense than that."

"But—but it was a moccasin. I seen it Will—it was a cottonmouth! Jessie say they kill you ever time!"

"There you go again—listening to that blabbermouth Jessie. I told you he needs to keep his mouth shut. Now don't worry, Jonas. I know what I'm doing. I'm going to bleed you so much there won't be no snake poison left. You just hold still now."

His words belied his own fear. He knew the snakebite could be fatal, but he was doing all that he had ever been told to do.

Jonas was becoming nauseated and William picked him up. He threw the boy's weight over his shoulder and struggled into a standing position. He stumbled toward the house. When he reached the cross-railed fence, he slid Jonas over it and then picked him up once more, moving as quickly as he could. He began calling for help when he got within shouting distance of the house and soon there was a crowd milling around.

"Take him on to the house and get my pa," he yelled.

Thomas took a look at the boy's leg, which now showed a swollen purplish color, and he directed George to bring the buggy. He drove the mare at a dead run into Newtonville.

Dr. Brandon gave the boy a dose of sassafras tea to purify his blood and a quantity of the herb, boneset, as an antidote for the venom.

Jonas was sick for three days, but his strong, young body overcame the effects of the poison. The flesh around the wound putrefied and sloughed off, and when it healed there was an indented spot on his leg the size of a hen's egg.

William checked on him several times a day, and the boy was delighted to have him visit in his cabin. The dank interior of the cabin was stiflingly hot, and William recoiled from the odor of rotting flesh, but he made a strong effort to be cheerful in his conversation with Jonas.

"Tell me about us going down that Sipsey to Mobile, Will… I mean Mist Will."

"Well, Jonas, it's like this. First, we got to get us a boat of our own 'cause old Captain Woodley—he got stabbed to death."

"Oh that be better anyway—a boat of our own!"

"Yeah… we can start building on it just as soon as you get well. How long you want it to be?"

Jonas grinned, the white teeth showing in the darkness of the room. "I spec it could be long as a cotton wagon and deep as a horse trough."

"I think that would be just about right," William agreed. "If we leave off the steam engine… we can just paddle it down to Mobile."

"Mist Will?"

"Yeah Jonas?"

"I done forgot all about seeing yo pa and Miz Serina doin it in the church cabin."

"Jonas! I told you…"

"I know," the boy said happily. "That why I forgot all about it—so we frens… jes like befo."

William grinned and nodded, shaking his head sorrowfully.

Chapter Twenty

The summer season moved into the fall and the cotton harvest began once more. There were busy times for everyone and little time for spying and gossiping—and certainly not in the earshot of young master William.

Cotton went to ten cents per pound and Alabama stepped ahead of Mississippi as the leading cotton producing state. The value of shipments out of the port of Mobile, according to the cotton factor, Horace Hall, exceeded ten million dollars.

Thomas Barkley was able to repay every dollar of credit extended by the factor, and the cast iron pot under the dinner bell post held every dollar that he had brought with him from South Carolina. He made his annual comparison between his production and the best year's harvest at Barkley Hall. He knew at last that he had beaten the record.

And then something changed the focus at the Barkley plantation. Dicey caught Elizabeth alone in the kitchen. "Wellum, the Creole woman done swallered a punkin seed!"

"Dicey... what on earth do you mean?"

"Ya'll knows what I mean... that woman gone have a baby."

"Oh... oh my word," Elizabeth managed feebly.

"That baby belong to yo pa, Miz 'Lizbeth, ain't no use denying facts. What us gone do now?"

Elizabeth fled to her room and wept. She had suspected but never dared to voice the thought that there was an intimacy between her father and Serina. She had truly come to care deeply for Serina and her child, Peggy, knowing what it was like to lose a parent. She had done her best to help brighten the child's world. She included her in every activity that she arranged for her own little sister, Katherine. Seeing the two little girls together had made her feel like a big sister to both of them.

But this other matter—how could she face it? What would the community think? For that matter, how could she ever go to church again? This child would be a real brother or sister... and... it would be illegitimate! She voiced her despair to William in secrecy. She felt he had been unfairly harsh in his criticism of Serina. Now it appeared he had known something that he had kept to himself.

"Why didn't you tell me this was going on?" she wailed.

"And what good would it have done? Would you have told her she had to stop seeing pa? Would you have confronted pa with the matter? Not likely!"

"But, but Will, we're going to have an illegitimate brother or worse... a little sister."

"And why would that be worse? No, I'll tell you what is worse... that illegitimate brother or sister is likely to be part... that is... a mixed blood."

"You mean it will be part Negro?"

He looked away from her now, startled that she should have the same suspicion as he. He jammed his hands into his pockets. "I think that is likely the case."

Serina was oblivious to the discord that her physical condition was causing. She was, in fact, serenely happy. She was wholly and totally in love with Thomas Barkley. He represented all the good qualities that she remembered about her own father. He was strong. He was brave. He was responsible and he was tenderly caring. Her lips moved into an easy smile when she remembered his strong arms around her body.

She waited for the right time to tell him, knowing in her heart that he would feel the same joyful sense of accomplishment that she felt.

"I suppose it might have been expected," he said, but there was no joy in his voice.

Serina's heart sank within her, and she tried desperately to see something that wasn't there. "Oh Thomas, please Thomas—tell me you want this child."

Thomas faced her squarely, and his face was lined and sad. "I can't say that, Serina. This child is a bastard. It has been conceived—"

"Don't tell me how it was conceived, for God's sake. I know fair well how it was conceived." Serina buried her face in her hands, and her body trembled with grief and with anger.

Thomas took her in his arms then, and she pushed at him, but he would not relinquish his hold on her. He shook her as he would shake a child in a temper tantrum.

"Stop now. You must understand—my concern is not for me—not even for you. My concern is for this child… how it will fit into this family, this community, this—this is my concern."

Serina backed away from him, and he let her go. She searched his face a long time before speaking. "How will our child address its father?"

Thomas took an equally long time to respond, and when he did, the answer struck her heart. "The child can address me as 'Sir.'"

"Sir? Sir? That's the extent of it?"

He nodded.

Serina began to laugh, a high-pitched hysterical laugh that brought tears to her eyes and continued until he slapped her sharply to stop her. She stared at him coldly through the tears, and he returned her gaze steadily.

"Serina… you have to realize there are matters here that go beyond what I feel for you. I must do whatever is best for all of us, including this child—which I know—is mine."

"But you can't allow it to call you 'Father'?"

"I can't recognize it that way. How would my children…"

Serina heard the words, and they burned into her heart. She wasn't good enough for him. Her child wasn't good enough for him. The white man's principles were different from the Cherokee's. Any bit of Cherokee blood entitled the owner to a place in the tribe. Having white blood did not make you a part of the white man's tribe. She was not accepted. That was the cruel truth.

His words came slowly now. "I will care for this child—because it is mine."

"Thank you for that, at least," she said coldly, and she turned away from him, struggling to swallow the despair that seemed to well up in her throat.

Chapter Twenty-One

Jeremiah Barkley was born on the seventeenth day of June, 1849. He came into the world with a lusty cry of indignation from the slap across his rump administered by the good Dr. Brandon. He was a Thomas Barkley of a different shade, but a Barkley, no one could doubt.

The baby boy captivated everyone from the outset. His disposition was pleasant, and his plump body invited hugs. Even Dicey, finally, became his devoted protector. Baby care was her specialty, and now that Katherine was wearing little girl clothes, her maternal instincts flowed toward the infant.

As he grew out of the toddler stage and was weaned from his mother's breast, he took up a place in the bedroom with William. William found himself unexpectedly fond of this little half-brother. He taught him to walk, to tie his shoes, and to dress himself. The boy followed William and Jonas to the stables and rode between them in a pony cart.

Serina was left now to her own affairs once again. Her built-in childcare service created time on her hands, and she reverted to her role of housekeeper and, inevitably, mistress. Thomas took her with him a few times on shopping trips to Newtonville, until the stares and whispers got to be too much for them.

Thomas' manner with the townsfolk became brusque to the point of hostility. He stopped going to church as well. The last time he attended, the preacher took his text from First Corinthians, Chapter Five. In Thomas' view, the preacher attached undue emphasis to the need to avoid the company of fornicators.

"Never again," he muttered to himself, and he walked to the opposite side of the doorway to avoid shaking hands with the preacher. He was reaching for the buggy seat when raucous laughter reached his ears.

"Kinda hit old Thomas right betwixt the eyes, by God!"

The cackling laugh identified its owner, old Thomas Murphy, village blacksmith and local gossip, who was standing with a small group of men at the hitching rails. Other church members passed by and seeing Thomas, looked away in embarrassment.

Thomas paused only briefly, not indicating that he had heard—started to move away, but then in a low and menacing tone, he faced the blacksmith. "I'm sure you were not referring to me—you damned old fool. If I thought for one minute that you were, I'd knock your damned teeth down your scrawny, flea-bitten throat!" In the total silence that followed, Thomas waited for a reply. Hearing none, he climbed into the buggy and drove away.

After that, he busied himself around the house. William and Elizabeth took the children to church. Aunt Dicey would not hear of the children missing a church service—that would have been a sacrilege to Sarah's memory.

Serina stayed at home also. The significance of Thomas' attitude toward the birth of the child was becoming clear to her now in light of the community reaction.

Thomas took his little brown son to the river to fish. Sunday was the only day that he hadn't worked in his entire lifetime, and he now felt free of church responsibility as well. The little boy became adept at setting the hook and pulling in small perch. By the age of five, he was bringing a string of fish up from the river by himself. Watching him carry his fish to the well house for cleaning, Thomas grinned at the boy's mother.

"Lord... he's a fine-looking boy!"

"Looks like his daddy, I suppose," she replied, and her wounded spirit began to heal. And indeed he did—the same gray eyes, the same strong chin—the same everything, except the color of his skin.

Now that everyone knew about their relationship, there seemed to be no further reason to disguise their meetings. They left in the buggy together and came back as they chose. None resented it more than old Dicey, who remained cold and distant from Serina, while lavishing affection on her son.

Jeremiah didn't know from his earliest awareness that he was in any way different from anybody else. He didn't feel different because his treatment by the family, if anything, was preferred status. Elizabeth tutored him. Dicey coddled him, William played with him, and his father—or "Sir" Thomas—was his idol. He followed Thomas everywhere on his plantation rounds.

It was Elizabeth, though, who became a second mother to him. Elizabeth wanted to send him to school, but Thomas would have no part of it.

"His place is here," he stated firmly. "I'll not have him embarrassed by some snot-nosed ignoramus that can't match wits with my dog!"

Elizabeth shook her head in dismay. "Pa... he has a good mind. He may be the smartest one in this family..."

"Then let him be smart enough to know his place is here. He will suffer less if he keeps to his place at home."

"But Pa—you can't keep him a prisoner! He's not a slave—he's... he's your son."

Thomas rose in fury, and his fist crashed down on the table.

"I have never denied that, by God!" The gray eyes were flashing fire, and Elizabeth trembled at the sight. Her father had never struck her in her life—but she sensed the enormous capacity for violence and she was afraid.

"I will tell you this one time—and once only. I will take care of Jeremiah. He is my responsibility—mine alone. I accept it and I will not share it—is that understood?"

Elizabeth fled the room in tears. She was bewildered by her father's attitude. It appeared that he gave no credit whatsoever to Serina—would share no responsibility with her. She didn't understand it.

She continued to tutor the boy at home, and kept his instruction at a pace equal to the school curriculum. He progressed so rapidly at times that she was hard pressed to find enough work for him.

"Libby," he asked, using the name he had chosen for her. "What does the word 'cartography' mean?"

Elizabeth looked in surprise. "Why that's the science of mapmaking."

"Ptolemy?"

"Yes, yes—you smart rascal! Ptolemy, the mapmaker."

Sometimes he would ask if he might sleep in her bed, and Elizabeth would tuck him in and watch contentedly as he drifted off to sleep.

Oddly enough, it was Lafe McGill who helped him discover his true identity—profane and unlettered Lafe McGill, who came upon Jerry at play with his daughter in back of Coe's Dry Goods Store.

Thomas had gone into the village for supplies, taking Jerry as was his custom. The boy wanted to remain outside to watch a teamster's wagon unloading merchandise. Thomas went on to make his purchases.

Little Mary Beth McGill slipped away from her parents and came outside the store. She saw the boy who appeared to be near her age and came up to him.

"What be yore name?" she inquired.

"I'm Jeremiah Barkley," he said. "But you can call me Jerry."

"I be Mary Beth McGill. Betcha can't ketch me," she said, making as if to run. The boy didn't respond and she tried a different tack. "I kin beat anybody at marbles."

Jerry doubted that statement. William had taught him the game to the point

110

that he frequently won. He had a genuine carnelian taw that he kept in his pocket for good luck. He produced it proudly and the little girl was impressed. She placed a hand on his arm.

"They's some level ground out back, and I got a sack full of nibs." She reached in a pocket of her dress and pulled out a small cloth tobacco sack bulging with marbles.

She led him by the arm to the back of the store and proceeded to draw a large circle on the ground, using the point of a stick. She drew two intersecting lines forming a cross and placed some glazed clay marbles on the lines. Next, she drew a pitch line and a lag line at opposite ends of the circle.

She turned to the boy in all seriousness, "No roundsters," she challenged.

"And no slippance," he replied.

She won the first shot with her taw a fraction of an inch closer to the lag line. She was kneeling down to shoot, when Lafe McGill came out of the store and called his daughter's name. She was so engrossed that she didn't hear, and Lafe came around the store looking for her.

The sight of his daughter at play with the dark-skinned lad moved the man to sudden anger and he jerked the girl up from the dirt and gave her a quick cuff to the side of her head.

"Don't never let me ketch you playing with no nigger boy agin er I'll stripe yore hide, by Gawd!"

Jerry looked about and seeing no one resembling a Negro at play, turned in puzzlement to the father. "She wasn't playin' with any nigger, sir. She was playin' with me!"

McGill nodded his head wrathfully. "Jist ez I s'pected... you don't even know you a nigger. Wal you stay clear uv my little gal, er I'll damn sure teach you who you are!"

"You'll teach who—Mister McGill?" The voice was low, more like a hiss, and the man wheeled to face the questioner. Thomas Barkley stood there, legs apart and arms stiffly at his sides.

"Wal, Mister Barkley, like I say—I think it time somebody told yore little pickaninny—"

He got no further. The ferocity of the attack was bewildering to Jeremiah. Sir Thomas had the man on the ground in one headlong rush and was striking him savagely in the face with his big fists.

A crowd gathered immediately. "Fight—FIGHT!" But there was no fight, only punishment, pure and simple, and the spectators finally pulled Thomas away from the man before murder was committed. Lafe McGill lay in the dirt at the back of the store until the strength returned to his legs. The little girl went wailing off to find her mother. Thomas caught Jerry by the arm and headed for the wagon. They rode back toward the plantation in silence until Jerry looked thoughtfully up at the man beside him on the wagon seat.

"Am I a... nigger... Sir Thomas?"

The man didn't answer immediately, and when he did, his voice was so low that Jerry strained to hear it.

"A man is what he thinks himself to be, Jerry. If you say to yourself, *I am a man*—then you are a man. Nobody can take that away from you. Remember this as long as you live—because it's biblical—and it's true. A man is what he thinketh himself to be!"

Chapter Twenty-Two

Alonzo Hogg had languished in the city jail at Demopolis almost five years. He knew he had been held unjustly, his charge being based on the thinnest circumstantial evidence, and he viewed with great suspicion the tall, wavy haired visitor now standing before him.

"My card, sir." The gentleman laid a card on Hogg's jail cot, and stepped back. The card read, James T. Honeycutt, attorney at law. "I'd like to offer you my services, sir."

Hogg stood up and looked keenly at the visitor. "Are you new around here?"

"Why yes, now that you mention it. I'm opening an office just down the street. I've been reviewing your..."

Hogg put a finger to his lips for silence and walked to the door. There was no other person in sight. "What can you do for me?"

"That might depend on your financial resources, sir."

Hogg kicked the door angrily and turned on the lawyer. "I've got money— in a money belt back in the Sheriff's office... if they haven't robbed me blind."

"My fee—for representing you..."

"To hell with representing me!" Hogg's voice rose. "Who can I pay to get me out of this pest hole?"

James T. Honeycutt adjusted the handkerchief in his coat pocket. "I believe that a sum of—let's say—one thousand dollars would be adequate."

"You're a damn highwayman," Hogg responded. "You get me out and I'll pay—but not one cent until I walk free."

It was the easiest money the lawyer had ever made. He spoke to the city prosecutor, emphasizing the very thin case and pointing out the man had already served more time than could be legally supported. The charges were dismissed, and Hogg collected his personal effects, including the money belt, which still held over two thousand dollars.

Hogg had spent many lonely hours contemplating his bad run of luck. It all added up to one person—a woman named Serina Malloy. Because of her, he had acted the fool—been jealous of her glances toward a man he learned was named Thomas Barkley.

There was a score to settle with the two of them, but he needed to develop much more information than he had, and his intuition told him his best chance for a thorough research would be back in Mobile—at a certain house on Conception Street.

He might, in the process, meet up with another bumpkin like the one named Tim that he had fleeced over many weeks during his previous trip. Hopefully, he would not have to kill the next one, but that fool had tried to attack him and deserved what he got. His luck was changing. He could feel it up and down his spine, like he felt when the cards were falling right and there was no way to lose.

The derby hat needed only a brushing, but the clothes had taken on a dank, musty smell from the jail storage room, and so he set out for a clothier. He emerged attired in a new woolen suit and booked passage on a steamer to Mobile.

Mobile had changed since Hogg's last visit. New manufacturing plants were in evidence, and newspapers were heralding a new day for the people of Alabama, if the trend continued. Mobile was now the second-ranking cotton exporting city in the United States.

Southern nationalism was being editorialized in the city newspapers. They emphasized the disadvantaged Southern consumer, who was forced to purchase his clothing from Yankee manufacturing plants, and grind his sugar cane in Northern mills. The South must free itself of such dependency on the North.

Hogg lost no time re-acquainting himself with the city's gaming facilities, and in less than a week, his premonition of good luck was proved justified. His adversary across the poker table was the scion of one of Mobile's oldest families. He had managed over the course of a few years to run through most of his inheritance. Seated in his customary chair, his face florid and bloated from drink, his collar unbuttoned and the remains of his dinner staining his waistcoat, he was an easy mark for a man of Hogg's abilities.

The game consumed the better part of the afternoon with only a break for dinner, which was served at the table. The chips were stacked in neat rows all around Hogg, and now the desperate player across from him tried one final effort to recoup his losses. He looked at his cards and determined that a Jack of Hearts could give him a Jack-high flush. He needed that card to fall or all was lost. He took the gamble and covered Hogg's bet with all his remaining chips, amounting to five hundred dollars.

Hogg dealt the cards face down on the table, and without looking at his last card, raised the bet to ten thousand dollars.

His opponent, in a desperate show of bravado, ignored his own hole card. Calling for a pen and paper, he scrawled drunkenly across the page "All my stock in Chickasaw Milling Co." He shoved the paper across to Hogg and in a hoarse voice said, "I'll see your ten and raise you ten."

Hogg looked at the paper and called the proprietor over for a quick conference. He seemed pleased with the conversation for he smiled a very thin smile and condescendingly replied, "I'll allow you to call for the paper—but raise it? I think not!"

"You're a dirty, thieving bastard!" the drunken man wailed.

"And you, sir? You're a yellow shit-eating cur," Hogg replied pleasantly. "Do you call the bet or slink off to the outhouse?"

"You're called and be damned!"

Hogg carefully placed his cards on the table, a pair of tens and an Ace high kicker. The wastrel reached with quivering hands for his last card. There was no Jack of Hearts.

Sometime after two o'clock in the morning, the loser left the bar and staggered down the street. Fog swirled around the gaslights so thickly that their posts were invisible. The lamps peered out of the fog like ghoulish eyes from hell. He followed the lights until there were no more, and he heard the lapping of water against the seawall. He lunged forward, his feet finding open air and then cold water.

Hogg prospered in the textile business. In fact, he found little time for gambling after winning the ownership of the textile mill. His good streak of luck just continued to hold from the first day that he visited his new company. He entered the old brick building north of the city, in the little community of Chickasaw. The foreman showed him around the premises, the interior dimly lighted by rows of lint-covered windowpanes, the air heavy with dust and the smell of sweat. Hogg hurried on to the administrative offices and the better breathing conditions.

He carefully studied the books left by the unfortunate previous owner. It was apparent that his lack of profit was due to poor administration. He found orders stuffed willy-nilly in various drawers and some that had never been passed on to the production plant. He fired the bookkeeper, a troll-like creature, and brought in one of the buxom young ladies that made application for work.

Hogg found his new position of power a tremendous leverage in attracting the opposite sex. He suspected the previous owner had spent more time seducing the female employees than he had spent at his ledgers.

He elected to present an aloof posture toward the workers; besides, he had gotten acquainted with a plump, young woman the girls referred to as Giggles, at Miss Della Devine's house on Conception Street. He spent much of his free time there and gradually learned all that was known about Serina Malloy.

Times were changing now. The South was on a hell-bent course toward secession and possibly war... and war was good for business. Hogg would need additional tooling and at least 400 looms and 10,000 spindles for the volume of business that was already available to him. His present capacity of 40 looms and 1500 spindles would barely support his orders for the coarse cloth called osnaburg.

Hogg needed to get to Baltimore and get his orders under manufacture before time ran out on him. He also had a side trip in mind that was almost as important to him. The years had not softened his rancor toward Serina Malloy and her companion, Thomas Barkley. Alonzo Hogg figured that his schedule could easily afford a little side trip off the north-south route to Baltimore.

The stage stopped at the New Lexington depot on the Byler Road. Hogg hired a rig to take him the short distance to Newtonville. He had the driver drop him off at the center of the village square and instructed him to wait at the Stough Livery Stables until he had concluded his business in town.

Hogg strolled up and down, spending time on the street, chatting with various townsfolk and soon took himself to Newtonville's only tavern. Any stranger passing through would have drawn attention in Newtonville, but Hogg gained celebrity status.

"The lines are pretty well drawn, folks. The South is going to secede because abolition will never be approved down here. You know why? Because the burden will fall heaviest on the poor white. Personally, I've always felt it better to have the Negro serve the white man—than for one white to serve another." Hogg smiled benignly at his audience and murmurs of approval could be heard.

Almost casually then, he mentioned that he had once known one of Newtonville's prominent citizens. "His name was—Thomas Barkley." Hogg chuckled. "The last I saw of old Thomas was when he took up with a nigger whore down in Mobile. He thought so much of her that he—by God—put her on a steamboat and said he was taking her back home with him!" He laughed loudly, and then ordered a drink. The crowd had made gasping noises but now grew silent. "He, by God, took her home with him!" He slapped his leg and laughed louder and then noticed his audience was not laughing with him. He took his derby off and ran his fingers through his thinning hair. "Well—hell— folks... we all got our vices, eh?" He walked down to Stough's and got into the hired rig and headed back to New Lexington.

Chapter Twenty-Three

Thomas hadn't been away from the plantation in almost two months of heavy spring plowing. He had matters of business and a need for supplies. He asked William to hitch the team to the brougham and they headed for Newtonville. They met several of the villagers on their way, and Thomas was surprised to see more than one person turn and make some whispered comment. An occasional burst of raucous laughter reached him as he moved out of hearing range.

William turned to his father and pointed at the crowd, a frown creasing his forehead. "What's going on here, Pa? Are those people laughing at us?"

"I'm sure I don't know," Thomas said. "But I intend to find out pretty damn quick." He knocked at the door of his old friend and fellow South Carolinian, Morton Franklin.

The law office was closed for the lunch hour, and Franklin himself opened the door. He seemed surprised to see them. He shook hands with William in mock formality and then turned to Thomas. "I've been meaning to send word to you, Thomas—that last tract…"

"You're the man to handle it—whatever it is," Thomas interrupted. "Will, wait out here for a minute—I want to talk with Morton privately." He turned back to Morton and nodded toward the rear of the office. "I've got some questions that you may be able to answer."

"By all means, Thomas—you come on to the back office." He closed the door behind them and turned to look anxiously at his old friend. Thomas' jaw muscles were knotted in rage, and his fists were doubled at his sides. Franklin walked over to his desk and sat down. He moved some papers from one side to the next, then cleared his throat and looked out the window. "Well, you have a right to know."

"You're damned right I have a right to know!"

"Now be calm about this matter, Thomas."

"Be calm—be calm? Every saintly son-of-a-bitch I've met today is snickering behind my back. What in hell is wrong, anyway?"

There was no easy way for Franklin. He knew Thomas well enough to know that he wanted nothing short of the facts. "Tom, there was a fellow through here last week—big talker—fancy dresser. He showed up over at Holman's Tavern and started running off his mouth. Worked the crowd up pretty good about the possibility of war..."

"Franklin," Thomas interrupted, "this is your old friend, Thomas Barkley—what has all this got to do with me?"

"Well, Tom, he said he knew you. Made sure everybody present heard the name—*Thomas Barkley*. Said he met you down in Mobile several years ago. Said the last he saw of you was when you took a nigger—his words—a nigger prostitute—home with you!"

"And they believed that? These miserable, small-minded hypocrites believed him?" Thomas felt as if he had been kicked in the stomach by a mule. He felt bile in his mouth, and he sat in the nearest chair.

Franklin glanced at him worriedly. "Tom?"

Thomas shook his head. Finally he stood and held out his hand, and Franklin took it, and Thomas looked him squarely in the eyes.

"That story is a damnable lie. You can pass that along for me. I think I know the man who told it. Last time I saw him he was in jail in Demopolis for the murder of old Woodley. The next time I see him will be when I shoot him dead!"

"I'm sorry, Thomas," Franklin said. "There's not much you can do when people are looking for scandal. You can say it's a lie, but they'll believe what they choose to believe."

"Then, they can all go straight to hell in a pile!" Thomas declared.

Rain struck the leather top of the brougham on the way back home and the sky was no darker than Thomas' mood. William realized that something very disturbing had taken place but he dared not question his father. Thomas said nothing, and when they reached home, he threw the reins to Jonas and stamped off to the river.

"What's wrong with Pa?" Elizabeth asked.

"Something happened in town," William replied. "Some folks were laughing at us, I think."

In the days that followed, all of the anger toward the villagers, and his rage against Alonzo Hogg, was directed toward Serina. He knew in his heart that he had been deceived—even worse—made to be a laughingstock in his own community! And the child—his child—was part Negro. He knew it now.

His only recourse was to avoid her. He was honestly afraid that he might strike her dead. He struggled, but it didn't work. She was there at the breakfast table, giving a tentative smile of greeting and then suppressing it before his glowering countenance. He ate in silence and the family as well. He would leave immediately after a meal, and the thought of the woman would go along with him.

Damn her to hell! She had been a common whore! She had passed herself off as a lady in distress and in his weakness and desire for her—he had let himself be deluded, made into a fool! She was a living lie and he had fathered a whore's son because of her—but he loved the son—and God help him—he still desired the woman.

He put off the inevitable confrontation, knowing that would bring the curtain down. The battle between pride and desire raged through his every waking moment. Eventually, it had to come out. He was standing at the family grave plot when he heard her voice behind him.

"She has the advantage, you know," she spoke quietly.

Thomas whirled on her, enraged at the intrusion. "What are you talking about?"

"I said she has the advantage. I am warm and alive—and full of love for you, and she is cold and dead, without feeling—and still you go to her!"

The rage within him became a cold and deadly weapon, and he spoke also. "She has the advantage because she was my wife, and because she was never a common, street WHORE!"

Serina recoiled as if struck by his fist. The ground moved beneath her, and she felt as if she could not stand. "Oh, please, dear God—Thomas, please—listen to me! I can explain—"

"No madam, you can never explain anything to me again!"

She watched him stalk away from her, and she turned and ran down the hill to the house. She took to her room and cried until her eyes were swollen shut. No experience in her life, not even the desperate flight from the Cherokee Nation, had approached this sorrow.

The strained relationship could only last so long. Serina went about her duties in a mechanical fashion, and if Thomas made an appearance, she left the room. She watched him in the distance in the fields, watched as he came into the house, ate in silence, and went back to the fields.

She saw him as he headed down to the Sipsey, and she followed him to the place where he sat on the upturned slab of sandstone, staring at the ripples on the water but not seeing them. "I think the time has come to talk," she said firmly.

"We have nothing to talk about."

"Yes, Thomas—we do. I did what I had to do to survive. You don't know—"

"And you sure as hell didn't say, did you?"

She looked at him quietly now, seeing his awful hurt and feeling a compassion for him in spite of her own hurt. "I did what I had to do—you didn't ask for a pedigree before bedding me."

"I thought you were Spanish—or part Indian. I didn't know you were part—"

"Negro—or NIGGER. That's the part that disturbs you most—it's not the Spanish—it's not the Indian—not even the whoredom. Nothing so much as the NIGGER!"

He looked away from her. The sight of her tortured features wrung his heart so that he wanted to take her in his arms and tell her it was all right, but he knew he could never do that again. A dark river of racial prejudice now flowed between them, and the headwaters reached back into his ancestry. "I guess it's like spilling a blotch of red wine on your linen napkin. The stain is there, and it ruins the napkin," he stated cruelly.

"So I have stained the Barkley name?"

"That's how I see it," he answered.

Serina spoke through eyes blurred with her tears. "Then—if that is the way you feel—I will have to take my children and leave." She waited for his objection, hoping he would not want her to go.

He looked at her then and his gray eyes were cold as ice. "You may take your daughter, madam. My son will stay with me."

"No! Please—Thomas, you can't be so cruel!"

He ignored her and drew out a folded piece of paper and handed it across to her. The words at the top of the page swam before her eyes. The words were in were in bold letters, and the signature of the judge showed the authenticity of the court document.

Thomas Barkley, Master.

Underneath the heading was a petition to the courts to have one Jeremiah Barkley, mulatto, apprenticed to Thomas Barkley as master—the petition saying there was no other person suitable for his upbringing. The bond money to the court had been duly paid.

She read the document through, unbelievingly at first, and then with resignation from the knowledge that all the cards were stacked in his favor. She looked then, directly into his eyes and her expression was just as cold as his. "May God forgive you, Thomas Barkley. I never shall."

"Nor will I forgive you," he said.

And so it all ended. Thomas never explained the departure to the family and Serina simply stated that she had to leave. Elizabeth was devastated—in fact all of the family mourned in silence, including William. He felt very keenly responsible for the outcome. He felt that his words regarding Serina's mixed blood had somehow doomed the relationship.

Thomas carried Serina and Peggy to the stage line at New Lexington. The parting was not prolonged. He handed her a small satchel. "You will find inside a sum that should be adequate enough to keep you off the streets." The implication was intentionally harsh. "The decision to leave is yours, but I will allow you to visit your son—if you choose."

She turned her tear-stained face upward, searching for any shred of hope, but found none.

"You know, as well as I, that he will never be my son again."

The young girl, Peggy, not knowing the reason for this calamity, reached out to him. He turned away, shaking inside but not sharing his grief. He watched them mount the step and go inside the stage. He caught a glimpse of Peggy's pale features through the glass and he felt as if his heart would break.

He got back in the buggy and drove the lonely distance home. He lay in his bed with his wounded pride and it was poor company. Even in his anger, he still desired her. There was such a void where his heart should be that he wanted to draw inward upon it. He curled himself in the bed and waited for sleep that didn't come.

Chapter Twenty-Four

The jolting of the stage had not interrupted the sleeping passengers. All the tension and anguish of the past few days had finally drained Serina's stamina, and she had fallen into an exhausted, if troubled, sleep.

Suddenly, the stage driver yanked back on the reins, and the coach rattled to a stop. Serina rose up immediately and looked from the window. In the dusky evening, the only visible object was the stage driver, standing by the front wheel and peering into the darkness ahead.

"Looks like they've had a storm lately," he announced. "There's a big tree of some kind thet's blowed across the road up thar. I reckon you folks will have to sit tight 'til I kin try and cut us a path around it." The driver got an axe from under the seat box. He took one of the lanterns from the side of the coach and moved out toward the obstacle blocking the road.

"Hold her right thar!" The voice came roughly through the darkness and then a grimy figure rose from the ditch alongside the road, rifle barrel pointed directly at the driver.

The horses snorted and reared as another man emerged from behind the tree that lay across the road. He grabbed for the reins and steadied the team as his accomplice came alongside the stage and peered inside the coach.

Serina clasped Peggy as the man looked inside. The only other passengers were an elderly man and his young grandson. The highwayman surveyed the interior of the coach and called out to his friend. "Nobody on this side—except a old geezer and a boy. But ye might be entrusted in what's on t'other side!" He leered drunkenly at Serina and her comely, teenaged daughter.

"Here now," the driver called. "No need to bother my passengers. You kin have the strongbox!" The grimy one turned, giving the driver a vicious kick in the midsection. The driver doubled over and retched into the dirt.

"You gon tell me whut I kin have air ye? I'll be the one to decide whut I kin have—and I jist decided!" He grabbed the door handle and swung the door wide, reaching inside for the woman.

Serina placed a hand over the mouth of her daughter, who had awakened in terror at the sight of the menacing stranger. The other hand came up quickly from the satchel on the seat, and the percussion derringer that Tim had taught her to fire was only a foot from its target. The sound of the gun filled the interior of the coach, and the grimy man still had a lopsided grin on his face as he slid lifeless to the ground.

"Hey now, Buck!" the other voice called from the darkness. "Did you shoot?"

Getting no answer he leveled his rifle at the coach, but the old man sitting across from Serina already had him in his revolver sights and the explosion from the .44 caliber pistol rocked the coach. The old man spat out the window and turned to the woman. "Life comes and it goes—don't it, ma'am?"

The driver straightened and looked about in awe. "I never…" he shook his head in disbelief. "I never woulda thought, that there was John Lee Cole and Buck Maddox—two of the roughest highway robbers in Alabama—and taken down by a woman and a old man!"

"Don't 'old man' me," the elderly passenger retorted. "'Pears to me this little lady and me held our own better than some other folks I could mention!"

The driver chuckled now in relief, and he unhitched one of the horses and hooked a chain around the fallen tree trunk. He slapped the horse on the rear, and the tree swung around, clearing a passage for the stage. The old man helped him load the two dead men into the baggage rack on the back of the coach. The horses strained into the harness once more, and the coach moved quickly down the rutted road.

The passengers checked into the Stagecoach Inn, but not before a crowd of curious onlookers had surrounded the two dead men. The old gentleman passenger pointed to Serina and then back to himself. "We done it, boys—we be the ones, me and that little lady!"

Serina found something worthwhile to remember about her lost husband, Tim Malloy. His foresight had saved her from a terrible fate.

"What air ye goin' to do with the reeward?"

Serina turned to face the old gentleman who had been her traveling companion on the previous day. "I don't know what you mean," she replied.

"Wal," the old man said. "Them two was worth five thousand dollars. I figger the way thangs turned out… you and me ought to split it… fifty-fifty."

Serina's head whirled. She hadn't thought of having such a sum at any one time. Coupled with the reserve account, plus the satchel that Thomas had given her, she was independent for the first time in her life. She and Peggy took a room at a boardinghouse a short distance from the stage depot. She had no immediate plans, but the reward money would not be available before the end of the week, and Marion, Alabama, seemed to be a pleasant enough place to spend their spare time.

The city was the county seat of Perry County and an important distribution center for goods brought up from Mobile. It boasted three colleges, one for men, called Howard College, and two for women: the Judson Female Institute and the Marion Female Seminary.

There were grand homes facing the streets belonging to cotton planters with large acreage outside the city limits. A dozen dry goods stores made for great shopping excursions. Actually, Marion seemed to be a good place for a widow and her daughter to settle. A chance conversation with the owners of their rooming house made them permanent residents.

The man and his wife had built the Simmons Rooming House some eight years earlier and had kept it clean and comfortable with many repeat guests on the ledger. A condition now existed that made it necessary for them to sell and move to Mississippi. Mr. Simmons' father was a man of considerable land wealth, but in failing health, and he advised his son to come home and claim his inheritance while an orderly transfer was still possible. Mr. Simmons looked about with a note of regret in his voice. "We will miss this place so much! We enjoyed the business, and we loved this city. Now, we shall have to sell—as soon as a buyer can be located."

Serina's heart fluttered. "What, may I enquire, are you asking for this place?"

Mr. Simmons' need was urgent. He allowed that a sum of two thousand dollars would be acceptable. Serina talked with Peggy that evening in the privacy of their room. It all seemed providential. After all the heartbreak, was it really possible that fortune would smile for change?

Peggy was as excited as her mother and immediately wanted to know if she could assist with the front desk. Serina readily agreed, so long as she maintained her studies.

The reward money was delivered to the rooming house at the end of the week, and Mr. Simmons introduced her to a lawyer who drew up the bill of sale. Within three weeks of that date, Serina Malloy and her daughter Peggy stood in front of their rooming house while a sign painter put the finishing touches on the billboard advertising "Malloy's Rooming House."

They pitched into the task of painting and refurbishing the two-story building. There were eight bedrooms, two sitting rooms, a large kitchen, and dining hall. Serina kept the cook and housemaid and reflected now on her good fortune. For the first time in her life, she had a sense of independent worth.

In time, she joined the Women's Temperance League and began to attend the Episcopal Church located two blocks down from her rooming house. The good people of Marion were impressed with her industry and her apparently cultured background. She didn't talk about her past, except to mention that she was widowed and that her family connections were "out West."

Peggy went off to school in her crisply starched crinoline and colorful bows. She was the envy of her classmates, having traveled on steamboats and stages and visited other cities.

It was a good feeling to be respected by the populace of Marion. The residents were proud of their city, and now Serina felt a part of the inner circle. There was little resemblance between the sophisticated owner of the rooming house and the naive, young girl who had learned her trade under the auspices of the notorious Della Devine.

Chapter Twenty-Five

Far off in the darkness of the Sipsey swamp, the howl of a coon hound reached the small group around the fire. Old black George cocked a hand to his ear and nodded his head. "Thet be old Nellie," he said. "Thet old 'coon leadin the pack tward Dyer's Sink." Young Jerry Barkley, Jonas, and William looked up from the campfire, and the laughter and joking immediately halted. There was a note of concern in Jerry's voice as he looked up at the old man. "You don't think old Nellie will—"

"Fall for that 'coon's game?" Old George shook his head, "T'aint likely. Old Nellie know this swamp better'n that coon do. She'll pull up 'fore they git to the shallows, and the rest uv the pack'll follow her lead."

The old man threw another limb on the fire, and sparks burst upward, reaching for the top branches of the trees. Thick fog surrounded them, and they instinctively moved closer to the comfort of the flames, relaxed now, listening to the music of the hounds.

"Uncle George, would you mind telling that story about the medicine man?" Jerry asked. William nudged Jonas and settled himself back against the big bay tree, knowing full well that George never tired of storytelling. The fact was, none of them tired of hearing the story, and the warmth of the fire, and their presence in the very swamp where it happened, made an ideal setting for the tale.

"Well, it wuz lak dis," the old man began. "It wuz when they wuz building that Byler Road, the one for the stagecoach line—north and south. They wuz choppin' down all them big trees in the Sipsey swamp and layin' 'em crosswise over the mud to make the road.

"They come to this section of the swamp thet look lak nothin' but some shallow water. They started layin' them logs across the mud, and the logs they jest kept sinkin' right out of sight. Well, they kept puttin' 'em down and they kept goin' under, and so they give it up and put the stage line road on t'other side of the river."

"Yeah, but what about—"

"I'm comin' to thet, Jonas… jest don't rush me," he grumbled. "There wuz this drummer come to Fayette. Had this wagon all outfitted with fringe curtains and he sold all kinds of stuff to make sick folks git well.

"He had a monkey, too, and the monkey would dance while the drummer played on a fiddle. Then, the drummer would hand the fiddle to the monkey, and the monkey would saw away on the fiddle, and the drummer would dance."

"Could that monkey really play a tune?" Jeremiah asked.

"Naw, but he ak like he kin. Then after the show, the drummer would get up on his wagon and advertise his remedies. He had all kinds—Dyer's Colonic, Dyer's Compound for Warts and so forth, but the favrite with everybody wuz Dyer's Grape Elixir. He sold thet by the bottle and also in big gallon jugs.

"He would pour a little sample in a cup and ask the folks to take a sip. Then, he'd pour a little sample fo hisself. Ever time he sold a bottle, he took another sip fo hisself. By the time he git ready to leave town he warn't in much condition to drive. Some folks say the monkey wuz driving when they went down the road toward Tuscaloosa County."

Jonas nudged William. "You don't believe that do you, Uncle George?"

George paused and thought seriously about it.

"They say thet wuz a right smart money—but he didn't know nothing bout them changing the road bed, so he kep on down the cleared line to the sink hole."

"So what happened next?"

"Well sir, thet horse come to the sink and thought it wuz jest shallow water and he started to cross—and befo you kin say scat—thet wagon up to the hubs. That Massa Dyer—he too drunk to keer, an thet wagon—an the horse… an the man… an all them tonics—went right under."

"Did anybody really see that happen?" Jerry asked.

"Naw, but they knowed it happened, because they found the wagon tracks—and they found thet monkey. He wuz screeching his head off, hanging on a limb of a big bay tree. After thet time, they name the place fo thet Massa Dyer."

Jerry shivered now, thinking about the medicine man and the unfortunate horse. He listened keenly for the sound of old Nellie's howl and then they all heard it—a long and a short—a long and a short—coming closer, leading the pack away from danger. George gathered up his charges and the dogs followed them back home.

Some time in the early hours before dawn, the pain came on him again, and George got out of bed and sat in his cane-bottomed rocker by the window. The first gray streaks of dawn gave him assurance of another day, and George Barkley was thankful for each day now.

He couldn't remember all the years he had lived on the planet, but a very long time ago, he had been a child in a different country. There was a village with straw-thatched roofs and walls made of mud and a large, round house in the center where the elders sat in a circle around their chief.

He remembered games with a gum ball and a curved stick and markings on the ground that no longer carried meaning for him. And he remembered the day the slave drivers came to his village, black men, who should have been brothers, but were mercenary and merciless traders in human life. He remembered the long lines of chained villagers, suffering and weeping on their way to the seacoast, and then the dark, stifling hold of the slave ship.

Before the perilous journey was ended, there was no prisoner on board who would not gladly leave the ship, no matter what sort of servitude was required. They did their best to look presentable to potential masters at the market in Charleston, South Carolina.

And the young black boy had appealed to Captain John Barkley, lately of the Continental Army of the United States of America. He had taken him back to Barkley Hall, and made him a house boy to his eldest son. He had served that son, William—and then his son, Thomas, since that time.

He dressed in the early light and made his breakfast, and shortly afterward, the young men—William Barkley and Jonas Watson, and the boy, Jeremiah Barkley—came by his cabin.

"Now what you young folks up to this mawnin'?"

"We're heading to the swamp," Jeremiah said.

"Now you ain't goin' back near thet old Dyer's Sink…"

William laughed and shook his head. "We're not going to Dyer's Sink… but we are going to bring back a mess of squirrel for supper."

Old George nodded. "And you want me to have one I guess."

"Tell you what. We'll shoot 'em, you skin 'em, and Dicey can cook for all of us."

"Thet be fine, young folks… yep, thet be fine."

George shuffled off to the shed behind the wood yard. He started work on the bookcase that he was building for Thomas' next birthday. It was an inspired work, and George had been working as the spirit moved him, but today he sensed an urgency to complete it. Each one of the boards had been rubbed to a soft sheen, and he started now to fit them into place.

129

Using the old spoon bit on the auger, he bored holes at either end of the slots where the shelves would fit and chiseled out a trough for the shelves in the thick sideboards. Next he cut the grooves in the top and bottom panels for the sliding doors and finally the case stood completed. The bookcase would make Thomas feel better, he figured. The Lord knowed he had been down in the dumps for some time. He raised himself up to admire it. He almost straightened to his full height when the pain hit him again—harder than ever before this time.

The boys found him lying in the woodshed when they returned from the squirrel hunt. All the color left William's face as he saw the old man lying in the wood chips. "Jonas, help me—help me get him up."

Jonas lifted underneath his arms but then laid him back again. "It ain't no use Mist Will. He done gone."

George was a loss to everybody and perhaps a greater loss to the slave families than to the members of the big house. To them he had been a symbol of permanence. He had preceded all of them into this country, and he had survived the bleak winters and the boiling summers. He had bridged the gap between fact and fantasy with his numerous stories of the swamp. All things were possible with George—his very presence lent credibility. Now he was gone, and each was aware of his own mortality.

Thomas was especially touched when the boys told him about the bookcase that George had been building for his birthday present. He had it installed in his bedroom, and there was a comforting feel to the boards—almost a form of communication when he rubbed his hand across its top.

Nobody knew for sure how long George had lived. The slave ship that brought him from Africa had docked at the port in 1796, and Thomas estimated the boy to have been about sixteen years of age. He carved a stone for him that read:

GEORGE BARKLEY
FAITHFUL SERVANT OF THOMAS BARKLEY

They buried George in the family graveyard, just below the foot of Thomas's plot. Thomas took over the ceremony this time and read from the family Bible. He picked the twenty-third psalm—all six verses—and when he had finished there was a long silence, and the slaves and the family waited for him to speak again.

He began to pray then, something he had not done in a long time. "Oh Lord, take this good and faithful servant and give him the long rest that he so much deserves, Amen."

Chapter Twenty-Six

William and his father reached a closer relationship after Serina and Peggy departed. Somehow the son was better able to sense his father's loss and he also felt a need to make up for the ill-chosen words he had used on that first meeting. William greeted his father in the early morning and always made it a point to wish him a good night.

The loss of old George, as well as the man Joseph, depleted the work force at the plantation. More work was required than the slaves could properly handle, and Thomas made a decision to purchase two field hands. He invited William to accompany him to Tuscaloosa. Jonas would drive the brougham, and there would be room for two slaves beside him on the return trip.

They spent the evening before the slave auction in the lobby of the Warrior Hotel. Profitable market conditions seemed to have lifted the spirits of everyone in the hotel. Thomas and William mingled with the guests and then entered the dining room. Long tables were crowded with men on either side, and the room was ablaze with the light of candelabras. Food was stacked on platters at each end of the tables.

A man was seated at the end of the large, central table, and he immediately got their attention. He had a large, florid face and white sideburns that exaggerated its width. His bald head gleamed in the light of the candle chandelier. He was talking about the racial differences of whites and Negroes. His voice was deeply mellifluous and his subject matter well rehearsed.

"My study of the Negro has proven that he cannot endure a frigid climate, just as the white cannot endure tropical climes as well as the Negro. The two races are just biologically different. The Negro has a thicker skull, and his skeletal composition gives him an elongated lumbar section. His skin coloring enables him to endure the sun to a much higher degree than the white, and his skin's texture is less sensitive to pain."

The speaker paused in his commentary long enough to guide his heavily laden fork into his mouth, and there was a murmur around the table as his audience pondered the declarations. Having swallowed loudly from the tankard beside his plate, the discourse continued.

"We all know that the typical Negro is habitually lazy and devoid of ambition. The qualities of energy and desire for betterment lie altogether with the white race." He smiled to the general murmur of assent from the group assembled.

For the first time in his life, Thomas Barkley found this type of rhetoric offensive. Perhaps, for the first time in his life, the degradation of the Negro affected him personally. Thomas Barkley had a son about whom some self-exalting white might evaluate in the same manner. "Let's get out of here," he said, and he pushed his chair from the table.

"What's the matter, Pa? Are we staying for the sale?"

"No!" Thomas called back, and William hurried to catch up with his fast stride.

They passed the slave market the next morning on their way back to Newtonville. It would have been hard to miss it, situated as it was under a grove of white oak trees just off Greensboro Avenue. There was a raised platform that extended some forty feet in length, with open sides, and a shingled roof.

The first lot of Negroes was now on that platform, and the auctioneer presented them as a group for the inspection by the crowd. They were then retired, and a single young male was led forward. He had leg irons that caused him to shuffle and his hands were tied behind his back. The auctioneer raised his voice and his eyes darted back and forth to locate a bid.

"We have here a likely looking male of twenty-two years. His name is Reuben, and his temperament is mild. His back is strong, and he has not been affected by fever or spasms. He has good teeth." The auctioneer pried the man's mouth open to display two rows of gleaming white teeth.

"What am I bid for this boy?"

"I'll bid 400," a voice pronounced and William punched his father.

"Look, Pa, it's the man who was speaking at our table last night."

"Pull up here, Jonas," Thomas directed.

The bidding continued with a bid at $450.

"Make that 500," the dinner speaker called.

"Going once at five... twice at five..."

Thomas raised his arm and got out of the brougham.

"I'll bid 600 even."

The dinner speaker looked toward them with disgust and shook his head.

"SOLD!" The auctioneer led the young man to the cashier's table.

Thomas motioned to William to climb the steps and take the man by the arm. William started toward the steps and the young man held back, his eyes wide and fearful, his mouth trembling. William noticed tears in his eyes.

"What's wrong?" he asked the man. He pointed back toward the platform where a young woman stood, waiting to be auctioned. "She my wife... my wife," he sobbed.

The dinner speaker was immediately on the platform. Without preliminaries, he yanked the woman's dress open to the waist, exposing her well-formed breasts, and then turned her around, checking the shoulder blades, thumping her rib cage. The man, Reuben, made gurgling sounds in his throat.

The speaker turned to the auctioneer and waved his money pouch. "I'll offer 600 for the wench."

William grabbed his father by the arm. "That woman is our man's wife, Pa. He's cryin'."

Going once..." the auctioneer called.

"Make that six-fifty," Thomas called.

The dinner speaker was now obviously upset. "I'll go 700!" he yelled.

"And seven-fifty," Thomas replied.

The speaker cursed and moved away from the platform, and the auctioneer's assistant brought the young woman to the table where payments were made.

The man, Reuben, kept murmuring, "Thank you, Massa—oh thank you, thank you."

Thomas realized that he had made the purchase because the speaker had offended him—because he didn't want a man with that philosophy to own these two slaves. He also knew that he was not free of the same prejudice. He knew in his heart that he was a product of his own heritage—but it was beginning to trouble him.

Chapter Twenty-Seven

When Elizabeth had come of age, Thomas arranged for her to attend the Tuscaloosa Female College, true to the promise he had made to Sarah. The timing was right—given the unsettled conditions around the big house after Serina and Peggy departed. Elizabeth was excited about the opportunity for higher education and the prospect of living in Tuscaloosa. She had long wanted to be a teacher and now it seemed a dream was to become a reality. She approached her father the day before she was to leave and was surprised to see the sadness in his face.

Thomas smiled but it was evident that he was melancholy. "So… I'm losing you now, young lady?"

"Not losing me, Pa—I'm just moving to Tuscaloosa, you know. I'd like to come back here and teach once I've gotten a certificate."

Thomas nodded. "That would have been Sarah's fondest wish."

Elizabeth was taller than her mother had been, with a more determined cast to her features. She was otherwise a copy of her mother. She exhibited the same coolness and detachment that made all decisions deliberate and well considered. She wrote happily to the family every week, and once each month William and Jonas made the trip to Tuscaloosa in the brougham to bring her home for a visit.

This time William and Jonas shared the open seat on the way down, but on the way back, William felt inspired to sit inside the carriage. The reason for his interest was Elizabeth's roommate, Loretta Dobbs. Now in their final year of studies, Elizabeth had invited Loretta to come home with her for the autumn holidays, and she had gratefully accepted.

Loretta had a directness about her that was sometimes disconcerting, but she meant well and was merely a product of the Dobbs' personality trait. If the Dobbs liked a person, they said as much, and if they didn't, it was wise to stay on guard. It was apparent from the outset that she liked William Barkley.

"I have heard nothing but, 'William, William,' ever since we became roommates," she laughed. "And I'm glad to see that much of it was justified."

William squirmed and reddened visibly, and this added to the girl's mischievous mood. "He has lovely brown hair and eyelashes that a girl would envy!" She mimicked Elizabeth's soft voice, and the girls traded affectionate blows that tended to ease the uncomfortable moment.

William hastily moved the conversation to horses. He was quite unprepared for the feeling that rushed over him at the instant when the girl's glance locked into his own. He babbled on without thinking, and before he knew it, had invited Loretta to ride his prize filly, weather permitting. As it turned out, the weather was gorgeous the entire weekend. Temperatures were in the high sixties on November 25.

William made good on his offer to take Loretta riding the next morning. Elizabeth cared nothing for this sport and besides, she sensed that some little spark had ignited between her brother and her best friend. She approved wholeheartedly.

The young couple took the trail along the south fields to the Linebarger tract, past the rows of slender cornstalks, still standing, but shorn of the ears and blades that had been harvested. From the cornfields, the trail led into the woods, and they walked their mounts along a pathway of evergreen pines where the brown needles formed a carpet on the ground so thick the sound of hooves was lost.

In the approaching days of winter, the hardwoods stood barren, and now it was possible to see deep within the forest. Clumps of blackberry vines covered with pine needles resembled rounded tents of some desert sheikdom. Above their heads, the bare branches of the mighty oak trees revealed huge brown nests for squirrel.

"Oh, it is a magic forest!" Loretta exclaimed. "I would be content to live in one of these berry mounds!" She turned to face William, face glowing from the ride and excitement radiating from her eyes. William felt his throat tighten, but he managed to speak.

"The really great thing is to lie here in the nighttime, listening to the hounds with the sound of a soft wind in the pine tops."

Loretta cocked an eyebrow and grinned impishly. "Do you really think we could do that sometime?"

The mere thought of such a thing left him certain that anything he said would sound foolish. He turned his horse abruptly. "Race you to the river!" he called over his shoulder.

Loretta gamely complied with the challenge but was no match in skill, and

William had already dismounted when she arrived.

"Help a lady down, will you?"

William was instantly at her side, reaching up and putting his hands around her waist, lifting every so gently and lowering her to the ground. The experience of touching her so legitimately bolstered his confidence. He reached out casually now and took her hand, mumbling about the need to exercise caution on the slippery river rocks. They walked for the better part of an hour, William pointing out a particular fishing spot or swimming hole.

"May I call you Will?" she asked.

"By all means—do call me that. All—that is—my friends do call me Will."

"And do you have lady friends as well?" she looked at him appraisingly.

"Well, that is—well I have friends, but no one in particular." He tried desperately now to carry the conversation forward. "Would you be my friend?" There... it was out.

Loretta smiled up at him, and she took his hand and placed it behind her neck, putting her weight on his arm. "Would you like to kiss me?"

William's mind whirled, and his body tingled all over. "Oh God," he whispered faintly and pressed his mouth to hers.

How long they stood this way, William had no idea. He could have leapt into the air, could have floated off into space. Instead, he took her hand once more, and they climbed to the large sandstone outcropping and sat on its warm surface.

"Will?"

"Yes?"

"Who is the beautiful, little brown boy?"

All of the magic seemed to be fading, and Will's face took on a sober mien. The question had caught him completely off guard, and he turned away from her, looking out across the water. "He is my brother," he answered simply.

"Thank God!" she exclaimed.

Puzzled, William turned back to her, and her sparking blue eyes held him in bondage.

"I was afraid—I mean he looks so much like you—I thought—you might be his father!"

William burst into laughter, and jumping down from the ledge, he held up his hands to lift her down. It was becoming easier and easier, he thought. He started to challenge her to another race, but something told him that he would never want to run away from her again.

Elizabeth and Loretta Dobbs remained good friends as the girls progressed toward their two-year certificates. Loretta also planned to teach, and as luck would have it, the Fayette Board of Education began interviewing prospective teachers the year the girls graduated. The board was very pleased to have Elizabeth and Loretta as applicants. Since Loretta's home was in Kingsville, some distance away, she decided to accept Elizabeth's invitation to board at the Barkley home. Everyone was pleased with the arrangement.

William and Loretta became more than friends as the months went by. It really was no surprise, and something of a relief to Thomas, that William and Loretta made an announcement of their engagement. The young couple, along with Elizabeth, made the journey to Kingsville so that William could formally request her hand in marriage.

Loretta's father took William aside and placed an arm over his shoulder. "She's a fine little filly," he said. "A little wild at times and might need curbing some—but my guess is that you'll be able to handle her. If you're the kind of man I think you are, she'll respect that. If you're not—just remember I'll be on HER side!" The words were softly spoken, but the implications were obvious.

"I love her, Mr. Dobbs," William stated earnestly. "I think she's the prettiest, sweetest girl in the whole world. I plan to take good care of her."

"Sounds like you mean it, son. I'll write a note to the judge asking him to grant the license." The note stated the groom was approved and that he was of legal age to marry. Preparations then began for the wedding. It was decided that the vows would take place in Kingsville, and then the wedding party would travel to Newtonville for an exchange visit.

William made a list of all the things he needed to accomplish before the wedding day. Along with the ring and the license, he needed to purchase tickets for the honeymoon trip downriver to Mobile.

He remembered a promise that he had made to Jonas that day on the docks at Newton's Landing—the promise that had given Jonas hope during his recovery from the snake bite. He had said that one day he was going to ride a boat all the way to Mobile and Jonas had questioned, "You gon take me witchu?" and he had answered, "Of course I will, Jonas."

William walked down toward the cabins and met Jonas at the chopping block. "I was just thinking, Jonas—considering the honeymoon trip—and the fact I'll be needing help with the trunks— "

"Mist Will, do you be thinkin' 'bout me goin' with you?"

"Well... yes I am, Jonas."

The young man let out a whoop and forgetting himself, grabbed for Will's arm, as he had in the younger days. They would leave from the docks at Northport, by way of the Black Warrior River. There was no longer a port on the Sipsey in Fayette County. There were too many sand bars from the soil that had eroded into the channel, and there was no longer a Sipsey River Navigation Company since Captain Woodley's demise.

There was something else that needed doing.

William and his father had a relationship based on mutual respect, but there had been a wall of reserve that dated back to the day Thomas had brought Serina to his home. Thomas had tried to overcome it, but William had not. Somehow, the time now seemed right.

He found his father standing by the fireplace in the kitchen. He was alone, and William noticed the brandy bottle on the mantel. Thomas poured himself a small quantity, and then turning to William, he poured a second glass and held it out to him. It was the first time he had offered spirits to his son, and William recognized it as a rite of passage and accepted it. He took a tentative sip, noting the warmth and bouquet of the liquor and touched his lips with his tongue. Thomas nodded his head and smiled without speaking.

They stood there for a time sipping the brandy, sharing the quietness and the importance of the moment. So lost in thought was William, that it came as a surprise to him when his father cleared his throat and prepared to speak. Thomas motioned to a chair, and both of them sat, balancing the brandy glasses on their knees and looking into the fire.

Thomas' voice came slowly, almost reluctantly. "If I had to sum it all up— it would just amount to a matter of timing." He stirred the coals and added another log to the fire. "Sarah was a saint, you see. I... I never really felt myself to belong in her world. There were times, accidental, I guess you could say, when the two of us seemed to be on the same planet, at the same time. A matter of timing—that produced you and the other children."

William stirred uncomfortably in his seat, looking not at his father, but at the bright new tongue of flame eating at the wood. "You... don't have to explain anything to me."

Thomas looked up then, almost as if he had forgotten his son was present. "No... I don't have to explain myself to anyone. But I want to explain, if I can— how things came about." Thomas poked at the fire and there was a long pause before he spoke again. "This woman, Serina—came along at a time when I needed someone—you know?"

William nodded and Thomas continued. "Men and women are different, of course, and the good Lord knew what he was doing when he made them that way. But sometimes it's hard for a man to figure it out. Sarah once said that the Sipsey was my mistress—that she was jealous of the hold that river had on me. In some manner of speaking, she was right.

"I retreated to that body of water when the body of my wife was not available to me. I lay in the leafy embrace of her and buried myself in the wetness of her. I slept on her rounded banks, still warm from the afternoon sun.

"And when this woman, Serina, came along—she had much in common with that river—wild and wet, and primal. There was no shame in her and no restraint. Her murmurings were the voice of the river, rushing in torrent—and whispering away into the shallows."

William had never heard his father speak in this manner and he was acutely attentive.

"I would not have taken her for a wife. God knows I would never allow anyone to take Sarah's place, but God also knows I wanted her—needed her—at the time." He paused now and looked into the fire, and William thought he had finished, but he spoke again.

"It appears to me that a man is made in such a way that his body just has a will of its own. His mind reacts to his body. He can be thinking on any subject at all and out of the blue, this feeling comes up in his groin and takes his mind off whatever he was properly thinking. His mind just reacts to his body.

"It's just the opposite with a woman. Her body reacts to her mind. She thinks about it first—and according to the way see sees it—her body either reacts or it doesn't.

"It was not in my conscious mind to take the woman for a mistress, but she had an effect on me right from the beginning—just brushing by me, or looking at me with that level, knowing look, like she could tell I was aching for the touch of her.

"I know that she had already figured it out. She knew what my needs were without my having to tell her. She had already made up her mind—and that's the way it is with a woman."

Thomas stood up and William got out of his chair also. "My whole point, I guess, is that I never meant any disrespect for your mother. It was just a matter of timing."

William searched for the right response, realizing that his father had possibly revealed more to him than he had ever admitted to himself, but he could only murmur, "I understand."

"Will?"

"Yes, Pa?"

"I want you and Loretta to have the Linebarger tract. It's got good pasture by the river and hills for an orchard. No finer cotton land around, I guess. I'll make a deduction from your inheritance for its value, but I want you to have it."

William was overcome. The land described was choice and the frontage on his beloved river was all that he could have hoped for. He put the glass on the mantel and walked toward his father, his throat too constricted to speak, so he just reached out for him and hugged him the way he used to do. "I love you, Pa," he said. It sounded strange to come right out and say it aloud now that he was grown.

Thomas clasped his eldest son as if he couldn't let him go. The crackling of the fire as the spent log broke in two brought the moment to a close. Each of them would have spoken, but there was no other thing that needed saying. William moved toward the door, and Thomas sat down once more in front of the fire and stirred at the coals.

Chapter Twenty-Eight

"Saints preserve us! 'Tis the widow Malloy!" The voice was vaguely familiar. Serina looked up from the registration desk and dropped the quill pen to the floor, mouth agape, as a smile broke across the face of Alonzo Hogg. "Don't the world turn about, though?" he asked casually. He strode up to the desk, taking the derby from his head and wiping the inside band with his handkerchief.

Serina was speechless at first but then spoke in a voice that shook slightly, in spite of her resolve to be calm. "You are not welcome here," she managed.

"Ah, but surely you would not deny a poor traveler the comforts of your lodgings?" He was obviously enjoying himself.

"I stand by my statement—you are not welcome here!"

The man's face darkened; the smile became a sneer. "Ah, but you will accommodate my needs, dear lady, you will indeed!" He dropped the valise to the floor, accentuating his words. "I plan to be with you for some time."

She didn't know how she made it through the day. All movement was mechanical under the swarthy man's scrutiny. When Peggy came in from school, Serina took her by the arm and rushed toward the stairs. She was frozen in her tracks by the voice of the intruder.

"Well, well, is this the young lady I've heard so much about?"

Alonzo came to the bottom of the stair and looked up toward the surprised young girl. "Hasn't your mother ever mentioned my name? Just call me Alonzo, my pretty, because you'll get to know me well. I'm an old... old friend of your mother's." He laughed loudly and went back to the easy chair by the window.

Peggy looked anxiously at her mother as Serina accompanied her to her bedroom. "Who is that man, Mother?"

Serina looked away from her daughter, hiding her concern as best she could. "He's a nobody—a troublesome nobody. He had some trouble—with Thomas Barkley—a few years ago, and apparently wants to take it out on me.

Don't you worry about it—things will work out in due course."

She said it, but there was little conviction behind the words. It was apparent that man had spent a great deal of time finding her, and she could not know to what purpose. Finally, she could stand it no longer. She strode defiantly to the easy chair. "What do you want of me?"

"Ah, now that's a good question, my dear—a very good question, indeed." He flicked the ashes from his cigar on the carpet by the easy chair. "The truth is… there is something that I want of you, seeing as how I'm a very big businessman these days and have little time to dally about!"

"Go on."

"Well for starters, there's the matter of a debt back in Mobile—for which I made the payment. A payment that was accepted under false pretenses, it seems."

"I can repay…"

"Oh yes, you can—and you shall—my dear. Make no mistake about that." He nodded his head for emphasis.

"Then there were those long months that I spent in a jail cell back in Demopolis. Months that could have been avoided by a simple testimony from my traveling companion. But she had unfortunately run away—with another man!" He smoothed the fabric on his lounging jacket without showing any expression.

"I was not responsible for your arrest…"

"Not directly perhaps, but indirectly—you have caused me considerable inconvenience, and I never allow such to go unnoticed."

"I want you out of my boardinghouse—at once!"

He laughed scornfully, glancing out the window at the loungers on the sidewalk. "I wonder… just wonder, what the good people of Marion would think of their highly regarded citizen—oh yes, highly regarded. I got the best recommendations when I inquired about you—but if they knew who you really are? Eh? Better still, I wonder what young Peggy would think if she knew her mother used to be a WHORE in a house on Conception Street?"

Serina's hands shook at the suggestion, and the veins stood out at her temples. Suddenly, the scene with Thomas Barkley flooded her vision, and she felt as if the floor was moving beneath her—the horror all over again.

"What's the matter? Cat got your tongue?" He grinned at her, his evil disposition now clearly revealed on his face. "Please don't fret, my dear. It doesn't have to come to that." He peered at her through the cigar smoke. "I have a proposition for you, dear lady. One that I'm sure you will find appealing, once you have time to digest it." He studied the ash on the cigar. "I would like you to become my wife." Alonzo smiled when he heard her gasp.

"I know how overwhelmed you must be. Wedding proposals don't come every day, do they?" His voice went on impassively. "The truth is, I am now a very rich man, rich and generous... to those who serve my needs. I have studied you very carefully these past few days. Admittedly, my first impulse was to punish you for your..." Hogg searched for the right words, "... wrongdoing—but then this other thing kept crowding into memory..." He paused, waiting for her comment and hearing none, continued.

"I like beautiful things—clothes... horses... women. I must tell you that your image—your naked image... has been constant in my mind."

"Hush! Hush you... you... VIPER!"

Hogg's controlled laughter was without mirth or mercy. "Don't allow your emotions to get out of hand, my dear." He drew on the cigar. "The fact is... you are USED goods, my pretty. Used goods, but still beautiful... still desirable, and I daresay I'm making you a better offer than the eminent Thomas Barkley."

His gaze turned hard now, and he advanced on her and grabbed at her hair, yanking her head backward so that she was forced to look at him. "I'm offering to MARRY you—you cheap little tramp! You WILL agree, or you'll never be able to hold your head up in this town again, to say nothing of how your daughter will feel!"

She agreed in the end, because there was no other course available if she wanted to shield her child from knowledge about her past. She remembered her options back then had also left her little choice.

Peggy could not believe her ears. The "nobody" that her mother had denounced was suddenly to be her stepfather. The very sight of him made her cringe. "Is this what you meant when you said things would work themselves out in due course?"

"Things will work out, my darling. Leave it to me!"

She knew now that it was Alonzo Hogg who had spoiled her life with Thomas. He had told the town about her past, and Thomas had listened to the gossip, and had believed it without giving her an opportunity to present her side. Well, Thomas could go to hell—along with Alonzo Hogg and all the men who had used her. Let Thomas Barkley believe what he pleased. It wouldn't matter. From this point forward, she would never allow her heart to be involved again.

Alonzo allowed Serina to keep the money from the sale of the rooming house. He was even solicitous toward young Peggy, doing his best to appear an interested, helpful mentor, but he got a chilled reception for his efforts.

He arranged for the wedding at a local Justice of the Peace office, and then he hired a rig for transportation to Selma, and they left immediately to board a steamer for Mobile. He appeared, in every respect, to be the gallant escort as he paraded Serina around the decks, nodding and smiling to fellow passengers. "Let us adjourn to our cabin," he spoke loudly at the end of the promenade. "A honeymoon, after all, shouldn't be spent in public ALL the time!"

A tittering of laughter came from the passengers, and Peggy fled to her separate stateroom, flinging herself across the bed, her sobs muffled in her pillow.

He opened a bottle of wine in their stateroom and poured two tumblers, gesturing a toast as he did so. She took the glass eagerly, anxious to dull the agony within her.

He gulped the wine and smiled malevolently. "Congratulations on your new station, Mrs. Hogg!" He laughed then—raucously, evilly. "You're still a whore—but now you can consider yourself private stock!" He flung her upon the bed and began stripping her clothes away. She kept her mouth shut so that the daughter in the adjoining cabin would not hear. Thus began her indentured matrimony. She was abused at the whim of Alonzo Hogg, and just as perversely, rewarded in cash for her services.

She was surprised to find that he had purchased one of the prominent mansions along Dauphin Street and appeared to be a well-known figure in the public eye. There was a full-time cook and a man to drive his carriage. A housemaid cleaned and waited on Serina's needs.

He entertained, but many of the guests appeared to be coarse and furtive in manner. Some wore uniforms, though, and some were obviously cultured men, from their manner of speech. There were also political figures that merited some refinement in hospitality.

That was Serina's function. He made her duties quite clear. "You will smile at the appropriate moments—whenever I nod in your direction—and you will dress appropriately for the occasion. You may bill your clothing choices to my account."

She even had her own bank account for household expenses, and she deposited any excess money into a special savings account. She was determined that Alonzo Hogg would pay a high price for the pain and humiliation that he heaped upon her. Publicly, he played the role of the perfect gentleman, pulling out a chair for her, or offering some delicacy from the table.

Peggy suspected the undercurrent of emotion, and she looked anxiously at her mother whenever she detected a bruised lip or a reddened splotch on her face. Serina brushed it off and continued to tell her daughter that things would work out in due course.

Peggy could see no indication, other than their newly found affluence, that things could possibly work to their benefit. She couldn't know that a plan had been forming in Serina's mind—a plan that helped her to overcome the pain of the present situation.

She was waiting at almost midnight, when Alonzo came in from his weekly meeting at the city's Commerce Club. Alonzo's face was flushed with drink, and he was obviously intent on tormenting her. She felt her stomach quiver in hatred as he approached.

"Has your daughter retired for the night, my dear?"

Serina rose from her chair in alarm. "Of course she has! It's near midnight—and I'll thank you to leave my daughter's welfare to me!"

"And I'll thank you to keep a civil tongue in your mouth!" He walked across the room and slapped her cruelly across her lips. He watched as a trickle of blood formed and spread down her chin. He fell upon her then, forcing her to the floor and tearing her garments away. He chewed at her nipples and entered her savagely—and in this manner was able to achieve the elusive satisfaction that he sought.

She looked at him afterward, her eyes brimming with tears of hatred and humiliation.

"I am your wife. You don't have to treat me this way!"

"You were my whore first—and quite frankly, I like it better this way!"

He laughed contemptuously, then reaching into his trousers pocket, he extracted a handful of bills and tossed them on the floor. "Your service was exceptional tonight, my dear, and as you know, I'm willing to pay for the best!" His laughter hung in the stairwell as he closed the door to his bedroom.

Serina sent Peggy away to a boarding school in Biloxi in the following weeks. The young girl was hesitant about leaving her mother, knowing that a probability for violence existed. On the other hand, she was thrilled at the idea of attending the private school and meeting other young ladies.

"Don't worry about me!" Serina admonished. "I have no doubt that everything will work out for the best. You just concentrate on your studies—and try to enjoy these young years. I'll be here when you need me."

At the end of the week, she paid a visit to Hogg at his office in the factory, playing the role of the devoted wife, needing his opinion on a set of china that she found to her liking. He was startled and suspicious at first, but then flattered at the attention directed her way by his employees.

Hogg strutted through the plant with his stylish wife on his arm and he introduced her to supervisors and staff, and then they returned to the privacy of his office. "Just what are you up to?" he inquired, grabbing her by the arm.

"I thought that it would be nice to see where my husband makes all his money." She smiled pleasantly.

"You're up to something," he said. "And I'm sure that you know just how much trouble you can get into… if you're thinking of running away from me again."

"Why, Alonzo! I'm surprised that you'd think I might do something like that. Do you think I'd give up all these fancy clothes—a fine mansion and servants and…"

"Just shut your mouth and get the hell out of my plant," he said. For some reason, her solicitous attitude angered Hogg more than her usual reserve.

Hogg pondered the visit after Serina's departure. Something was afoot. His instincts told him that, but he was also quite positive that he held all the trump cards, whatever game she wanted to play.

Chapter Twenty-Nine

1861

War between the states was now imminent. The Southern states had already sent delegates to a convention in Montgomery, Alabama, to vote on seceding from the United States. He suddenly had a new customer—the Confederate States of America.

Hogg had purchased influence on all sides. He stood to become one of the richest men in the city of Mobile. He shipped raw cotton to the North and imported finished cloth from the factories in New England. He sold this, and all that he could produce in his own factory, to the Confederate Quartermaster.

He looked over the shipping schedules and made allotments to the English ship anchored in Mobile bay. He had a unique arrangement with the British Captain. While the rest of the South withheld shipments of cotton to both the North and the English, Alonzo Hogg was making a fortune working all of the political ends. The English ship plied the coastal waters, and the Captain enjoyed the greatest hospitality in ports north and south. Hogg could see limitless opportunity ahead.

His situation at home was not as rewarding. The more Serina played at being the doting wife, the more difficult it became for Hogg to be physically attracted to her. Finally, Hogg retraced his steps to Della Devine's house for a more compatible setting for his perverted pleasure. And Serina carefully measured arsenic into his coffee each morning before he left for work.

Alonzo Hogg shortly began to have frequent bouts of weakness and terrible stomach cramps. He wondered if he was coming down with some ship-borne plague from his foreign contacts. He considered the possibility of the Yellow Fever and rationalized that he would feel better in cooler weather. He didn't feel better, and in fact, continued to deteriorate, and he took to his bed, sending his driver to bring a doctor.

The doctor came, and continued to visit over a period of weeks. He developed little use for the man in the upstairs bedroom, and Alonzo was not timid in his criticisms of the doctor's capabilities. "You are a villainous old fraud!" he berated. "I wouldn't trust your medicines on my worst enemies—and I have a few!"

"Doubtless you do, my good sir," the doctor replied. "But in my opinion, you are suffering the consequences of your own excesses." He adjusted his waistcoat over his ample paunch and peered over his spectacles at the stricken man. "There seems to be very little liver function, and your coloring has worsened since my last visit."

"Don't stand there reciting what's killing me, you heartless old bastard! Figure some way to cure me, for God's sake!"

"God may well be your last resort," the doctor replied curtly. He nodded his head toward Serina, and she escorted him to the door.

As if fearful that he might expire before he got the chance to inflict more pain on Serina, Hogg finally brought to light the secret he had held so long. Leaning back on his pillows, he smiled cruelly in her direction. "Tell me, my dear, about your esteemed first husband."

Serina was caught off guard. She hadn't thought of Tim Malloy in a long time. Oh, he was evident in the child they had created and in the zest for life that Peggy displayed in her letters home, but Serina had not consciously considered her life with him. It was a dead page in history—and deservedly so from her point of view.

"What... whatever makes you bring up the subject?" she asked, the warning signals of possible hurt already striking in the pit of her stomach.

"You haven't spent much time talking about his virtues as a husband," Alonzo leered.

"He was a good husband; at least, he was a good man before he came to this Godforsaken city!"

"Ah, but one cannot blame the city, my dear. The potential for good and evil lies within each of us... it merely depends upon which option we choose to exercise."

"Well, you had no problem deciding which option you would exercise!"

Alonzo laughed in spite of his pain, and then scowled as he looked at the useless medicine bottles on the table. "At least he didn't spend much time wondering how he was going to die!"

"How could YOU possibly know what may have befallen him?"

Hogg paused now, relishing the moment, taking his time as he pronounced the words. "Because, my pretty, I shot the son-of-a-bitch dead!"

Serina could not believe she had heard the statement. All of those long years she had wondered—no, suspected—that he had merely forsaken her and his infant daughter. And now this personification of Satan admitted that he had killed him!

"You are lying—lying!" She screamed at the hateful figure on the bed, her heart rejecting what her mind had recorded. He had ruined her in every way possible, killed her husband, and had killed any chance she had for happiness with Thomas Barkley. He had tormented her into giving up her one chance at independence back in Marion.

Hogg smiled now, gloating over his victory. "Not lying—just giving you the benefit of the facts. I doubt very much that I have to worry about it now. How you must have wondered what happened to him—how could he have deserted his loving wife and child?"

Serina crumpled into a chair, and Hogg smiled once more. "No—he didn't desert you—at least not intentionally. He just made the mistake of picking a fight with the wrong man! Face the facts, you must have known he was a loser! You must have known it and tried to overlook it because he was so big—and strong—and handsome... eh?" He laughed fiendishly and then grimaced in pain. "He WAS a loser! You know, my precious, there are only two types when the cards are laid down—the winner... and the loser."

Serina's face was ashen, and she trembled visibly. "You... you kept this from me... all this time?"

"Well, let's say for some time now. It's amazing the amount of information I gained through my affiliation with Della Devine's girls. You should know all about that!"

Serina looked at him in a different way now. She no longer felt the fear that had stricken her speechless so many times. The look was pitiless—and more. There was pure venom now.

Alonzo Hogg recoiled when he saw the look, and she delivered his death warrant. "The cards are laid down, Alonzo Hogg. There is a winner, and there is a loser. This time... the loser is you. I arranged it, Alonzo—do you understand what I'm saying?" She smiled now, and the chill of it reached the dying man on the bed, and he understood now the source of the cramps, the nausea, and the pain that racked his body.

"You POISONED me!" He screamed in futile rage, and struggled to rise from the bed but was unable to do so. His eyes only delivered the hatred that consumed him.

Serina felt neither fear nor pity. She turned coolly away from the man and left the room.

She discovered that he was unconscious the next morning and summoned the doctor once again. He gave the man a cursory inspection and turned to Serina. "Could we step outside?" She nodded silently. "You can never tell what they might hear. I hate to be the bearer of bad tidings, Mrs. Hogg, but I seriously doubt that your husband will last through another night."

Serina hid her face in her handkerchief, and then appearing to regain her composure, led the doctor toward the front entrance. She gestured toward the furnishings. "Whatever will I do with all this… and no one to share…"

"There, there," the old doctor comforted. "You are a young, and may I say, attractive lady. I'm sure…"

"No, no," she corrected. "I am too distraught to think about it!"

"Well, in any case, I'm sorry, Mrs. Hogg, that we couldn't overcome. I feel certain, however, that no medical science could have saved him."

"I am sure that you did your very best, Doctor," she said softly.

Alonzo Hogg died during the late hours of the night. Serina slept peacefully for the first time in many months in her downstairs bedroom.

Chapter Thirty

Thomas Barkley sat with his daughters, enjoying the hour before the evening meal. The weather was warm and it had been a totally beautiful spring day. The girls were planning a weekend trip to Fayette and Thomas was reading the last edition of the *Fayette Gazette*.

The twelve-year-old boy, Jerry, came running up from the river road with news of an approaching visitor. "I see a rider coming," Jerry announced. "It looks like a soldier."

Thomas rose from his chair and looked down the roadway and then recognizing the rider, he walked down the steps to meet him. "This is an unexpected pleasure, Drew Hall," Thomas said. "That officer's uniform is right becoming to you."

Drew removed his hat, and the freckled grin was the same as in his teenage years. "They've got a storage room full of these uniforms down at the regimental headquarters in Tuscaloosa."

"I don't think they've got one with my name on it." Thomas replied. "Come on up to the porch and greet the girls, and the boy Jerry. If you'll be patient for a bit, Dicey will be calling us to eat."

"That's very kind of you, Mr. Barkley." He shook hands with the children and took an empty chair. He motioned to the flowerbeds. "I've always thought that your house presents the loveliest view in the county—especially with all the flowers."

"My wife was responsible for them," Thomas said. "I've tried to keep the beds growing since she passed, and of course, Elizabeth has added the roses."

"And a beautiful addition they are," Drew said.

Thomas looked at the visitor and raised his eyebrows. "I suppose you didn't come out here to talk about the flowers."

"No sir, I didn't. I'm afraid the news I've brought will not be as pleasant a subject."

"If you mean Shiloh, Tennessee, son, we've already got the news. I think

151

folks are going to realize now that this war is not the great adventure it was cracked up to be."

"No sir, it's no longer expected to be that. We've had our troops spread too thin trying to cover every mile of the borders. The Yankees just bunched up and poured through our lines into Virginia and Tennessee."

"They captured the Mississippi River forts?"

"I'm afraid so—and now the bad news from Shiloh. What we've got now is the Tennessee River separating us from an invading army, and as you know—the Tennessee loops right down into Alabama."

Thomas stared off into the distance and spoke almost in a whisper. "So, the war has come home to us."

Drew nodded, "I'm afraid so, sir."

He stayed for dinner, and afterward, Thomas walked with him to the hitching rail. He looked the young man squarely in the eye and spoke softly so the girls couldn't hear. "Drew—your intention was to talk about William joining up. That's what the visit was about in my judgment."

"I won't lie to you, Mr. Barkley. The South needs all the able-bodied men it can get. I'm signing up men for my company for a period of one year or until the war ends. Nobody expects it to last long. The Yankees have the advantage right now, but Colonel Murfee says General Braxton Bragg is going to give them a taste of their own medicine—right up through Kentucky."

"Have you talked yet with William?"

"No, sir. I wanted to talk with you first."

Thomas nodded. "But you plan to talk with him tonight?"

"Yes, sir. I think William would be an able man to have in my company, and I want the best I can find."

Thomas's shoulders sagged a little now. "William is a grown man—a married man, too, and I suppose you know how this will affect his family. Loretta is pregnant right now, and she needs her husband with her."

Drew placed his campaign hat back on his head and pulled the horse around to mount.

"I know, Mr. Barkley. I wish we could all just wait for the whole thing to blow away. I suppose we both know that's not going to happen."

Thomas shook his head in anger and frustration. "I never believed in splitting off from the Union. We've let hotheads like Yancy…"

"The state's voted, Mr. Barkley."

"Yes, they voted—and the two representatives from Fayette County voted against secession, didn't they?"

Drew's face darkened. "Fayette County is not representative of the State of Alabama. I hate to tell you this, Mr. Barkley, but Fayette County sent a full company of cavalry to fight with the YANKEES!"

Thomas shook a finger in Captain Drew Hall's face. "That's just what I'm talking about, Drew. This war is not right! We've got brother against brother…"

Captain Hall mounted his horse and touched a finger to his hat. "And you've got an invading army just across the Tennessee—ready to burn your plantation to the ground."

Chapter Thirty-One

1862

William Barkley's mother Sarah had once said that "Spring is God's celebration of life." William had occasion to think of those words on a glorious, shimmering, fragrant day in the spring of 1862... the day he rode away to war.

William and Loretta spent their last night together in fitful sleep, sharing the same aching knowledge that the physical presence of the other might never be shared again. They lay in the darkness, committing to memory the warmth, the passion and the tender caresses... a memory that would have to suffice in the uncertain days ahead.

They left their modest house that William and Thomas had constructed on the Linebarger tract and traversed the short distance to the big house for the farewell meal. Each member of the household had a gift ready.

Elizabeth presented a Bible with copper corners, bound in leather. Katherine offered a warm scarf, and Jeremiah, the lucky rabbit foot that William had given him. "You'll need it more than me," he said, and his eyes brimmed with tears.

Thomas gave him the gold watch that he had inherited from his own father, and Loretta presented a locket inscribed with their names.

Dicey was efficient during the meal preparation, hiding sorrow behind a gruff exterior. But it was Jonas, among the servants, who displayed the greatest concern.

"Please take me with you, Mist Will," he begged. "I be watching dem Yankees while you be sleepin'. You KNOW you gon need me!"

William shook his head sadly. "Pa needs you more, Jonas—now, more than ever," but Jonas was not consoled by his words. He rode out of the yard, and when he reached the bend in the road, he turned and took a last look at the home place. It was a view that would have to last a long time. Lavender blossoms of wisteria hung in grape-like clusters on either side of the roadway and white petals of dogwood shimmered among the newly formed leaves of the hardwoods. In the background there stood the house that had sheltered them all, and the family stood in front of it, still bravely waving goodbye.

William lifted his hand, waving also, and he didn't fight the tears any longer. He wheeled the horse then and set off along the river road to Tuscaloosa.

The Forty-First Alabama Regiment was being organized by Colonel Henry Talbird, president of Howard College. He had enlisted the aid of his good friend, and military expert, Colonel James T. Murfee, Commandant of Cadets at the University of Alabama, for the purpose of training the troops. It was to their encampment on the east side of the city, adjacent to the University, that William proceeded for his formal enlistment.

One of the first men he recognized was Loretta's brother, Loren Dobbs. They were about the same age, but Loren was still a bachelor, still the lady charmer, with a ready smile and a golden thatch of blonde hair.

"Will! You old dog! The war's going to be over before we get ourselves trained!" He laughed in high good humor, the war a glorious adventure to his mind. He grabbed William by the arm and took him on a tour of the grounds.

The headquarters was in a grove of trees next to the University's observatory. It was here that Loren and William reported to their company commander, Captain Drew Hall. Drew shook hands warmly, and then released the young men to explore the grounds.

"Would you like to see some Yankees?" Loren asked eagerly.

"I guess we'll be doing that sooner than you think," William replied.

"Nah, not in combat. We've got Yankee prisoners in a compound right down the road by the paper mill. Part of our troops are pulling guard duty right now."

He was off again with William in tow, and they shortly reached the edge of the barbed-wire compound. A row of tents ran the length of the enclosed area, and in back of the tents a long ditch had been dug with wooden platforms extending over the opening. William was surprised to observe the bare posteriors of several men hanging over the pit.

"Don't look much different than rebel asses, do they?"

The air reeked with a sulphurous smell, and William looked about quizzically, causing Loren to slap his leg in merriment. "You don't need to hunt for smell. It's Yankee shit—or the paper mill!"

The food was worse than William had imagined. There was a basic ration of cornbread and beef, the former cooked in thick, soggy portions and the latter stringy and tough.

"We never set a nigger down to rations this bad," Loren said, shoving his plate aside.

"It sure won't compare with Dicey's cooking," William agreed.

The regiment, consisting of 1,250 men, was ordered to join General Braxton Bragg's army at Chattanooga. They marched to Marion, Alabama and took rail cars to Selma. Many of the troops had never seen a train, and they viewed the experience with high spirits.

The trip from Selma to Montgomery was to be made on the Alabama River by means of the steamboat *James Dellet*. This vessel had the misfortune to strike a submerged sandbar, and began to take on water. The Captain decided to evacuate the troops, and they made an orderly transfer to shore in small boats without incident.

They camped that night in the swampy ground by the river, sleeping on tangled masses of moss and roots, fighting mosquitoes and cursing the inconvenience.

"So, this is what it was like to be a swamp fox!" William grinned. Loren had lost some of his good humor. "The damn fox can have it, as far as I'm concerned."

The regiment languished throughout most of the summer doing picket duty in middle Tennessee. They moved then from Chattanooga to Knoxville and on to the Cumberland Gap to join Bragg's army, now withdrawing from the Kentucky campaign. Then it was back to Knoxville, where William's company had the duty of arresting stragglers and holding them in detention until they could rejoin their units.

On the morning of the 25th of October, the Forty-First boarded rail cars under a blanket of early snow for transport northward to a town called Murfreesboro. The regiment was assigned to General Hanson's brigade, which was attached to a division commanded by a former Vice-President of the United States, General John C. Breckinridge.

On the 16th day of December, the regiment had the signal honor of being reviewed by the President of the Confederate States of America, Jefferson Davis. There was no prouder soldier in the Southern army than Loren Dobbs. He and William stood within three yards of the President and were able to overhear conversation between Davis and Breckinridge.

Loren wrote to his parents that evening by the light of the cook fire, using an upended cartridge case for a table. He showed the letter to William.

The State of Tennessee
December 17, 1862

Dearest Family,

 I take pen in hand to advise that both Will and I are well, and we hope that you are. I experienced the high point in my life today. Will and I stood at attention, and our company was reviewed by President Jefferson Davis.

 We were so close that we could hear General Breckinridge tell the President that our brigade was ready and willing to give a brave accounting.

 I think if the Yankees attacked us tomorrow, we would put them to rout. Everyone here was much heartened by the President's visit.

 You are all in my prayers, and I know that I am in yours. May God bless all of us and our glorious cause.

 Your loving son,
Loren

On Monday, the 29th day of December, the regiment took up position one mile from the town of Murfreesboro and to the right of the Nashville Pike. They were in an oak grove with a large open field in front of them.

Early in the day, there was a sound of distant firing, and as the day wore on, cavalry passed them on their way to the rear, having slowed the advance of the federal troops.

Just before nightfall, with nerves taut as fiddle strings, the men of the Forty-First were ordered to advance a half mile and throw up a breastworks. They were digging industriously when the federals sent in their skirmishers.

William and Loren dove into the trench, their imported British Enfield rifles resting on a log at the top of the embankment. The darkness revealed an occasional flash from en enemy muzzle, and they heard, for the first time, the eerie music of a Minnie ball.

"You go on and get some sleep, Will," Loren insisted. "I'll wake you if the Yankees get serious."

"I'll do the same for you," Will replied. "Wake me up in two hours."

He tried to sleep, but it was impossible. They talked and joked and tried to calm the butterflies in their stomachs. The first light of dawn found the men eating from the pre-cooked rations they had been ordered to prepare the previous day. William and Loren were cleaning the last crumb from their mess kits when the command came to "load at will!"

General Hanson rode into view. Their Colonel Stansell rode out to meet him, and then came back to alert the color bearers on the direction of the attack.

"Are you scared, Will?" Loren's face was pale in the early light.

"Damn right, I'm scared," William said. "I'm scared they're going to ask us to charge, and my legs won't get up and move."

Sharp and clear—the sounds of the trumpets cut the frosty air, announcing the advance. William and Loren saw Captain Drew Hall rise to his feet, sword drawn now and looking in their direction. "Let's go men! Give 'em some Rebel music!"

Through the sage fields they ran, and soon a sound unlike anything William had heard before grew in tone and volume, and the famous Rebel yell took all the pent up emotion of the night and vented it on the air. The sound of it was overpowering, and the enemy massed at the crest of the hill began to fall back.

"They're running Loren! We've got 'em running…"

William fired and dropped to one knee to reload. Loren ran on, yelling and firing as the enemy continued to retreat. William was now on his feet again and running when he saw Loren fall. The way he fell… not trying to catch himself, but falling flatly, face first to the ground, let William know the worst.

When he reached him and turned him over on his back, he saw a round, dark hole over Loren's right eye. The blood covered his face and stained the blonde hair a dark crimson. William held him in his arms… not believing… until the voice of his sergeant rang through the din of musket fire.

"Fall back! Fall back! Fall back to the lines!"

The Federal counterattack was on all sides, a surging sea of blue. He dragged Loren's lifeless body as the company retreated back to the breastworks with the whistle and whine of bullets all around them.

The pain he had thought was a scratch on his right arm turned out to be a bullet hole, and there was blood mixed in the mud on his scalp where shrapnel had torn a furrow.

William's wounds were treated by Dr. Thomas W. Spruill, and it was in the field hospital that he learned that General Hanson and several members of his staff had been killed.

"We got cut to pieces," the man in the next cot reported. "They got the Captain, the Major…"

"What outfit?" William whispered.

"Wright's Battery—every officer and man either killed or wounded. "You with Stansell?"

"Yeah."

"Lose anybody special?"

"Someone very special," William replied, and for the second time since he had left home, he turned his face to the wall and allowed himself to cry.

"Happy New Year!" a raspy voiced patient at the end of the hall cried bitterly.

It was January 1st, 1863, and back in Fayette County, Alabama, Loretta Barkley was giving birth to William's son. She named him Thomas.

Chapter Thirty-Two

The weeks passed slowly in the hospital. It was difficult to sleep at night due to the groans from the amputees, and by day the screams of the unfortunate victims in the operating area sent cold chills down William's body.

He was determined to keep his arm, and he practiced using it daily, clenching his teeth from the pain. It took the better part of a month to draft his first letter home, and he spent several days perfecting the writing before he deemed it legible.

And then, Captain Drew Hall came striding into the ward with an orderly behind him. He informed William that he had posted a dispatch to Loren's family after his death. "I also want to inform that you that as of this date—you are now the second sergeant for Company B. Take a furlough home, and get that arm healed up. I hear there's a baby boy back there that needs to see his Pa. A visit now will do you more good than another month in this place."

The road south to Dalton was still open, but subject to enemy fire from cannon mounted in the hills. The sutler's wagon bumped and jarred around the shell holes, and William braced his right arm between his knees. On occasion, a puff of smoke appeared in the tree line and then a shell would burst down the roadway ahead. The driver seemed oblivious to anything other than guiding the mule team and making conversation with the young soldier who had hitched the ride south with him. "I reckin you'll be gittin out at a good time."

"I'm not getting out; I'm just on furlough 'til this arm gets healed up."

The driver laughed. "Thet's a good 'un son."

William shook his head and frowned in his direction. "Of course I'm going back. I'm not a deserter."

The grizzled driver yanked on the reins, and the wagon wheel on the right front narrowly missed a deep hole in the shoulder of the road. "Take a word of advice, young feller. Once you git home—you jist fergit to come back. It won't make no difference in the end. Fact is—you'd be doing the South a favor if you never came back."

160

"What are you talking about?"

"There ain't goin to be nothin' to eat. I'm telling you it's all played out. I'm in the supply business, and my supplies are running out. The South ain't going to be able to feed the troops it's already got."

The driver spat over the side and slapped the reins across the rumps of the mules as they started upgrade. "A soldier can't fight on a empty belly, not fer long, anyways. One of the sutlers from the Kentucky campaign said he saw soldiers picking corn kernels out of cow dung and roasting em fer their supper."

William shook his head. "For all that fellow knows the Yankees are in as bad a shape as us. We ain't turning the South over to Abe Lincoln just yet."

"I don't blame you fer trying, young feller, but it's jest a question of time."

William left the sutler's wagon in Dalton and caught a ride with a farmer to Rome, Georgia. The trip on to Fayette County was spent walking in the mud and rain, shivering in the blustery winds of March.

It was a tired and mud-caked soldier who came around a bend of the road and saw the Barkley land stretching before him, the pastures greening now with spring grass and fat cows grazing placidly in the morning sun.

He reached the fork that led to the Linebarger tract, his pulse quickening so that his chest hurt. Finally the dirt road to his own house came into view, and the dusty feet moved faster. The legs that he thought were too tired for double-time were running toward home.

He set down a rule, the first day—that he wanted no conversation about the war. "I want to forget there is any place on this earth that is different from here. I want to lie on my back in the sun and play with my boy. I want to fish in the Sipsey with Jonas. I want to work in the fields again with Pa…" He looked around carefully but he and Loretta were all alone. He kissed her warmly on the lips. "… and I want to love my wife at any other times, day or night."

Loretta tried to protect him, and she also passed the word that William wanted this visit to be like the old days, that he didn't want to be reminded of the war or the hunger and suffering he had experienced. It was impossible. At every turn, the questions were fired like bullets.

"How long before the war will end?"

"Did you take my rabbit foot into battle?"

"How many Yankees have you killed, Mist Will?"

161

And so it went… and he did the best he could to reassure them, and himself, that it would all end very soon now, and he'd be home for good.

He got behind a plow once more, feeling the smoothness of the plow handles, thrilling to the sights and smells of growing plants, enjoying the smell of sweat and leather and freshly turned earth. Thomas was in the fields with him on a daily basis and they got the crops in the ground at the Linebarger tract.

The arm healed quickly. Old Dr. Brandon checked it on a regular basis. "I'm surprised they didn't amputate," he said.

"Oh, they would have in any other regiment. I told the doctors I wouldn't hear of it, and Captain Hall backed me up. He said I had a good chance to save it, if I kept it clean—one big problem there, but I managed."

"You've got a good constitution, son. That's the main thing. Healthy folks heal better. Well, I've got calls to make—never seem to catch up…" the doctor coughed, and William heard the rattle in his chest.

"Listen, Doc, you need to take care of yourself. Why don't you go on home now?"

"Cant' do it son. Got folks depending on me."

And so he went off in his buggy, denying his own afflictions to care for others. William was reminded of another time, when that buggy followed him at breakneck speed on a lost mission.

The time to go back came all too swiftly. The arm was now completely healed and the news from the Forty-First was not encouraging. William went with Thomas to the courthouse in Fayette for the weekly list of casualties report. That number grew steadily as the unit was engaged time and again.

"I'll be leaving tomorrow," William said.

"Son, I'd go in your place if they'd let me."

"Pa, you're doing what the South needs to do—raise food crops. If we can keep the troops supplied with grain, we've got a chance to press them back into Virginia. The South needs food supplies as much as it needs men right now."

"But the South needs you—more than we do?"

"Yes, it does, Pa. It needs me to replace Loren Dobbs and other men from Company B. Drew Hall depends on me, Pa. I'll be moving on tomorrow."

They walked together through the fields that afternoon, and they talked about the crop rotation for the next year. He helped Thomas repair a section of fencing, and then they shook hands, smiling at each other, and said goodbye.

He kissed his sisters and old Dicey, gave Jonas some joking advice on women, and went home with Loretta and little Thomas. Early the next morning, he mounted the fine saddle horse that Thomas provided him. He looked a long time at his wife and son, knowing everything had been expressed—and then he slapped the riding quirt on his mount's flank and galloped away. He didn't look back.

Chapter Thirty-Three

1863

Slick, red mud and the soured smell of his own unwashed body made sleep difficult for Sergeant William Barkley. The pain from the leg wound was so constant that he was almost conditioned to it, and his wakefulness was not solely the result of it.

His unit had encountered the Yanks in a small thicket. It was apparent the enemy hadn't suspected that they were so close to Rebel lines. General Bragg had counted on just such confusion when he had ordered infiltrators to breach the Federal lines. The infiltrators had informed the enemy that Bragg was giving up the fight.

"Ain't nuthin' left of the Southern army," young Private Samuel Gray told his captors. "All our lines around Chattanooga done been vacated—'ceptin some rear guards to hold back a Yankee advance."

"Wal now, if you're telling it correctly, I guess you won't have no objection to leading the way when we advance," the Union Captain responded.

"Naw suh—no objection at all, suh," the private grinned innocently.

When Private Gray came striding from the ticket in advance of the Union patrol, he was dressed in the blue jacket the Yanks had forced him to wear. William recognized him, even so, as the tousled haired boy from Millport. They had spent many an evening sharing a pipe and recounting stories from home.

"Hold your fire!" William had screamed at the top of his lungs, but young Sam Gray had no chance at all. The Yankees fired and the Rebels returned it, and Sam Gray was caught in the middle. The cornered Yankees fought like wildcats. Bullets cut through the air like angry swarms of bees.

William felt the thud against his thigh as the leg went out from under him. Dr. Spruill checked it, clucking in that admonishing way of his—running his probe cleanly through from the entry point to the exit. William felt himself fainting from the pain and heard the voice of the doctor to the orderly. "Hold this man up," he said, and he poured some fiery liquid through the wound and placed a bandage around and over it. "No broken bones. You can keep the leg until it gets infected."

"I've kept an arm before and I'll keep the leg," William retorted. He returned to his own campfire.

The day was ending and in the west a large thunderhead appeared on the horizon. Lightening streaks played around and inside of it. William laughed as he thought about Jonas and a story he had told about counting from a lightning flash until you heard thunder. Jonas said George told him it would reveal the distance to the storm. It dawned on him that he had never gotten the formula, and it bothered him not to know how many miles applied to each count. Still, it was soothing to think about home—about Jonas, about his childhood—and he finally drifted off to sleep.

He awakened from a fitful slumber to find a cold rain pelting his tent flap and blowing in on his chest. He eased himself further back and closed the flap. The campfires sputtered and died away, and blackness descended over the forested campsite. The gnawing hunger in his belly returned and an increased awareness of his hurt. Lying there, cold and soberly awake, his thoughts returned as always to Loretta, and to home. He longed for the serenity of the river, the solid, timeless stance of the big oaks, and the smell of the boxwoods by the front porch steps.

Out of the blackness of the night, William constructed a scenario of his life on the Sipsey. He could envision the fireplaces all lighted, red embers glowing underneath the logs. He could feel his quilt of thick, cotton batting, colorful with the scraps of various textile dyes. He could smell the hot coffee brewing and biscuits cooking.

The sound of the rain changed from a spiteful patter to a muted drumming and then to a vision of ripples on the surface of a river. He could see it was the Sipsey, and he saw the big trout break the water in a silvery splash as the line yanked tight in his hand. "I got him!" he called into the blackness. He saw the giant fish swinging aloft now, the cane pole bent almost double.

"Did you call, Will?" The sentry stopped by the tent flap and getting no answer, returned to his post. And William slept once more, a peaceful smile on his face.

In the morning there were horse sounds, and harness sounds, and human sounds as the men in William's company moved into position south of the city of Chattanooga on Chickamauga Creek.

"You'll never get out of here alive," the Yankee prisoner told Lieutenant

Hawkins of Company B. "We aim to clear a path to the ocean so wide and clean that a jackrabbit couldn't hide hisself."

"That so? Well, in the meantime, you can get your Yankee ass back there and start digging redoubts," the lieutenant answered cheerfully. The man was hustled away and hooked to a chain with other prisoners. He was given a shovel and put to work digging the fortifications south of the city of Chattanooga.

The Forty-First Alabama Infantry at Chickamauga had been reduced to 325 fighting men. Many of them, like William, were wounded but on duty that Sunday morning, September 20, 1863. They were attached to Gracie's Brigade and Longstreet's Corps and they held the center of the line in the proposed attack. They had fought all of the previous day in a vain attempt to turn the enemy left, through woods and thickets so dense that it was impossible to communicate effectively.

Now sunlight streamed through the trees, and the day began. There was softness in the air, a touch of fall in the mountains.

William felt an enormous sense of purpose as he gazed about on the glorious morning. Men were moving through the trees, and sunlight glinted on the barrels of their rifles. "There's a smell of victory in the air today," William said and smiled toward his captain. The officer looked at his sergeant intently to see if he was lucid.

General Bragg divided his army into two wings with Longstreet in command on the left and Polk on the right. The men under Longstreet were to charge with everything they had directly into the Federal forces under Rosecrans. The Union General had received misinformation to the effect that a breach existed in his line. He moved a division right on top of one already in place, but concealed in the brush. The hole that was created by this move was directly in front of Gracie's Brigade and Company B of the Forty-First Alabama.

The battle trumpets sounded, and the glistening gun barrels swept forward, the Rebel yell rolling between the cannon bursts. The men of Company B were running now in the warm, September sunlight—and William couldn't even feel the pain from the leg wound anymore. Smoke swirled over the yelling men and the terrified, neighing horses.

The Yankees were running, too—away from the troops of Company B— away down the slope, running in retreat. There was a solid wave of blue ahead and then the Rebel guns roared, and part of the wave lay on the ground.

William ran toward the wave, and he exhorted his men to charge the retreating enemy. He reached the top of a ridge, and the wind suddenly swept away the smoke of the battlefield, and down below the federal troops were in full flight.

The September sun was high in the sky, and white clouds billowed one upon the other with streaks of orange light on their edges. He heard something and turned in surprise, but he didn't see anyone at first.

"What kind of a day do we have here, Will?"

It was his father's voice, and he looked about in wonderment and then— he saw his father and himself, walking through a field lush with growing crops and clouds towering above them. He felt his father's hand on his shoulder and he smiled, remembering the statement his father had made on that early morning so long ago... "It's a day when the sun is shining, and your work is all caught up—and you have the vision to see God's entire universe!"

The artillery shell screamed its way across the sky, but he didn't hear it. He heard instead the sounds of the mockingbird and the blue jay, and he smelled the aroma of freshly turned earth. He struggled with the vision. It was beginning to fade now, and he desperately wanted to have it back. He ran, hunting the vision—toward the descending shell—and he laughed aloud in jubilation as the vision came back to him. "It's a Glory Day, Pa! Today is the Glory Day!"

Chapter Thirty-Four

The casualty lists were posted at the courthouse in Fayette whenever couriers brought them. Word of their arrival would spread throughout the community in rapid order. Thomas went each time to hear the names read. People lined benches on either side of the hallway, tensely and fearfully waiting. The clerk appeared with a sheaf of reports and the courthouse became very quiet. The clerk cleared his throat and began to speak. "We have here the casualty lists for the action at Chickamauga, Tennessee. I will read each name twice—and I ask you to conduct yourselves with consideration for all present."

The clerk began to read them slowly—the dead, the wounded, the missing in action. The names started with Allen, then Anders, Appling, Ashcraft.

Thomas suddenly felt he must suffocate from the closeness of the packed hallway. The clerk's voice sounded far away but he read each name and paused, and the name was Barkley—the name again—Barkley, William—dead.

Thomas staggered from the courtroom and made his way to the buggy. He drove off down the Columbus road, a road that was not familiar to him. He stopped the buggy and he dropped down on his knees in the dust. He looked heavenward from the unfamiliar road to the sky above him and he spoke to God.

"My name, God, is Thomas Barkley. I introduce myself to you because it is evident you have turned your face from me. First you took my infant child, then my beloved wife—and now God, you have taken my son. For what purpose, God? For what purpose did you bring me into this world—only to rob me of everything that I ever held dear?" His chest heaved with great tearing sobs and the pain threatened to stop his breathing.

He looked at the indifferent sky, and a rage began to burn inside him. He shook his balled fists at the sky and he cursed God. Finally, he climbed back into the buggy and wheeled it about and drove through the town and down the road to Newtonville.

Jerry and Dicey were on the porch and they viewed with alarm the reckless speed of the buggy and the fearful rage of the driver, and they knew the worst. They all tried to comfort him—Elizabeth and Katherine, Jerry and Dicey—but it was impossible, and they went away to handle their own grief. Loretta sat motionless in her chair, the baby crawling on the floor around her, and she made no sound at all when Elizabeth gave her the news. Loretta crumpled to the floor and Elizabeth ran to find Jerry. Together, they carried Loretta and the baby to the big house, and Elizabeth watched over her until sleep finally overtook them.

Thomas went to bed late in the evening, but he could not sleep. He got up and walked in the darkness to the river, and he was tempted to just keep walking into the water and allow it to carry him away. He considered this for some time until the chill of the night led him back to the house. He sat down in his chair by the bed and covered himself with a quilt. Later he suffered a violent attack of nausea. He attempted to rise up from the chair and fell heavily to the floor.

When Jerry knocked at his door to announce breakfast, there was no answer, and so he opened it and found him, unconscious but breathing still. He struggled to get him on the bed and called the girls to watch over him while he went to get Dr. Brandon. When he returned with the doctor, they were pleased to find that he had regained consciousness, but it was obvious that he was suffering, and he was unable to speak.

The doctor noted the unequal size of the pupils of his eyes and his rapid pulse. He motioned to Elizabeth and Jerry to follow him to the hall.

"I don't want to alarm him unnecessarily at this moment, but it appears to me that he's a victim of apoplexy."

Jerry grabbed the doctor's arm, the loss of his half-brother now overshadowed by the desperate condition of his father. "Will he die? Say he won't die!"

The doctor patted the boy's hand where it held on to his arm. "Not now, anyway, but he needs to be kept as quiet as possible. You will need to keep his bowels regular. I'll leave a purgative for that purpose if needed." He took a bottle of the dark-colored liquid from his satchel and handed it to Jerry. "I expect you'll be the one to handle his physical needs, son."

He closed the satchel and placed his hands on the boy's shoulders. "I've watched you grow up in this house. I suppose you know—better than me—how much depends on you now." He got back in his buggy and went off down the road to Newtonville.

Thomas' recovery was slow. The left side of his body was useless, but his power of speech returned over a period of weeks. His manner of speech was different after the stroke. He resorted to the crudest terminology at times. He would, in short, call a spade a spade or something much worse. The girls would beseech a visitor with their eyes to overlook his behavior.

"God damn them all!" he told the visiting preacher. "God damn the Yankee sons-of-bitches, and *damn that old scarecrow-looking bastard, Lincoln!*"

Chapter Thirty-Five

1865

The Corps of Cadets at the University of Alabama in Tuscaloosa, along with a remnant of reserves under Confederate General Garland, put up a gallant defense of the city. They lost to overwhelming odds and suffered 150 casualties. And so, five days before Lee's surrender at Appomattox Courthouse in Virginia, the war ended for the folks in Tuscaloosa and Fayette Counties—in the Sipsey swamps.

Those left in the decimated ranks of the Confederacy came home at last. None had given more than the Forty-First Alabama Regiment. Its 1,250 men had marched away to war, filled with excitement and a sense of responsibility to defend their native soil. They had drawn the last rations that would be given them on April 2, 1865, at Southerland Station, Virginia. Each soldier's ration had consisted of six crackers and a small piece of rancid meat. They survived on that until Palm Sunday, April 9th, when Lee surrendered his army. The men wept then, because they would have fought on. The starved and ragged remnant of that valiant regiment, consisting of 250 old men and boys returned to the desolated land in defeat. Major Drew Hall was not among them. All the good men that he had recruited perished beside him long before. Those who returned, regardless of rank, took up whatever means availed to sustain themselves and their families. Generals walked behind plows, alongside the rank and file.

Men who had killed took up the ministry, others the practice of law. Some became politicians and some became teachers, and the South needed all of them. Theirs was the task to rebuild a civilized society—to make some sense of it all. It was a hard undertaking.

Some, like Mrs. Stevens' son, Leviticus, came home physically, but the four years of hell left him devoid of all emotion. The Yankees had put him on a river steamboat bound for Columbus, Mississippi, and he walked home from there.

171

He came in the door and walked over to the kitchen table and sat down as if he had never gone.

He hitched a mule to the turning plow and went into the field the next morning, but oftentimes he would forget where he was, his eyes staring off into space and seeing an endless replay of the debacle called Chickamauga.

Blight spread across the land—and its name was poverty. It sapped creativity and numbed the sensibilities. It spawned the twin evils of ignorance and meanness. The pre-Civil War culture had aesthetic values and refinement, but no such world existed for the children of the vanquished South. A Yankee general named Sherman burned and pillaged a path to the sea, determined to spread a punishment so severe that the South would never again consider secession. Genealogical records were burned; family connections were forever lost.

And so the South closed in upon itself, reverting once more to a frontier status. The great plantations were sold off to pay debts and taxes. The emancipated blacks were displaced and dependent on Federal dole, and the fields grew over in briars and pine seedlings. The dark days of Reconstruction settled upon the land. Sharecroppers moved from one place to another, wearing out their families and the land itself, searching for the one good crop and moving on when the spindly stalks of their labor proved unrewarding.

Life went on at the Barkley plantation, but it was a continuance of momentum. Thomas sat in his chair and drank from his jug. When he was sober, he played with his grandson, but the likeness of the small child to the son he had lost would overwhelm him at times. Almost overnight, Thomas Barkley had changed from a vital contestant in the game of life to an embittered old man, resigned to his fate but cursing it nonetheless.

The former slaves moved into the fields because the work was a habit that was binding. Leadership was lacking, with the old master often oblivious to the demands of the day. They went about duties they had customarily been assigned to do, and the most authoritative voice on the plantation belonged to Dicey. She harangued the lot of them for their slothfulness.

And then one day, there began to be mutterings of some new system, a new order with free land and money, offered up by a Federal agency called the Freedman's Bureau.

Chapter Thirty-Six

They filed up the hill to the big house in the early mists of the morning, walking two by two—black faces set in determination. There was a gap in the file near the end of the line. It was a short space that divided determination and reluctance. In this small group walked old Moses and Chloe and Jonas.

Jerry saw them coming from his perch on the porch railing and he went inside the big house to find Sir Thomas. He helped him into his clothing and positioned him in the rocking chair, and using the rockers as runners, pulled the old man out of the door and onto the porch.

The group had marched with their eyes fixed straight ahead and they had gotten almost even with the graveled walkway that led up to the steps before they noticed the boy and the old master. There was a perceptible shuffling of bare feet in the dirt and the whole procession ground to a halt.

The lead man set his tow sack down and removed his black felt hat. Thomas saw it was the man Reuben. He was standing there beside the wife that Thomas had purchased for him—standing there now with their three children, born on Barkley land. The man looked up at his former master and was at a loss for words. He turned toward the group behind him, seeking some support, and found none. They stood there with heads down, looking resolutely at the ground in front of them.

Thomas eyed them all in silence, waiting, and when no spokesman emerged, he shouted at them, suspecting their purpose. "What in the plu... perfect hell... is happening here?"

Reuben looked up to the man on the porch, and his face contorted with the effort at speech. "We be a'goin'now... Marse Thomas, sir."

Thomas stared at the man as if he didn't exist. The group behind Reuben and the wife and children beside him, all shifted from one foot to the other. There was a general clearing of throats and an unintelligible murmur of assent.

"What... did... you... say?" The words were slow and reasonably quiet, but in the vacuum that surrounded them, the words seemed insufferably loud.

"We be goin' now, Marse Thomas, sir." Reuben raised his head now and dared to look Thomas in the eye and this vexed the old man even more.

"Going where, for God's sake?"

"We be free now, Marse Thomas, sir."

"I know you're free... Goddamit! Have I said that you weren't free? Haven't I paid you to work by giving you food and clothes and shelter?"

Reuben nodded solemnly, opening his mouth, finally speaking again. "That a fact, Marse Thomas, sir—but the man—the man down at the courthouse—he say they pays you jus to vote the vote."

"Man? What man? What sort of man has filled your head with lies of that sort?"

"Ain't no lie, Marse Thomas, sir. It be that Yankee nigger... the one from the Freedman's Bureau. They calls him a field agent."

Thomas beat his fist against the porch rail. "Are you going to listen to this poppycock, Reuben? How about you back there, Moses... or you... is that you, Jonas?"

Jonas turned his head upward and looked at Thomas with his big, round eyes looking even larger than normal in the blackness of his face. He reached into the pocket of his ragged trousers and removed a crumpled bank note. "He done paid us, Massa Thomas. We powerful sorry to leave, but we be FREE now, Massa Thomas. With Mist Will gone and all—I ain't got no bindin here no more. We gon do whut the white folk do now. We gon colleck our money and vote the vote!"

"God in heaven help us all," Thomas muttered under his breath.

"He sho do," Jonas responded, and he grinned then and turned back the way he had come. The others followed him, their bundles of rags tied about the end of a stick, inspired by the promise of freedom and an easy life.

Thomas shook his head in dismay. "There goes the new South, Jerry—a bought vote and a government dole. God help us all!"

Jerry watched as they shuffled away, swinging now into an easy rhythm and breaking into song. "They're like little children," he said.

"Eh? What's that you say?" asked Thomas.

"I said they're like little children. They have learned no more than children—only what the white man has permitted them to know."

Thomas was astounded at the boy's clarity. "Aye, God, you're right!"

He looked at the boy and then spoke aloud—not to the boy—but to the lost and vacant world around him. "What purpose can there be in setting them free? Can this be God's purpose?" He sat silent for a moment. "Not God's," he answered himself. "The devil's maybe. The whole damned country is going to hell in a bucket."

He pulled the flask from his coat pocket and took a long swallow. "Left me, by God, in the middle of the growing season! Didn't I feed them all their worthless lives? Didn't I put clothes on their backs and give them shelter? Did I ever mistreat them in any manner? *Hell no—I didn't.*" The injustice of it all was overwhelming. He shook his head in disbelief and pulled once more on the flask.

Chapter Thirty-Seven

1866

Jerry hadn't seen Mary Beth McGill since that day as a child when she had invited him to play marbles. He drove down to the village in the wagon to pick up a barrel of flour, which had become available once more, now that the war had ended.

He didn't recognize her. The girl was a young woman, as far as he could tell, and he was surprised when she shyly smiled at him from underneath her bonnet.

"Bet you don't remember me," she greeted, as she seated herself on the porch railing outside the store.

"No ma'am," Jerry responded. "I don't believe that I do."

"No ma'am, I don't believe that I do," the girl mocked, but in a laughing, giggling sort of way.

Jerry felt his face burning as he climbed the steps to the porch, watching as Mary Beth removed her bonnet, allowing her blonde tresses to fall naturally to her shoulders.

"My Pa ain't here today, so you don't need to worry about talking to me. I come to town with my Ma and she's inside the store."

Now it dawned on Jerry that he did indeed know this young person, and it also made him angry to recall the words the father had spoken to him that day long ago.

"Are you sure you want to be talking with a nigger boy?" he asked scornfully.

"Them's my Pa's words, not mine," Mary Beth answered. "And I'm sure I'd like to talk with you if you have the notion."

Jerry scuffed the worn sole of his shoe against the rough end of the top porch step. "My brother, Will, got killed in the war."

Mary Beth nodded her head, and her eyes were looking gravely at him from behind the wisp of hair that hung over her face. She raised an arm and brushed the hair aside. "They's lots of brothers that got killed... lots of daddies, too, I reckon. My uncle got killed at Shiloh."

"Will died at Chickamauga. I guess you heard about that battle."

"I heard about a lot of them, but they didn't mean nothing to me, 'cause I didn't know where they was, anyway."

"Don't you study about geography in school?"

Mary Beth shifted uncomfortably on the porch railing. "My Pa don't let me go to school. He says women got no business gittin' educated, and besides my Ma needs me around the house."

Jerry shook his head sadly. "Everybody should be able to read. My Pa wouldn't let me go to the regular school either, but my sister, Elizabeth, she's a teacher, and so I got to learn reading, writing, and arithmetic as good as any of her students."

Mary Beth looked at him admiringly. "Could you teach me to read from a storybook?"

"Well sure, but..."

"I'm not talking about in front of folks." Mary Beth thought a minute and then looked at him shyly. You know that old Davis place on Beaver Creek? The one where nobody lives?"

"I've seen it when we go 'coon hunting, I reckon."

"If we could meet there some morning, my Pa wouldn't never know, because he goes to the sawmill real early and don't git back home 'till late in the evening. My Ma always sends me to the fields in the morning and I gather up vegetables. I mean, you could teach me a little while—and then I could run back and still git my chores done."

"I'll think about it," Jerry replied. "But I wouldn't know how to tell you..."

Mary Beth caught a glimpse of her mother coming toward the front of the store. She hastily put the bonnet back on her head and jumped off the porch railing. "Next Tuesday," she whispered and walked toward her mother.

Jerry stood aside to let them pass, and Mrs. McGill gave him a stare of possible recognition, but he couldn't be sure. He walked to the back of the store and asked Carl Newton for the barrel of flour; Carl helped him roll it to the loading platform at the back of the store.

"How's Thomas getting along?" he asked.

"About the same. Some days he gets pretty low."

"And the girls?"

"Oh, they're all right, I guess."

"I was telling Mrs. Newton the other day, it sure is nice that Thomas has himself a grandson now. Little Thomas will be taking over the plantation one of these days."

Jerry felt a hard lump settle in his throat. He had envisioned himself as the man in charge, now that Sir Thomas was incapacitated. He was doing all the work in the fields, doing all the shopping, helping old Dicey bathe and dress the old man. It seemed Mr. Newton was overlooking all of this... waiting for the day when the credit could all go to little Thomas.

I'm nothing, he told himself on the way home. *Nothing but a little nigger errand boy.* He didn't eat supper that evening, telling Dicey he had a stomach cramp.

Dicey immediately dosed him with some sassafras tea and honey.

The next Tuesday arrived almost before he was aware of it. As he drove old Emma down the lane, pulling the Georgia stock plow, he got an image once more of Mary Beth in her bonnet and the long blonde hair hanging off her shoulders.

She might be waiting at the old Davis place, even as he started old Emma down the first row of the cornfield. He decided he would not think about it and he plowed on for an hour, but his mind kept working, seeing the girl waiting there alone, possibly looking for him at that very moment.

He tied the mule to a shade tree and walked back up to the house.

"You forget to take water?" old Dicey asked.

"Yeah, I got in a hurry, I guess," he replied.

"I'll fix you a cold jug from the well and the biscuits is still warm there in the ovem. Put you some 'lasses in a few and take 'em on before I throw them out to the chickens."

"I'll do that," Jerry said, but he ran instead up to his room and got a copy of the *McGuffie Reader* and stuffed it down in the bib of his overalls.

Mary Beth McGill didn't prove adept as a pupil. She listened as Jerry pronounced the words and she would repeat them after him, but there was no relevance to the word when she saw it in print.

Jerry decided to try spelling words at random. He would pick out an object—a tree, a rock, or a bird. Mary Beth would try, but the very next time she would forget what he had told her.

"It ain't no use," she declared. "I ain't no good at learnin', anyway."

"We'll try it again next Tuesday," Jerry said. "It's just a matter of practice."

They made their way out of the house, stepping over the cracks in the floor where boards had been taken up by coon hunters to light their fires in the woods.

"Will you come back for sure?" the girl asked.

"I'll be here," he answered. "We'll try arithmetic next time, just for a change."

He watched as she lifted her skirt to climb over the rail fence, watched her run as fast as her slender, white legs could carry her, over the crest of the hill.

Old Dicey was concerned on the following Tuesday when Jerry failed to show up for lunch. She called to Katherine, who was lazily arranging her hair in front of the tall mirror in the hallway. "You hear Jerry say anything 'bout going someplace special today?"

"He was going to the field the last time I saw," the girl replied. "He had a plow on a slide... went off toward the Davis place."

"Toward the old Davis place on Beaver Creek?"

"That's the direction he was headed," Katherine replied nonchalantly.

Old Dicey shook her head. "Somepin ain't right. We ain't got no cornfields in that direction... that land all in pasture."

Katherine seized on any possibility that might involve misfortune to her unwanted half-brother. She never got credit for anything. It was always Jerry this and Jerry that, until she was sick and tired of the sound of it. You'd think her father considered him as good or better than her. "I'll go check on him, if you like," she offered brightly.

Old Dicey was pleased... and surprised. She didn't find Katherine willing to do anything helpful around the house on most days. She spent most of her time primping in her room, or complaining about the food or the lack of proper clothing.

Jerry and Mary Beth were not aware that anyone had missed them. The arithmetic lesson had, if anything, presented more difficulty than the reading experience and Mary Beth had grown bored with it. "Let's don't fool with this old stuff," she said. She stepped across the broken boards and over to the ladder that ran up the side of the wall. "Let's see what's up there," she called and began climbing up the vertical ladder.

Jerry watched as she went, the white legs flashing under the petticoats, and a surge of excitement went through him. He mounted the steps and looked over the opening into the loft to see Mary Beth curled up on a mound of hay. The hay had probably been left there by some coon hunter, he thought, had probably gotten caught a rainy night and decided to sleep inside the abandoned house.

She smiled at him and patted the hay next to her. "Why don't we forget about that old studying and just lie here and talk a little?"

"We don't want to stay too long…"

"We got lots of time. My Pa left early for the sawmill, and my Ma, she went over to the Peabody's to help with the babying, so ain't nobody knows when I'll git home."

Jerry sat down beside her; he felt the strange excitement return and his face flushed. He felt the girl's eyes on him, saw a sly grin tugging at the corners of her mouth.

"Have you ever seen a girl's titties?" Mary Beth inquired.

Jerry felt a shock as palpable as a mule kick go right through his chest. He looked at the slanted ray of sunshine coming through the hole in the roof, watched the dust from the hay floating in the shaft of light. The scent of the girl's body reached him, a vaporous sort of damp, sweet, apple odor. The tumescence between his legs was something beyond his control—urging, seeking ahead of him—and he fumbled for words.

"I… I reckon so," he mumbled.

"You reckon so," she giggled. "I'll bet you'd remember it if you'd really seen any."

He knew then how idiotic he must seem to this worldly-wise young woman. His mind told him that he should get up and run, but the thing down there wouldn't let go of the opportunity at hand.

"Have you got titties?" he asked, not believing the words as he heard them coming from his mouth and knowing the answer full well, without asking, because of the way her dress rounded out over the front.

"Of course I have," she answered indignantly. She studied him intently for a moment and then grinned mischievously, "Would you like to see mine?"

Jerry couldn't speak. He was overwhelmed with the directness of the question. His face burned even hotter, and the girl giggled.

"I'll bet you'd like just a little peek," she whispered.

Jerry nodded his head, his eyes round with wonderment now, watching as she began to unfasten the buttons at the top of her dress. He watched the mounded flesh rise as it was freed from the restricting cloth of the bodice. He was only slightly aware of a distracting noise in the distance.

They both heard it then, Katherine's voice, in the distance, yelling now in anger as she tired of the search.

They scrambled down the ladder and across the broken boards of the floor, the girl running without saying goodbye and Jerry hurrying to retrieve old Emma and the slide.

Their movements were hastily made, but not beyond the keen eyes of Katherine, who saw the flash of the girl's skirts and then recognized the McGill girl climbing over the fence.

Dust swirled, rising from the tapered, wooden runners as Jerry lashed old Emma into a trot, pulling the slide at perilous speed along the dirt path to the pasture. "I'm going to tell Pa about what you were doing," Katherine informed him as he approached.

Jerry's face contorted in pain and embarrassment. "Please don't do that, Katy."

"Oh? Why not?" she asked. "I think Pa would like to know the name of the little hot wench you've been hiding in the old house."

"No, please, especially not that... not the name. I... I promise I won't ever go there again if you won't tell Sir Thomas."

"The name must really be special, huh? Why do I care what you promise? What good does that do me?"

"I'll do whatever chores you want... saddle your horse, bring in wood for your fireplace... anything at all..."

"I'll think about it," she replied. "But if I decide to keep your secret, you'd better jump any time I call, you hear?"

Jerry nodded, miserable in his plight. He detested having to knuckle under to Katherine but the terrible consequences of his meeting with the McGill girl became all too clear to him. Katy would likely tell Lafe McGill also. The father would probably come with a gun to kill him. Yes, he would certainly come after him with a gun because of the beating he had gotten from Sir Thomas.

The father would know that he had nothing to fear from the crippled old man, and so he would boldly stride into the yard and most likely shoot Sir Thomas, also. His mind wrestled with all the worst possibilities that might occur, and in comparison, the servile role he must play to prevent it seemed the lesser of the evils.

Katie took full advantage of her dominant position. "Here Jerry, run these clothes down to Dicey, will you? ... By the way, Jerry, my horse needs a currying before I can expect to ride to the village... Oh yes, Jerry, you can clean the mud from my boots..." It went on and on, until her insufferable disposition got the best of him. "You can go to hell, Katy," he stormed, and waited for the disaster that was sure to befall him.

Finally, he could stand the suspense no longer, and so he found a quiet moment with Sir Thomas and told him that he had been tutoring the McGill girl.

"What did you teach her?" Sir Thomas asked.

"Well, we tried *McGuffie's Reader* and then *Webster's Speller*, and a little…"

"And what did she teach you?"

"Well, you see… she wasn't teaching me…"

Sir Thomas studied the boy, felt the embarrassment in his voice and understood it, but he needed to know how far the thing had gone. "Don't lie to me, boy."

"Honest, Sir Thomas, she didn't teach me anything…"

"But she would have… you can count on it. Anyway, don't worry about Lafe McGill. He's got a yellow streak right down his middle and if he ever sets foot on my property, I'll put a bullet right in the yellow spot, by God!"

He reached up with his good hand and caught the boy's arm. He held on to it, feeling the proud strength in his son, and his face softened. "Watch yourself when you go to town, though. The bastard's not above sneaking up behind you."

Jerry felt better getting the matter off his chest and particularly knowing that Katy didn't have blackmail power any more. He surely resented Katy for showing up just when one of the mysteries of the universe was at the point of being revealed to him. You could count on Katy to do something like that. The way Mary Beth had run away, without even saying goodbye, made him doubt that he would ever see her again.

He tried to think of something appropriate to say to himself—something that would equal one of Sir Thomas's descriptive pronouncements. *Damn you for a meddling, uppity she-dog bitch,* he thought. He believed that Sir Thomas could not have said it better.

Chapter Thirty-Eight

1866

The Johnson grass competed with the corn plants for survival, and the grass had the genetic edge, but Jerry Barkley toiled on from sunup to sundown. Sweat drenched his body, and his clothing carried lacy circles of salt, evaporated from his sweat by the blazing sun. He gathered what he could of the harvest that the former slaves had abandoned in the fields. He figured they would have enough grain to feed the household and the farm animals.

It was the best that he could do, the best any one man could do, and he was now the man of the house in all matters that required a man's physical effort. He still referred all decision-making to Sir Thomas, and he faithfully carried out whatever instructions he was given. The old man was cranky most of the time, but Jerry never took offense.

He gave Sir Thomas a degree of mobility. He took the old man's favorite chair one day, while its owner was sleeping off a pint of whiskey, and carried it out to the woodshed. He cut the two rear legs off so that they were shorter than the front. He braced them well and then bored horizontal holes through which he ran an iron rod for an axle.

Selecting a section of log that was as completely round as possible, he sawed off two slices that would form the wheels. When the wheels were attached, the rear legs were again at a level with the front. When the chair was tilted, Thomas could easily be rolled from bedroom to porch or down a wide board ramp that he constructed next to the steps.

"Aye, God, you're a boy with imagination," he said. "Look at this, will you? Elizabeth... Katherine... come here everybody!"

He had Jerry parade him about the grounds to the very edge of the river bank, the wheels digging deeply into the soft earth so that they refused to turn, and he dragged the old man back to the house with a revision in mind for the chair.

Again, the rear legs were sawed shorter, and he removed the spoked wheels from the little pony cart that had served William and Jonas and himself, and attached them to the chair. He put a small-diameter wheel on the front and between the front legs of the chair. He made it swivel by adding a handle to it. Sir Thomas could actually propel himself about the house, from room to room, to porch and back, by pushing on the right spoked wheel with his good right hand, stopping to change the direction of the guide wheel as needed.

The old man celebrated his mobility with several pulls on the jug, and it was only Jerry's swift action that prevented his missing the ramp off the porch. After that, Jerry put rails alongside the ramp.

Thomas was proud of it, prouder still of this dark son who bore his image. He watched him from the porch as he went about his duties, nodding his head approvingly. He thought about his conception and of the woman that had borne him.

When he thought of the woman, he thought about her body—the beautiful curves of her flesh were etched like a painting in his mind. It was a painting without life, because his body no longer yearned for her, which was a sad and sorrowful thing. He tried not to think of her. He thought instead of the dark son, the only son that God had allowed him to keep. He thought of the irony of it all— that God would have chosen his bastard, part-Negro son, and doomed the other son to death on the battlefield. But he no longer questioned God's judgment. He was grateful for what he had left.

The sixteen-year-old boy was large for his age. His handsome, muscular stature was familiar to all the merchants in Newtonville. His quiet, respectful manner merited immediate approval and made him a welcome customer. He purchased all of the household supplies on weekly trips to the village, swapping freshly shelled corn for ground meal, or a crate of frying-size pullets for a sack of flour, sugar, or coffee. He was referred to as the 'Barkley boy' behind his back, but always "Jerry" to his face.

"That's a real devoted boy there," Mrs. O'Reilly confided to her husband who operated the gristmill. "They say that he takes care of that old man just like a regular nurse."

"He's carrying out a son's duties, I suppose."

"Well… whatever… he's just a nice boy," she commented as she watched him drive away in the wagon.

He stopped by the post office on the way out of town, as was his custom.

"Good morning, Jerry," the postmaster greeted. "I've got a piece of mail for your old Thomas."

"Just so long as it's not a tax bill!" Jerry laughed. "He gets real upset when one of those comes in the mail."

"He sure ain't by himself!" the postmaster sympathized.

Jerry enjoyed the shopping trips to town. He put the mail in the bib of his overalls and climbed back in the wagon. He watched a horsefly settle down on old Emma's rump, and he carefully lifted the leather rein and snapped it down over the insect, smashing it and causing the mule to snort and kick back in indignation. Jerry laughed aloud as the offended animal lurched into her collar, and they were off. Two hours later, he unloaded the wagon and brought the letter from the Newtonville post office to Thomas.

Mail, other than a tax bill, was a high point of adventure for the chair-bound old man. He could not imagine who would be writing to him from a post office out in the Indian Territory, but the envelope bore a seal from Tallequah, Oklahoma.

He carefully slit the flap open with his pocketknife and looked to the signature before reading the letter. It was the only written communication that he had ever received with that particular signature. He sat for a long time with the letter folded in his lap. He was afraid of what the words might say to him, afraid to resurrect the demons that had driven him almost to insanity at times.

At last he unfolded it again and started to read, and his hands shook before the page was finished, and then his tears made a blot on the bottom of the page. He hurriedly shook the paper and blotted the moisture with his sleeve. He folded the letter and placed it back in the envelope, then he rolled himself over to the nightstand by his bed. He carefully placed the letter inside the cover of his Bible and rolled out on the porch. He gazed down the slope toward the river. As always, he sought the comfort of the river in his pain and solitude.

He watched the current moving swiftly due to the early spring rains. The water was a muddy color and he was vexed to see the topsoil rushing away from the farms upriver. The good soil and the good days of his life merged together in the rushing current, and he felt no purpose anymore.

Jerry came for him and saw that no words were needed. He recognized Sir Thomas was in one of his moods and so he got him ready for the evening meal. Later, in the lamplight, Thomas removed the letter from the nightstand and unfolded it once more.

Tallequah, Oklahoma
Indian Territory
March 4, 1866

Dear Thomas Barkley,
I have never written to you, but I have thought many times of you—and of the son that we created. I could not have written this before because it would have been too painful. The pain is now past—dead history, like the dead Confederacy.

I have moved to the Indian Territory. Peggy has married a railroad engineer that she met in college. He is involved in planning the rail line through the Territory. I moved out here to be near them and to locate my relatives. I have found the Parker family—my family—in the Cherokee lands and have been well received by them.

My purpose in writing is to tell you that I am well off financially. I was married for a time to a wealthy textile businessman and have inherited his fortune. I would be able to take good care of Jeremiah, if you could ever find it in your heart to allow him to come out here.

I will tell you now that I loved you, Thomas Barkley, more than any man I have ever known. Because of that truth—I must forgive you.

Serina

He read and re-read the letter, and then he put it in the yellow pine bookcase that old George had made for him. Many times later, he would extract it and read it again. He felt that there was a purpose about the letter that merited its safekeeping… but he wasn't sure what it was. He put it aside, as he put most things aside these days, and reached for the jug under his bed.

The whiskey came from a bootlegger in North River. Jerry picked it up for him every month. The whiskey eased the old man's suffering and restored some of the humor that his sober mind rejected. He became more tolerant of everyone and less concerned about God's purpose when under its influence.

Chapter Thirty-Nine

1868

Sharecropping was the new way of life for the inheritors of the wasted South. Small dirt-farmers and ex-slaves alike worked the fields of the old plantations and shared the fruits of their labors with the landowners. Thomas Barkley was not in favor of sharecropping. He felt it showed disrespect for the land. He had always believed a man should own his acreage. Only then could he appreciate the land's needs and protect it for his future use.

When the widow McNalley broached the subject of farming the Hollimon tract, his first reaction was to refuse; but the widow had a sad story to tell, and he was in a mellow mood at that moment—so he listened.

Sean McNalley had died in the battle at Stone's River, Tennessee. The hardscrabble farm on which he had eked out a miserly existence had been sold at auction by the county for non-payment of taxes. The widow had her own mule and wagon and had salvaged a plow and handtools. The Hollimon tract hadn't been worked in over three years and had grown up in bitter weeds and Johnson grass. No harm could come from tilling of any sort, so he told the widow she could move her belongings into the small house two miles down the river road.

"I sure would be obliged if'n you could spare me that light-colored boy … jist to help with the big things?"

Thomas nodded to Jeremiah, and he climbed up on the back of the wagon. The woman's little girl turned around in the wagon seat to stare at him, and he spoke, but she didn't say anything. They proceeded down the river road that led to the Hollimon house, the wheels of the wagon squeaking from lack of grease.

Jerry started lifting the cane-backed chairs off the wagon and then the rickety table that had lost one leg in the journey. He tapped the leg back into the auger hole at the top and wedged it with a sliver of wood. The widow smiled in appreciation.

"You're a right handy boy, ain't you?"

Jerry smiled uncertainly, and the little girl stared at him with one thumb stuck in her mouth. Mrs. McNalley backhanded the girl and her voice rose slightly as she admonished her.

"If'n I told you once, I told you a hundred times—quit suckin on that thumb! You as goin' on eight years a'age!" The little girl crimped up her face as if she might cry but then placed the thumb back in her mouth, and the widow seemed not to notice.

"Come on in now, boy. I'll show you where to put things. I'll sweep out the place. Got to knock down all them spider webs before we place the furniture."

Jerry nodded politely, and the woman smiled again. Her face was thin, and the smile sort of peeled it back from her teeth like it was an effort, but she wasn't an ugly woman. Her body seemed a bit thin under the gingham dress, but the bodice strained from the fullness of her bosom.

"You don't talk much, do you, boy?" she inquired.

"No ma'am," Jerry answered.

"No ma'am," she mimicked. "Now ain't that nice and polite, though? You musta been one of the house niggers... now ain't that right?"

She smiled again, but the boy felt a flush of anger mounting, and he turned away from the woman and headed for the door.

"Hey now," she called. "You ain't mad or nothing, are you?" She moved across the room so rapidly that he didn't make it to the door. He was surprised at the strength in her. "You a fine-looking boy, if I ever see one." The widow pulled on his arm and sort of squeezed it a little.

Jerry stood there, shifting uncomfortably before he spoke. "I guess I'd better be getting on back now."

The widow looked around and saw the big-eyed little girl gravely watching from the shadowed kitchen door. "Ain't you got nuthin' better t'do than stand around watchin' me every minute?" The little girl disappeared, and the widow smiled again. "You just have to keep after these youngins, you know."

She let her hand slip down to his hand, and she sort of lifted it up so that the back side of his hand mashed against the fullness of her bodice. "You just about a white boy, ain't you?"

Jerry looked away from her and down the dusty tracks of the road. "Yes, ma'am," he answered, and then he broke away from her and fled down the road, cutting off through the field toward home. When he reached the shelter of the woods, he stopped and sat down by the rail fence and looked at his hand, remembering how soft the woman's breast had felt.

An excitement stirred in him, and he put it off, getting to his feet and running once more to the end of the fence line.

The new wheels on Sir Thomas's chair made the trip to the river an easy and delightful experience for him. Jerry pushed him regularly, but one day the old man negotiated the path, which was downhill, all by himself with the right hand. He sat by the riverbank and watched the water flow over a sandbar that he didn't recognize. He noticed that the river was spreading out into small channels, separated by the eroded soil from the farmlands upstream.

When Elizabeth returned from the school and didn't find him, she naturally assumed that Jerry had taken him on one of his field trips. "When did Jerry leave with Pa?" she inquired of Dicey.

Old Dicey rolled her eyes in surprise and fear. "Massa Thomas was settin' on the porch when I left for the garden. I ain't seen Jerry since lunch."

Now the household was turned upside down, and nobody could recall seeing Thomas since the middle of the day. With confusion and alarm reigning throughout, old Dicey saw the struggling figure, pushing the pony cart wheels up the path from the river. "Lawd have mercy... look what coming up the path," she cried, and everybody ran at once.

Sir Thomas was in rare form. He felt triumphant, and he celebrated his victory over circumstance with several pulls from his jug. "Don't stand about eyeing me like I'm some damned freak or something. Get the hell busy and fix some supper. A man could starve to death around here!"

Jerry came in from the fields, from the Hollimon fields to be exact, and Elizabeth talked with him about the problem.

"Jerry, he could have just rolled right into the river, and we wouldn't have known until it was too late. You've got to take those wheels off his chair, for his own safety."

Jerry shook his head stubbornly.

"I'll take care of it, Libby, but I won't take his wheels away. That chair has given him new life, and I won't let anybody spoil it for him."

"Then, you must assume responsibility for what may happen."

Jerry hugged her, laughter crinkling the corners of his mouth.

"I accept that challenge. Ain't he a sight, though?"

"Don't say 'ain't.'"

"Yes, Miss Barkley, I'll try to remember..."

Over a period of weeks, during the tilling and planting season and on into the harvest, the widow found it necessary to solicit Jerry's services. When the old man was in his cups and feeling mellow, he would allow him to go.

"Lordy mercy!" the woman exclaimed as she mopped the sweat from her face with the tail of her apron. "Let's git outa this heat and into the shade yonder." She walked toward the cluster of trees at the edge of the field.

Jerry was agreeable. They had been picking black-eyed peas, and the widow had gone back to the house to bring him some water. The fresh spring water from the stone jug looked refreshing, and the widow held a covered basket in the crook of her elbow.

The temperature under the water oaks felt at least 20 degrees cooler. He removed the wide-brimmed, straw hat and tilted the jug upward, letting the cool water trickle down his throat and dribble off onto his chin.

"I guess you was powerful thirsty, now wasn't you?" The widow busied herself spreading a cloth over the thick carpet of green grass and then opened a jar of pickled peaches.

"Made these last summer," she stated proudly. "I'm sure going to miss them peach trees from our old place. Lord, how the times have affected us all! Mr. McNalley… he was a great one fer peaches. Peach pies was his favrite."

The thought of Mr. NcNalley brought sadness to her face, and she looked off through the trees as if searching for him somewhere in the shadows. A kind of sob caught up in her throat and she turned to Jeremiah with eyes that were misted. "They ain't no men left from the damned war—just a gaggle of starved-out widow women with kids to raise and no man to comfort them."

Jerry listened sympathetically, feeling it would be improper to reach for the bowl of black-eyed peas. He hoped the widow would stop talking before the cornbread got cold.

"My goodness, boy! Do get yerself some of that hot cornbread. I put a slab a'butter in each piece."

Jerry found the thin-crusted bread to be excellent. He ate with relish from the bowl of black-eyed peas, and he dipped his cornbread in the dark juice from the peas, soaking it up and sucking it into his mouth.

The widow offered a towel, and he wiped the butter and pea juice from his fingers.

"I got a cold jar a'buttermilk… if'n you'd like some," the widow invited.

"I don't mind if I do," he said, and he got another piece of the cornbread to go with the buttermilk.

His hunger sated, he stretched himself out on the grass and placed his hands behind his head. He watched two blue jays quarreling over a morsel high in the branches above him.

The widow sat and watched him, and she smiled with satisfaction at the contentment in the boy's face. "If they's anything thet pleasures a woman, it's to see a man eat," she said. She took the towel and wiped a bit of buttermilk from the front of Jerry's shirt.

Her touch was electrifying somehow, and Jerry closed his eyes in case the widow could read his thoughts.

She continued to wipe at his shirt, and then, she put the towel down and ran her fingers inside his shirt, tickling his rib cage. "You ain't ticklish, are you?"

She laughed, and Jerry laughed, and she kept it up, only now it wasn't so much a tickle as it was a rub. She rubbed under his shirt and on down to where his trousers were buttoned.

Jerry knew that he really ought to get back to the pea field, but he felt the widow's fingers working at the buttons on his trousers, and he knew now that she didn't have to read his thoughts. She could tell what he was thinking by what was poking out through the fly of his trousers. He squirmed and thrust himself upward, and the widow settled herself astride him, and she moaned in her need for the man in him.

Chapter Forty

Jerry approached the house from the back and circled around to the front steps. He walked up on the porch and knocked at the door.

The widow's daughter came to the door, her large, blue eyes appraising him, her thumb fixed firmly in her mouth.

"Who's there?" the widow called from the kitchen.

"It's Jerry, ma'am."

"Well, you have a seat there on the porch. I'm taking a bath. You there, Maudine, get on down to that garden and pick a mess of peas... and stay there until that bucket's full!"

The little girl left with the bucket on her arm, and the house was quiet except for the splashing of water from the washtub in the kitchen.

"Come in here, Jerry," the widow called softly.

The widow sat in the large tub used for washing clothes, and the soapy water came up just under her well-formed breasts. The breasts were outlined on the surface of the water by tiny bubbles, and the widow smiled at Jerry in such a way that his blood coursed through his veins like a runaway mountain stream.

"I need you to wash my back," she held up a cloth.

Jerry took the cloth and rubbed it over her back, and then her arms, and then her breasts, and then he threw the cloth aside, and his soapy fingers moved across the erect nipples.

"Git in the tub, and I'll do you," the widow offered.

He threw his clothes off and slipped into the warm suds, and the widow bathed him tenderly. She sat then, on the edge of the kitchen table and spread her legs for him, the soapsuds clinging to her body. She lay back on the table, warm and slick, and soft and yielding.

He couldn't have been more shocked in later months to find a buggy parked outside the widow's door. He saw the little girl, Maudine, watching him come up the path, and her mouth was stretched around the thumb into a grin.

"Your Ma has company?" Jerry inquired.

Maudine removed the thumb and inspected it carefully. "My Ma is seeing somebody else."

Jerry felt himself tremble, and he looked at the girl in some alarm. "What do you mean—someone else?

"She got herself another man... that Mr. Boshell from the cotton mill."

Jerry felt a sense of betrayal and then a rage that blinded him to caution. He started to walk toward the house when he heard the widow's voice. She was speaking in a very formal manner that he hadn't experienced in his relationship with her.

"It's been so kind of you to call, Mr. Boshell. My little daughter and I ain't got much company way out here from town. I must say I do miss seeing folks."

Jerry slipped around to the side of the house, and watched the man come out on the porch. He was dressed in his Sunday suit and had a black felt hat, which he held in his left hand. He looked like an old man to Jerry, but in fact, he was only approaching his middle years. The war had made him old before his time, robbed him of his youth and opportunities.

The man held out his right hand to the widow, and she caught it and made a sort of curtsy, smiling up into his face. The gentleman brushed the back of her hand with the tips of his large mustache and got into his buggy.

Jerry watched the dust settle on the road, and then he went around the house and knocked at the door.

The widow McNalley came to the door, surprise registering on her thin face. "Why Jerry, what brings you at this time of day?"

Jerry felt the blood rush to his face, and he forced himself to be calm. "Who was that man?"

"Oh, you saw Mr. Boshell?"

"I saw him... saw him kissing on your hand... saw you grinning up at him like a Chessy cat!"

"Please, Jerry, don't be mad at me..."

He wanted to strike her, but he held his arms rigidly at his sides. "Don't be mad at me," he mocked. "Why wouldn't I be mad at you—you've betrayed me..."

"No—Jerry, please... you need to understand." The widow pulled him inside. "You there, Maudine, fetch me a bucket of water from the well."

Jerry resisted the chair she offered, and so she put her hands on his shoulders. Her face was very sad, the tears hanging on her lower eyelids and then spilling over. "I'm a widow, Jerry—an older woman. I can't never have no future with you. It wouldn't be allowed nohow. Them Ku Kluxer's would git us sooner or later.

"I need me a provider. My little girl needs a daddy. You got to admit you can't do those things for me. You ain't old enough to be my girl's daddy... and you ain't white enough." She paused then, trying to pull him to her, but he flung her arms from his shoulders and ran down the path to the big house.

They sat on the bank of the river, the old man and the dark son. The man in his wheeled chair, the wheels fixed so that he couldn't accidentally roll into the river.

Jerry had made a sort of brake for the chair. It was a stick made from oak, and it had a rope tied to one end, and when Sir Thomas reached his destination, he could push the stick through the spokes of the pony cart wheels, and it would lock against the legs of the chair and make it stationary.

Sir Thomas held a cane fishing pole in his good right hand, and Jerry had baited his hook with one of the red wigglers from the barnyard.

They fished together often now. Jerry had more time for fishing these days, and Sir Thomas seemed pleased, but he was also puzzled at the melancholy attitude Jerry displayed. "Is there something you'd like to tell me, boy?"

Jerry moved the cork float on the surface of the water. "I... don't know what you mean."

"Yes you do, boy. You've got a burr under your saddle blanket, for sure. You can tell me... or you can keep it. Sometimes it helps to talk."

Jerry looked thoughtfully at the cork float. "I guess you know the widow..."

"I guess I do," Sir Thomas replied. "But I suspect you know her a lot better, eh?"

Jerry looked at him, and Sir Thomas kept his gaze on the water.

"I knew her," he said.

"You knew her," Thomas repeated, "but you don't know her now?"

"I don't know her now. She... she... got somebody else." His voice caught in his throat and he had to exercise control over his tear ducts.

Thomas nodded silently, moving the float with his good right arm, watching the ripples on the water. He looked up now, facing the boy with his face tired and sad looking. "It's a sorry day in a man's life when he loses a woman," he said. "It kind of robs a man of his credentials, you might say. He's not complete anymore."

Jerry waited without reply, and they sat there.

"God knew that. He looked at the man he'd made, and he saw he wasn't complete—saw he wouldn't have much purpose—without a woman beside him. It seems sometimes—that's really all that life's about—the relationship between a man and a woman. I lost both of mine."

When Jerry looked at him, he saw the old man's shoulders start to shake, and he realized that Sir Thomas was lapsing into one of his remorseful moods. They seemed to hit him more often these days. Jerry couldn't take that. He couldn't allow Sir Thomas to break down like that. "You got a bite there," he said.

Sir Thomas yanked on the line and the fish broke the water, its silvery scales flashing in the sun. "Aye, God... you're right!"

He swung the cane pole and the fish landed on the bank. Jerry got it and ran a line through its gills. "We'd better get on to the house," he said. "Old Dicey will be pleased to see what you brought for supper."

They were coming up the path when they saw the wagon sitting in the front yard. The widow's meager furnishings were in the bed of the wagon. The little girl, Maudine, sat beside her mother and watched them come up the path, but the widow sat looking straight ahead, waiting for them to come closer.

"Good afternoon, Mrs. McNalley," Thomas said.

"Good afternoon to you," the widow said, in a wooden sort of way.

"It appears you are leaving us," Thomas said.

"I left your share of the pea crop in the corncrib, Mr. Barkley," She kept staring straight ahead, not even glancing in the direction of Jerry and the old man.

"Well, I appreciate that," Thomas responded. He looked at the wagon and the furniture and noticed something missing. "I don't see your plow, Mrs. McNalley."

"You can have it," the widow said. "I won't be using it any more."

The little girl looked directly at Jerry, the thumb in its usual position in her mouth. She took it out then and shared the news with them. "We're moving to town," she said. "We ain't going to be picking peas..."

"Hush your mouth," the widow said sharply. She clucked to the horse, and the wagon moved out of the yard, and the little girl turned back to look at them. She had the thumb in her mouth but she grinned around it and waved to them with her left hand.

Thomas waved back, but Jerry held his hands rigidly on the back of the chair. He started to propel the chair forward but Thomas held up his good arm and they paused. "I'm sorry about what happened," he said.

Jerry felt awkward and embarrassed. He hadn't counted on a face-to-face farewell scene with the widow and especially not in front of Thomas. "Who cares about her anyway," he said.

Thomas nodded, "Women can be right peculiar at times, and there's not much a man can do but accept it. Sometimes a man just has to look at the bright side of things." He looked back at Jerry and grinned, "I'll bet my hat there ain't a man in Fayette County who's had more fun with a crop of peas, eh boy?"

Jerry managed a rueful grin, and the old man chuckled.

Chapter Forty-One

1869

It was a time of leave-taking—everything happening so fast the old man found it hard to accept the changing season. First, it was Katherine, off to the Tuscaloosa Female Academy, and then there was Elizabeth, who found reason for a new life away from the plantation.

Elizabeth surprised all of them. It had come to be accepted by the family, and especially by Jerry, that Libby was a permanent fixture in the household. Somehow, they had forgotten to ask Libby. She had never found the right person, but this condition changed almost overnight.

Her happiness came in the guise of a traveling evangelist. His name was Obadiah Day, fair of complexion, with golden hair glistening in the sun. He reminded her so much of Loretta's brother, Loren Dobbs, that Elizabeth caught her breath on meeting him. She told Loretta about the preacher and encouraged her to come with her to the next service. Loretta was also amazed at the resemblance.

When the preacher's piercing blue eyes first encountered her own, Elizabeth just melted inside. The man drew people to him as if he were magnetized, and the conviction in his voice when he preached the Holy Word brought many a sinner down the aisle of the church.

Elizabeth attended every service during his revival meeting, sitting as close to the front row as possible without appearing to solicit his attention. His attention was attracted, nonetheless, and after the third evening service of the week, the Reverend approached her and asked if they might converse after the crowd had dispersed. She nodded her agreement.

He drove her home in his buggy and turned to look at her in the moonlight. There was an Irish lilt to his voice that she found charming. "I can't know the days of your life that have escaped me so far. I am only concerned that I not miss any more of them!"

The directness of his courtship swept her off her feet, but his words made sense when she had time to recall and digest them. He had lived through the years of the lost cause, a flag-bearer fighting a war that he didn't understand. God had spared him, he was certain, for a special purpose. Now he needed the assistance of a wife, and he was certain that providence had again intervened and pointed him to Elizabeth. She came to feel the same way.

He stayed at the Barkley house for a week after the conclusion of the revival. Elizabeth warned him that he might find antagonism or drunken rage— or any of several emotions that she had come to expect from her father. What she had not counted on was the tender and loving conversation that took place at the announcement of their betrothal.

She thought it was to be a lecture, a reprimand for taking leave of his house, to go off to Selma and become a pastor's wife, but it was none of that. The old man took her hand, and the tears trickled down his face. "You have been all that I could have ever wanted in a daughter, so much like your saintly mother." He reached down by the chair to retrieve a small bag that he had directed Jerry to bring from the iron pot at the base of the cedar bell post.

"I have here the dowry that your mother brought into our marriage. I have kept it all these years for you. Please take it."

"But that might deprive Katherine…"

"Katherine will have what she needs. This is beyond that—and is mine to dispose." His voice had an edge now, and she recognized he would not tolerate argument.

"Thank you, Papa."

She ducked her head and knelt beside his chair, her tears concealed. His moods and his rage, his rough stories and criticism—she had been able to handle those things. It was his tenderness that made her vulnerable. And in that—she was also very like her mother.

In due course, Loretta married again. She had continued teaching at the same school as Elizabeth after William's death. She was able to do that with old Dicey looking after little Thomas during the school day.

Her new husband was Ashton Richards. He had family land holdings in Pickens County and was engaged in the sawmilling profession. She moved in the spring of 1869 to the Palmetto community between Newtonville and Columbus, Mississippi. She came by the big house with the boy to say goodbye.

"Papa Thomas," Loretta began. "I want to talk with you about the Linebarger place. There was nothing, outside of the family itself, that William loved more. I would never feel right to sell it, and I want to give it back to you."

The old man's eyes misted over, and he lifted his good right arm from the chair, clasping Loretta's hand. "I've never been an Indian giver; the land belongs to you."

Loretta shook her head firmly. "No, not to me... perhaps to my son. You keep it for him."

"There was a time," the old man's voice broke. "There was a time... when I would have given the world... to have my mother see things as you do." He nodded his head in agreement. "Yes—we will keep it for him." The young boy, Thomas, held his grandfather's hand and felt it start to shake. "What's wrong, Grandpa?"

Thomas swallowed and composed himself. "It's your face, boy, looking up at me just like your daddy used to do. You know he wasn't much bigger than you when we left South Carolina. It's, I don't know... it seemed for a minute there..." his voice trailed off.

"We'll be back soon," the boy said.

"I hope so." Thomas held the young man at arm's length. "There's land here, boy," he said softly, "Barkley land... cleared and plowed and purchased and fought for by Barkley men.... There should be a Barkley to watch over it." The boy didn't comprehend the significance of the statement, but he thanked his grandfather anyway.

Loretta gathered up her belongings and said goodbye to Dicey. She met Jerry on the way to their buggy, and she reached out and pulled him to her. "William would have been so proud of you," she whispered. "Nobody could have done a better job than you."

Jerry was pleased. He hadn't considered his work extraordinary, but it was always nice to be appreciated. "Let Thomas come back for vacations," he said. "I'll take good care of him."

"I know you will," she replied, and then the buggy was on its way, the little boy waving from the passenger seat.

Jerry watched them go and thought about Loretta's compliment. He was proud of what he had accomplished. He had done a good job with the cultivation. His strong body had provided the occupants of the plantation with most of their food. It had been a test of his mettle, and he had risen to the challenge. He considered himself a man, and he remembered Sir Thomas's advice—that *a man is what he thinks himself to be.*

Chapter Forty-Two

1870

Adversity hung on the man like a sodden blanket. His shoulders drooped and his arms hung long and rope-like to his big hands. His back was bent, and his neck stiffened, so that he was forced to turn his entire torso to glance from one side to the other.

The face was another matter. There was a beatific cast to his features when he smiled. His white teeth gleamed in his angular, deeply lined face. His eyes reflected a spirit within that was disarming, even to a stranger. His hair was gray and shoulder length.

His wagon and sway-backed mule made a rather pitiful appearance with spokes missing from some of the wheels and rusty farm implements hanging from the sides of the wagon. "Mr. Barkley, sir?"

It was not Thomas's habit to be disarmed on meeting strangers, and even with the mellifluous effects of the whiskey still circulating in his crippled body, his tendency was to be cautious, if not abrupt, with the stranger.

Thomas nodded, without speaking from his vantage point on the front porch. The stranger shifted his feet and smiled in Thomas' direction.

"I was wondering, Mr. Barkley, sir, if you had any land…"

The voice from the porch was immediately hostile. "I've got over three thousand acres and not one damned acre for sale, if that's what you mean."

"Yes sir, thank you, sir." The man backed away from the porch and lifted his hat back to his head, his torso turning now as if to leave.

"Confound it, man," Thomas said. "You didn't even give your name."

The man smiled again and removed his hat. "Excuse me, Mr. Barkley. My name is Renfroe Jackson, Reverend Renfroe Jackson."

"Well, I hope you didn't come here to preach," Thomas said.

"No sir," the man said softly. "I do my preaching in God's house—that is, I plan to… if I can find a place around here. That's what I was asking about.

I need to sharecrop with somebody that would allow me to hold church in my house."

"What sort of church do you mean?" Thomas inquired.

"The African Methodist Episcopal Church, sir."

Thomas seemed startled, and he looked closely at the stranger.

"That sounds like a mouthful to me. Is that some sort of a nigger church?"

The Reverend Renfroe Jackson smiled his beatifying best, nodding his head in confirmation. "We are a Negro church," he said.

"And are you telling me that you're a..."

"Negro. Yes—that is my race. I am, in fact, a quadroon, sir."

"Well, I'll be teetotally damned," Thomas said. "You sure could have fooled me. I considered you to be a white man."

"That mistake has been made many times, sir."

Thomas eyed the man carefully, remembering his last sharecropper. There was something different about this applicant, something that demanded consideration. He took another pull from the jug while he thought about it and the Reverend waited patiently with his hat in his hand.

Presently, Jerry stepped out on the porch and looked at the stranger in surprise. He looked at Sir Thomas and back to the stranger, and Thomas nodded in Jerry's direction. "This is my boy, Jerry."

Thomas looked up at Jerry, the whiskey improving his disposition. "This here," he inclined his head in the Reverend's direction, "is a preacher man. He wants to sharecrop and hold church to boot. I was thinking of a place where he might kill two birds with one stone, so to speak." He winked at Jerry. "And I thought... well... there is a place that sort of lends itself to that idea. I thought you might go along with the preacher and show him the Hollimon place."

Chapter Forty-Three

"I think I'll go to church today," Thomas announced at Sunday breakfast.

Jerry looked up in surprise, and old Dicey almost dropped the coffee pot. "You want me to drive you to Newtonville?" Jerry asked.

"No," the old man answered. "I had my fill of church in Newtonville... a long time ago. I think this time, I'll attend the African Methodist Episcopal church—down at the Hollimon place."

Dicey shook her head in disbelief, and Jerry grinned over his coffee cup.

Thomas was enjoying his little melodrama, gauging the effect on his household, which now consisted only of Jerry and Dicey, except on the odd weekends when Katherine drove home from the Tuscaloosa Female Academy. "Come on, Dicey," he called. "Get into your Sunday clothes. Jerry—you too, but help me with my bath first. Lay out my suit. We don't want to make a bad impression."

They were ready within the hour, and Jerry pushed Thomas out onto the porch and laid some boards up to the tailgate of the wagon. He rolled Thomas' chair into position behind the driver's seat and locked the wheels. Dicey sat beside Jerry, and the unlikely threesome headed off down the river road.

There were a few wagon teams at the hitching rail by the barn when they pulled up. It became evident that the services were being conducted in the barn, for a mixed chorus was singing *Glory to God on High*.

There were murmurings as the wheeled chair was pushed into the center of the open space between the stables. Black faces looked in astonishment and then away, but none of them looked familiar to the Barkley visitors. Thomas figured they might have been some of the Hall Plantation Negroes come back from freeloading at the Freedman's Bureau.

The ground was covered with fresh hay, and a row of benches was formed of flat timbers across short sections of oak logs. The pulpit was made of a corn bin, standing upside down at the opposite end of the barn.

The song ended, and the deformed body of the preacher rose up now and turned from one side to the other, smiling and nodding at each person in attendance. He opened his Bible and laid it on top of the bin, but he didn't read any text. He looked at them all, and then he began to speak.

"I am called by many names," the preacher said. "On this day," he looked up at the hay loft, "in God's house, you may call me Preacher, or Reverend, as you prefer.

"On the white man's plantation where I was born, I was just called... Nigger. I do not care what name I am called." His face was lighted by the open door of the hay loft as he gazed upward and the beatific smile was upon them. "I do not care... just so long as they also call me a child of God!"

"Amen. Praise God."

"I see your needs, brothers and sisters. I see your needs—the hunger in your bodies—the hunger in your hearts. I can see all of that, and let me tell you something. The Son of God did not come into the world as a mighty conqueror. He came—as you have come—to a stable. He is no stranger to the poor and the oppressed. He came as one of you."

The preacher held the Bible aloft now, raising it to his face and touching it to his cheek.

"This is a precious book, brothers and sisters. It is from this book that you will learn how to use your newly won freedom... for the glory of God.

"It takes no talent to hate; it takes no education to hate, because hatred is a raw and human emotion." He held the Bible outward to them, turning his stiffened torso to look at each one in turn. "This book teaches us to love. God says we should love our neighbor... even as ourselves. Love is a learned emotion, and it comes from a study of God's Holy Word."

He opened the book to Corinthians, thirteenth chapter and thirteenth verse. "And now abideth Faith, Hope, and Charity, these three, but the greatest of these is Charity. That is the Biblical word for Love, brothers and sisters. You don't have to know how to read—the Bible says, 'He that hath ears to hear... let him hear.' Listen to the words in this book, for they hold the answer to all of life's problems."

A mockingbird suddenly began to sing from the roof of the barn. The preacher smiled and waited for his song to finish, and then he spoke again. "Our land is drenched in blood, and its color is red. Whether spilled from white skin or black skin, its color is red. The blood was shed because of hatred, and our land must be cleansed by love. Love must apply to our neighbors. It must apply to a black skin as well as a white. If a man looks at me and sees only the color of my skin, then he does not know me. If a man has a name for me and that name is Nigger, he does not know me. If he has a name, and it is just Preacher, then he does not know me. If a man has a name for me—and calls me a child of God, then he knows me."

The crowd was quiet and expectant. The Reverend's face was lit with his beatific smile. "My God in heaven knows me, and he knows that I know him. He knows each of you… what is in your hearts… and he knows your need for comfort. 'I am the way,' saith the Lord, 'the truth and the light… no man cometh unto the Father, but by me.'"

A chorus of Amen's came from the assembly, and the preacher looked now directly at Thomas. "The Son of God came into the world to redeem all of us, to take away our cares and problems, and restore our souls, and to give us peace. That love of God extends to all of us, white and black, and all the colors between. Believe that we are children of God. Know that we are here at his disposition and that we leave when he decides."

Jerry looked at Sir Thomas and saw a rapt expression on his face. He saw the good right arm struggle with the wheel of the chair, and then he was rolling himself toward the altar.

"Have hope, brothers and sisters, for life without hope has little purpose. Have charity, which is love, the greatest of all gifts. Finally, have faith… in the word of God, and all things will be made possible… and now abideth faith, hope, and charity."

Thomas had reached the pulpit, and the preacher lowered himself down to his knees and placed his hand on Sir Thomas' shoulder and looked upward toward the hay loft, and he closed his eyes and prayed silently, and the audience was silent also.

Jerry walked down to the front when the preacher stepped back, and he turned the chair around and pushed Sir Thomas back toward the wagon. They heard the sounds of singing as they drove away. Sir Thomas was quiet on the way home, and Jerry and Dicey shifted uneasily on the driver's seat. They sensed that something had happened but were unable to define it.

Jerry walked down the path to the Hollimon place a few days after the service. He saw no sign of the preacher or his wagon and mule. The house stood empty just like the widow had left it, and he found it hard to believe the preacher had ever been there at all.

He walked down to the barn, and all the benches had been removed, and the corn bin was back in its place, right side up. It all seemed very strange, and he hurried back to tell Sir Thomas. He figured that the old man would be pretty upset over the loss of his sharecropper.

Thomas listened in silence to Jerry's story, and then he looked thoughtfully at his own broken body. After a time he looked up and searched the sky, and Jerry wondered if the old man could really see the cloud formations or if he was seeing a vision of something beyond.

"He was a messenger," he said softly. "And I suppose he was directed to carry the message some other place." He folded his good right arm over the left and sat and contemplated for a while, and then he spoke again.

"You know, I think God sent a mixed-blood messenger—just for my benefit. You heard what he said about hate—what he said about love. Now, I never hated my slaves—but except for George... and Dicey, I sure can't say I loved them. I looked after them—in the same manner as I looked after my livestock. I fed them and housed them and treated them well—but I didn't, so to speak, accept them as members of the family of man. I wasn't brought up to think that way."

His face took on a sort of mystic aura that was uncommon to him, and Jerry was strangely moved by it. "It took the messenger to convince me that all men are brothers beneath the skin—such a simple truth to be so hard for people to accept. We have laid waste to this glorious land of our fathers, stained its earth forever with the blood of our children—trying to resist that fundamental truth."

His face saddened now, and he looked off again, seeing something that Jerry couldn't see. "And my own prejudice has caused my life to shrivel like a pea pod in the sun—has left a drought in my soul—has caused me to wrong someone. I wronged your mother, Jerry." His shoulders sagged and Jerry was afraid he might be settling into one of his depressions. He suggested they roll down to the barn and feed the livestock.

A gust of wind swept across the yard, and a collection of multicolored leaves blew down around them. They were near the end of the Indian summer. It was a time for change, for a new order to things. The widow was gone from the Hollimon place and living in town with the cotton mill worker. Jerry could imagine Mr. Boshell hugging the widow in the cool nights, and he felt sad about the change.

The messenger had come and had gone again—but in his own unique way, had left an ineradicable mark on all of them. Jerry felt in his own mind that he was undoubtedly sent by the Almighty because nobody short of God's own special emissary could have made such an impression on Sir Thomas.

The house that once sheltered Sarah and William, Serina and Peggy, Elizabeth and Loretta, little Thomas and Katy—now held only three: a crippled, old, white man and an older black servant, and a young man of mixed bloodline whose courage and devotion was beyond question.

The young man carried the genes of his African and Indian ancestry, as well as the blue blood of Sir William Barkley, General of the English army, Knight of Bath, and Lord of Mount Barkley, Ireland. He didn't know that, of course.

Chapter Forty-Four

She had been a motherless child, and many times she felt a fatherless one as well. Katherine, or "Katy" as they had come to call her, had suffered a deprivation that was difficult to put into words. She had hoped her father might turn toward her once Elizabeth had married and moved away. Without acknowledging it, she had looked forward to Elizabeth's marriage with this thought in mind.

It didn't happen that way. She had finished the first semester at the Tuscaloosa Female Academy, and finding that cloistered atmosphere a far cry from the adventure she was seeking, she returned to Newtonville, expecting to assume her rightful position as lady of the house.

She returned instead to a crippled, old father who was critical of her every move. He always relied on his servant Dicey for small favors, and on his bastard son Jeremiah for anything of importance. The jealousy that she felt toward her half-brother was understandable.

Thomas had always shown a partiality toward his sons without himself being aware of it. His rejection of his child, Katherine, was an insidious thing, borne of his own guilt and suffering. Thomas had blamed himself for the pregnancy that had caused Sarah's death, but finding that burden too awesome, he unconsciously shifted much of it to the child. Somehow, this child had cost him the life of his wife. He wanted to love her as much as the other children and would have defied anyone who stated that he made a difference, but that didn't alter the fact.

And so the girl's natural petulance became more pronounced as the years went by. Now that her finishing school experience had foundered, her personality gravitated toward rebellion. She found fault with the slow-paced Dicey. She found fault with the whiskey-drinking, crippled father, but more than anyone, she found fault with the illegitimate half-brother.

She wanted love. She wanted affection, but her attitude predisposed an opposite response from the household. She came to hate the Spartan existence of the post-war period, the sacrifices that were called for and which she was unwilling to make. She was fair game for anyone promising a better standard of living, and as fate would have it, he came her way.

Jed Akins was a railroad bond salesman. He rode in a fancy trap around Fayette County seeking investors for a prospective rail line that would link the people of Fayette County to cities such as Chattanooga, Tennessee; Columbus, Mississippi; and Elyton, Alabama.

The Miss/Ala Line, as it was named, would bring prosperity to the farmers by providing easy access to interconnecting rail lines and would further the development of vast mineral resources, moving coal east and west and iron ore to the big furnaces at Elyton.

This was the presumption and it was an appealing proposition. In actual fact, Jed worked for a group of sophisticated con artists, well rehearsed in the art of using other people's money. The total motivation was the fleecing of the rural population. The timing was right for such fantasy because reality didn't offer much solace to residents of Fayette County.

Jed Akins stepped out of his hotel on his way to the livery stable. He found himself walking directly toward a young blonde lady with an imperious carriage and obvious high spirit, for she looked him up and down without any sign of modesty. He found this most intriguing. He doffed his hat politely, remarked on the fine weather, and she smiled but went on her way.

Jed hurried into the first business door he came to and inquired as to the name of the young lady, still visible as she continued her stroll down the boarded sidewalk. The businessman, who happened to be the newspaper publisher, looked out his grimy window and recognized the young woman.

"Why, that's Miss Katherine Barkley," he stated. "She's from Newtonville… father owns a plantation there—if you can call three thousand acres of briars and Johnson grass a plantation. She's a fine looker!"

Jed agreed and later that week he planned a little trip down her way. He sought directions as he went along, surveying the boundaries of the estate. He noted the rich, tilled land by the river and also the fields that lay fallow for lack of laborers. He rode in the direction of the house and had another opportune "chance" meeting. He found Katherine gathering flowers from the beds on the front yard.

"Why, I do believe you're the young lady I met just yesterday in Fayette!"

He registered complete surprise as he dropped down from the buggy and bowed in front of her. Katherine was immediately taken with his appearance. His clothes were clean and recently pressed. His face was clean-shaven and smelled of bay rum.

There was no hint of somberness or frugality in the style of his clothing or the fine, leather interior of the buggy. The arranged encounter went very well for both parties and the man came back often. He told the clerk at the hotel desk that he had discovered a "perfectly formed fruit in a blighted orchard."

He took the girl for rides in the buggy, and he courted her with gifts. He learned that she had an older sister, but she didn't mention the dark, young man who appeared at times to gaze steadily at the stranger.

Jed rightly assumed the old man was on his last legs. He seemed comatose much of the time. Jed figured also that this girl was inheritor to a plantation that he might convert into a windfall opportunity of his own. He possibly overstepped himself when he inquired about the property at the Fayette Courthouse.

"I would like to check the tax standing on the Barkley place," he mentioned casually.

"And who might you be?" the clerk asked warily, being none other than Thomas' old lawyer, Morton Franklin, who had become the Fayette County court clerk.

"Someone who will shortly be responsible for those taxes," he replied huffily.

The clerk was not swayed. He looked sourly at the stranger. "I can assure you that Thomas Barkley pays his taxes, and he wouldn't appreciate such inquiries." He later made occasion to mention the stranger's visit when he dropped by to check on his old friend.

The old man was furious when he discovered the man's description matched his daughter's newly found suitor. He gave her a sound tongue lashing when he saw her at the dinner table. "I'll have no part of that jackanapes meddling into my affairs. You tell that Fancy Dan to keep the hell off my property!"

She didn't tell Jed, because the man made complimentary remarks to her. He told amusing stories and appealed to her physically. In short, he made life enjoyable once more, and so she welcomed his advances.

Thomas had rolled himself onto the porch earlier in the afternoon, and from his position, he could hear the sound of laughter and hushed exclamations from the driveway. Jed's buggy was concealed by one of the large magnolias framing the drive, but he knew that Katherine was still seeing the bond salesman.

"Get in the house—you young hussy!" he called toward the sounds and hearing nothing, he called again. "Get off my property, you miserable, sneaking son-of-a-bitch!"

The man's laughter reached Thomas' ears, and in his own good time the man appeared from behind the magnolia, Katherine hanging onto his arm. He bowed in front of the old man on the porch as Katherine giggled her way into the house.

"Get off my land, I say, or I'll blast you with my shotgun, by God!"

The man didn't laugh this time. With Katherine inside the house and out of range of his voice, he snarled wickedly. "Don't get too fired up now, old man. I'm willing to make believe I didn't hear what you said, and I'm one to make allowances for cripples, but don't push your luck with me!" He walked to his buggy, and then called mockingly as he drove away, "Good day, Mr. Barkley!"

Thomas cursed at the retreating buggy and called for Katherine, but she had gone up to her room and didn't respond.

The open front door had allowed much of the conversation to reach Jerry's ears as he helped old Dicey tidy up Thomas's bedroom. Jerry left the room abruptly and ran to the barn. He bridled the mare and jumped astride without bothering to attach the saddle. He used the shortcut through the orchard to reach the main road just below the point at which Jed's buggy approached. He dismounted and waited by the side of the road.

Jed Akins pulled up and grinned down at him. "Well, well, you're one of the farm hands, I take it?" Jerry looked at the man without acknowledging the greeting. Jed's face began to purple at the slight, and he raised his voice. "I like an answer when I ask a question!"

"I'll give you an answer." Jerry's words were evenly voiced, and he didn't change expression. "You'll do well to keep a civil tongue when you address Sir Thomas, or you'll answer to me."

Jed Akins couldn't believe his ears... a blasted field hand having the impertinence to address him in such a manner. He raised the buggy whip threateningly. "Why you goddamned, half-breed nigger! How dare you confront me! I know some boys who can teach you some respect for your betters!"

"Well, you'll need all the help you can get, Mister Akins." The gray eyes never wavered from the man's face, and the jut of the Barkley jaw indicated his readiness for combat.

"Who the hell are you?" Jed Akins asked.

There was no reply, and Jed popped the whip over the horse's head and tore out down the road, cursing under his breath.

Jerry found Katherine in the kitchen on his return from the barn. He walked through the door, and the quiet rage that consumed him caused her to retreat, but then she became defiant and whirled around. "What do you want?"

"I want to know why, in God's name, you would allow that... a man of that caliber... to insult your father!"

"And what caliber of man is asking the question?" she retorted.

"I suppose your lover would refer to him as a bastard nigger," he said without emotion.

"Well, if the shoe fits..." she taunted as she flounced out of the room.

Jed Akins was in his usual place at Holman's bar, polished boots casually at rest on the brass foot-rail. He finished a bottle with two other customers, and ordered a second round for the three of them. The local men had become known to him, at first, only as fellow patrons at the saloon. As time went on and they got better acquainted, he learned something regarding a social club they had recently joined.

The club was called the Ku Klux Klan, and it had originated up in Tennessee, headed by an ex-Confederate general named Nathan Bedford Forest. The organization was quickly spreading over the South because it offered some security from conditions imposed by the occupation troops. Its principal purpose, regardless of its flamboyant charter, was to scare hell out of the former slaves, so none of them would dare impose themselves upon the now vulnerable citizenry.

The evening wore on, and during the conversation, Jed mentioned that he had run across a "smart alecky" nigger boy, light colored, who had dared to make threatening comments to him. "I tell you, just let something like that go unchecked, and they'll be pushing us off the sidewalk any day now!"

"Like hell they will."

"Show us the sombitch!"

"Well," Jed stated thoughtfully. "It seems to me I see that boy about once a week, usually on Thursdays, driving a wagon into Newtonville to pick up supplies."

"He'll have a welcoming party next Thursday, by God! You just let us handle it from here."

Jerry came as usual the following Thursday. The weather was hot, and on the return leg of the trip, he pulled over into the shade of some chestnut oaks by the side of the road. He wanted the team to cool off and he wanted to drink from the natural spring that gurgled out of the rocks at that point. It was a natural point for intercepting a traveler.

"Git down frum that wagon, boy!"

Jerry looked about in surprise and saw two men walk out from behind the trees, wearing white-peaked hats that came down to the shoulders and eye holes cut in the front.

Jerry held up both hands to show he was unarmed. "What do you want of me? I've got no money, just some good staples…"

"You don't hear too good, do you, nigger?"

Jerry knew there was no way but to fight his way out, if possible. He cleared the side rail of the wagon in one quick leap and lunged for the first man, striking him between the eye holes in the mask and hearing his nose crunch under the impact of his fist.

"Damn!" the man screamed. "You broke my damn nose, you son-of-a-bitch!"

Jerry whirled to confront the other man and was met with the solid end of an oak club over his right temple. When he came to, he was traveling blindfolded, head and feet dangling across the back of a mule. He kept silent, trying to regain his senses and decide his best course of action.

The rope around his right wrist led under the belly of the mule and up to his left ankle and seemed to reduce his options sharply. They moved on through the woods, and the motion of the mule made it difficult for him to breathe. At last they reached a clearing, and he felt the rope being released by his foot, then a rough hand yanked on his arm and he fell heavily to the ground.

"What we got here, Arnie?" The voice came from across the clearing.

"Don't use my name, you dumb bastard!" Jerry's captor replied.

"Well, all right, your Scribeship, sir!" The man laughed roughly.

Another voice broke in, a voice of authority, and the men grew silent.

"What is this man doing here, Scribe?"

"He confronted a white man, Grand Cyclops—insulted and threatened him."

"Where is the white man who makes this charge?"

"Well, that railroad guy—you know, Jed Akins is his name."

"You're just as bad as your friend over there. Don't use names."

There was silence again, and then the voice of authority. "Has this nigger boy ever insulted or mistreated any white person to your personal knowledge?"

Jerry recognized the voice of authority. It belonged to the man who owned the hardware store—a Mr. Brad Tyner. He realized also that Mr. Brad Tyner knew that he was Jerry Barkley.

Jerry could hear some inaudible muttering within the group, and then the voice was speaking again. "Scribe, you have waylaid this young boy on hearsay gossip. You have no proof that he has ever insulted anybody."

The muttering started up again, and Jerry was afraid Mr. Tyner was losing control of the situation. "This is the sort of thing that will not be tolerated in this Klavern. Take this boy back where you got him, and don't let anything like this happen again."

"Ah shit, Brad!"

Jerry heard a noise, as if someone had struck someone in the stomach. It made a "whoosh" sound. Then, Jerry felt himself being lifted once more and laid across the mule. The rope was retied, and they were off again through the woods. Sometime later, they stopped and Jerry was thrown to the ground. Rough hands jerked the dangling rope from his wrist, and then he heard feet moving away. He raised the blindfold in time to see a retreating figure, but there was no further conversation. His team was still standing where it had been tied by the club members, and he got back in the wagon for the trip home.

Old Thomas saw the bruised bulge over Jerry's right eye and demanded to know the particulars. He knew about the hoods and the sheets, the invisible society that had been formed in Fayette. The avowed purpose was to "protect the weak from the lawless, the violent and brutal, the relief of the oppressed and injured, the protection and defense of the Constitution of the United States, and to aid in the execution of all laws passed under it." It sounded mighty fine—but he knew there were members who would embrace violence for its own sake. It would take strong leadership to weed them out.

"Strap a gun under your coat from now on," Thomas advised. "If you are going to get killed, take some with you, by God!" He was thankful, of course, for the Grand Cyclops—the one named Brad Tyner.

Chapter Forty-Five

"I guess I'll be moving in with you for a while, old man!"
Sunlight slanted between the outstretched legs of the man in front of him, and Thomas Barkley jerked awake from his nap to view the intruder. Jed Akins stood there, valise in hand, an insolent grin on his angular face.

"You'll do *what?*" the old man thundered.

"I guess you heard me after all," Jed replied easily. "For a minute there, I thought you was dead drunk!" Jed set the valise on the floor and pulled up a vacant rocker. He reclined in the chair, putting his feet up on the rail and pulling a cigar from his pocket.

Thomas stared at the man in disbelief.

"Seeing as how Katy and me are getting hitched up one of these days, I just thought it would be the family thing to do!" He chuckled in high good humor, slapping his trouser leg to free the dust from the ride.

"You can go to hell, you insolent bastard. Jerry! Oh Jeremiah!!"

Jed Akins grinned easily, flicking the ash off the cigar. "If you're calling that half-breed, nigger boy of yours, I saw him down in the cane bottom as I drove up. But I wouldn't involve him in family affairs if I was you. I'd hate to have to hurt him!"

"Damn you for a son-of-a-bitch." The old man shook in his anger. "When I can get my hands on a gun…"

"Now that ain't likely, old man. I had Katy hide your guns after your last threat to me. Told her you were too old and senile to be fooling with guns— you could get yourself hurt." He let his feet down from the rail and picked up the valise, ignoring the old man who was now speechless in his rage. He walked to the front door and called to Katherine.

"Oh Katy, tell your old nigger woman to bring Mr. Thomas some cold buttermilk. Looks like he's about to overheat!" He laughed as he swung through the door to meet the surprised Katherine.

"Why Jed, what—what are you doing here so early in the day?"

He grabbed her up in his arms and gave her a resounding kiss on the cheek. "A little change of luck is all—I need a place to stay for a few days. Damned railroad held up my commission checks and the hotel threw me out!"

"Oh, I'm so sorry. You... of course, you can stay, but..."

"No buts... my dear young lady. It's time I got to know the family better anyway, don't you agree?" He laughed and pinched her on the buttocks; she slapped at his hand and looked around for Dicey.

"Please show Mr. Akins to the guest room, Dicey. He'll be with us for a few days!"

Old Dicey scowled at the man, but she did as she was told and showed him to the room. He plopped down on the bedspread with his boots on and ordered her to bring a cool glass of water.

When Jerry reached the porch in the late afternoon, he was alarmed at Thomas' condition. He shook visibly when he tried to speak and Jerry started to go for the doctor, but the old man held him by the arm and finally got the words out. "Get me a gun, Jerry. We've got a snake in the house and I'm going to kill it."

Jerry finally learned the full story from old Dicey, who had overheard it all. Jerry got the old man undressed and settled in the bed.

"May God strike me if Katy ain't crazy." His already stricken state didn't diminish the vehemence of his statement. "I want you to bring me that gun," he insisted, but Jerry soothed him and told him not to worry.

"We'll get it all settled without that, Sir Thomas!"

Jerry was plowing near the end of the corn rows, alongside the road, when the buggy came careening down his way. He heard the laughter of the man and the shrieks of the girl as she implored him to slow down. And he did. Slowed to a stop right by the road where Jerry stood.

"Are you taking care of the farming, my boy? Well, I sure hope so. You've got an extra mouth to feed now!" He laughed uproariously, slapping his leg, and Katherine looked away in embarrassment.

Jerry's gray eyes drilled into the man, and Jed's laughter faded out, his face turning into a scowl. "You are beginning to smell up this place," Jerry said, his voice low. "You remind me of something... a buzzard, I think, a filthy, carrion-eating buzzard!"

Jed's face purpled, and he twisted the leather reins. "Some folks just can't learn how to treat their betters," he said. "Guess the boys didn't do a good enough job on you the other night!"

"You hush now, Jed!" Katherine said.

215

"Don't hush me, woman! You think I care what your nigger brother thinks of me?" He turned back to Jerry. "You better walk a chalk line from now on, or you and me will have some settling up to do!" He slapped the reins across the horse's rump, and the buggy jumped forward.

Jerry watched them out of sight, and he turned back to the plow. "We'll have some settling up to do all right," he muttered, "and the sooner the better!"

It was amazing, he thought, how a man could just be tending to his affairs in the same way as he normally would, and right out the blue... a new circumstance could develop to change his life. Because that is what Jed Akins had done; he had changed Jerry's life forever. He found himself thinking of him when he wanted to think of something else.

)

Chapter Forty-Six

Jed Akins was drunk. His loud argument with Katherine earlier in the morning had put him into a surly mood, and the whiskey bottle now lay empty on his bed. The argument started because Jed had not gone to work since he moved in with the Barkley's, and Katherine questioned him about it.

"My work is my business!" Jed declared.

"I believe you have been giving me the impression that your work was directed toward our mutual benefit," Katherine replied.

It went on from there, the gist of it being that Jed finally admitted that he had been fired. "But, it's nobody's damn business if I never work again!"

He began to drink, and she began to pout, and when she'd had enough, she asked Jerry if he would hitch a horse to the buggy and bring it around so that she could do some shopping in the village.

Jerry did as he was asked, and then went back to the apple orchard to bring one of the full baskets to the kitchen. Dicey was making jelly, and the kitchen was given over to the project. He knew she'd need him to peel a fresh batch of apples.

She had not called the stranger to breakfast because she had overheard the argument upstairs. She wanted to avoid any involvement with the unwelcome boarder.

Jed, believing that he had been slighted, and being drunk and unreasonable, came down the stairs demanding to know why he had not been called. Old Dicey had no response for him, and this angered him even more. "I said you didn't call me to breakfast. Why didn't you do that?" he demanded.

Dicey was frightened now. She had never dealt with a situation like this—a guest talking to her this way. "I… be… making jelly now," she stammered.

"I didn't ask you what you were doing, you stubborn old bitch." He glanced about the kitchen, and seeing the broom by the fireplace, picked it up and advanced on her, the long handle held menacingly above his head.

Dicey, who had never received a blow from her owners in all of her long life, was terrified. Her high-pitched scream reached Jerry in the apple orchard, and he dropped the basket and started to run.

The thud of Jerry's boots on the kitchen porch caused the man to whirl around, and the venom in his voice was now directed toward the young man. "Well, now… if it ain't the master's nigger boy! Come here, nigger boy. I owe you some of this broomstick!"

Jed broke the broom over his knee and now held the broken handle as a short club, its jagged end a lethal wooden dagger. He advanced on Jerry, jabbing with the broom handle, and Jerry easily sidestepped the thrust. Again Jed lunged, and Jerry grabbed at the broken handle. The jagged edge ripped into his hand, and blood ran down over his fingers.

"Got you, by God,' Jed leered. "But you ain't out of the woods yet, nigger boy!"

The two men circled the kitchen, and Dicey's muffled sobs could be heard as she cowered in a corner behind the stove.

The apple juice was boiling now, and the long, wooden handle of the boiler was within easy reach. The old woman considered the distance, and waited….

Jed lunged again and Jerry spun around, the wooden lance catching in the fabric of his shirt. Now, the bond salesman had his back to the stove—within easy striking distance. Dicey lifted the boiler and threw its contents at Jed's back.

He screamed as the hot, syrupy liquid splattered over his head and down his shirt collar. He whirled to find the source, and seeing the old woman holding the empty boiler, raised the broken broom handle to strike.

Jerry grabbed him from behind, putting a chokehold on him. Jed twisted, dropping to his knees, breaking the headlock. Streetfighting was a talent he had learned at an early age, and he was good at it. The pain of his blistered back and the thought of being bested by Negro servants put him into an animal rage. His only thought now was revenge, and he grabbed an iron poker from the fireplace and swung with all his might.

Jerry ducked the blow and caught the man's arm at the end of its forward motion. The muscles developed in the months of hard work in the fields responded easily. He yanked the man forward and swung him in an arc. When Jerry let go, Jed struck the rock facing of the fireplace, his head banging against the iron support for the cooking pots. Jed Akins lay where he fell, and a trickle of blood ran from his left ear.

"Oh dear GAWD!" Dicey wrung her hands and would have fainted dead away if Jerry had not reached her in time to seat her on a kitchen chair.

"What'll we do… what will we do?" she wailed. "We done went and killed a white man; we done went and killed a white man!"

Jerry bent over the man's prostrate form. Jed's eyes seemed glazed over, and he didn't appear to be breathing. "We'll ask Sir Thomas what to do," he replied calmly.

"First, let me bandage that hand," Dicey said. She washed his hand and put a clean strip of cloth over the ragged cut.

Thomas was delighted with the news of Jed Akins' accidental death. "I glory in your spunk," he said. "I would have killed him myself, but that son-of-a-bitch had Katy steal my guns." The thought of Katy caused him to pause, and he looked down the road for any sign of her buggy, but there was none.

Thomas' good hand tapped on the arm of his chair. "Now, in my opinion… that man was a thieving carpetbagger to begin with. There's little likelihood that anybody will be inquiring as to his whereabouts… but if they do—we'll tell them the truth. The last we saw of him… he was in his buggy headed away from here. Now then, Jerry, this is how we'll handle it."

He dismissed old Dicey and then gave Jerry specific instructions on the disposal of the man, his buggy, his horse, and personal effects. All of which added up to a boggy place in the swamp that the locals referred to as Dyer's Sink.

Jerry hitched Jed's horse to Jed's buggy, and he loaded the man into the seat. He tied a rope around his torso and secured it so that he appeared to be in a sitting position. If anyone should accidentally see them, it could appear the man was asleep or drunk, and he'd pass it off that way if necessary.

He put the old Springfield rifle in the back, along with the man's valise, and drove the buggy right down through the apple orchard, following the same tracks the wagon had made with the full baskets of fruit.

He cut across the edge of the woods, down behind the peanut field. He kept off the dirt roads that might risk a chance meeting with a neighbor, or one of the peddlers that sometimes canvassed the back roads for sales of pots and pans or medicinal compounds.

He looked at the surroundings for any sign of another person, but there was none. The man's body swayed back and forth in the seat with each jolt of the wheel, and Jerry had to admit that he looked for all the world like someone who had a touch too much of the red eye.

Once they had reached the swamp itself, there was no way to conceal the tracks of the buggy. He decided he would come back with the wagon and cover them, perhaps chopping a tree to account for the trip.

He stopped the buggy and tied a tow sack around the horse's head for a blindfold. The horse reared and shied a bit, but he held on to the bridle. He led the horse forward, a step at a time, until they reached the edge of the sink. Its black, liquid surface rippled with the thrashing legs of whirligig beetles.

He walked back and secured the reins to the seat and took the old Springfield rifle out of the baggage rack. He clucked with his tongue and slapped the horse on the rump, and it moved forward. When its front hooves began to sink in the muck, the horse became frightened and tried to lunge, but his momentum only carried him further into the quicksand.

Now the buggy itself began to sink, and the horse neighed in terror. Jerry took the old rifle then and shot the poor animal cleanly between the eyes. The horse collapsed into the mire, taking the buggy with it, the bottom of the buggy now resting on the surface like an odd sort of flatboat.

And then, a strange thing happened. The man, Jed Akins, came back to life. He straightened in his seat, and he looked about his surroundings in confusion. He head began to twist from side to side and he struggled with the ropes that bound him to the seat. His eyes got large and round, the whites glowing in the gloom of the swamp. Then, in horror, he watched the dark, shimmering glue rising above his ankles.

Jerry was totally astounded at the turn of events. He looked at the man now holding his mouth open in a noiseless scream, his eyes wide and disbelieving. Jerry looked at the Springfield in his hand, knowing he should offer the man the same sort of merciful end that he had given to the horse. He couldn't bring himself to do it. He watched in paralyzed fascination as the buggy settled and the muck rose higher and still higher. Jed began to scream then, in a strange, inhuman sort of way. "Help me… help m…" The muck began to flow into his open mouth, and then only his white eyeballs showed.

Jerry looked at the eyes and the eyes looked back at him. He saw them even after the surface of the ink shuddered and became slick again. And he watched the whirligig beetles begin to swim around where the eyes had been.

He thought about what he could have done and what he should have done and about what Sir Thomas would probably have done. He decided that Sir Thomas might have shot the man, given the same conditions, and he hated to have to tell Sir Thomas that their plan had not worked exactly as he had laid it out. The end result, though, was the same, and he could see no good reason to reveal the unexpected side of it.

He decided that it must have been God's purpose to allow the man to see his punishment. After all, God could have just let him go on being unconscious and he wouldn't have known how he came to pass. He decided that if God had allowed the man to awake at the precise moment when nobody could save him, then it must have been the way that God wanted it. Thus reassured, he shouldered the old Springfield and made his way back to the house.

Chapter Forty-Seven

The way things turned out with the MISS/ ALA LINE, nobody doubted that Jed Akins had skedaddled out of the county with the rest of the carpet-bagging thieves. The bond salesmen, the sales manager, and the fake surveyors—all left town in a bundle. They took with them a goodly slice of the tax monies provided by a duped legislature and all of the savings invested by small farmers and townspeople. The only reason anybody could have wanted to find Jed Akins would have been to string him up.

"I hope to hell you've learned your lesson!" Thomas told Katherine. "That man was a born crook, a fancy pants son-of-a-bitch, out to turn the heads of simple-minded females, and you just fit the bill!"

Later, Jerry and the old man would marvel at the way things turned out. Sir Thomas was sober enough to have given it considerable thought.

"The way I see it," he told Jerry, "it's the unexpected event that molds and shapes a man. If all of us faced the same conditions every day of the week, then we would all be pretty much the same. When something comes along like this Jed fellow... now that's what you'd call an unexpected event... and we had to deal with it in the best way possible.

"We could have stood back and allowed that no-good bastard to bully us around, and we would have molded ourselves into the shape of an egg-sucking dog, dragging our tail between our legs, so to speak. We didn't do that. We stood up for ourselves, and for old Dicey, and we can feel good about that. We molded ourselves into manly shapes, so to speak."

As usual, Jerry was inclined to agree with the old man's thinking. It was comforting to have Sir Thomas share the responsibility for what had happened.

Katherine never asked for specifics, and Thomas didn't give her any. She felt that Jerry had a hand in the disappearance of Jed Akins, but in light of their last encounter, she had already deduced that Jed was a loser. Katherine intended to have better. Somehow, she gained a new respect for her dark-skinned half-brother, and on occasion, he would find her looking at him with a semblance of affection.

Katherine decided a change was in order—that it was time to move on to newer and better opportunities. She wrote to Elizabeth detailing the hopeless conditions in Newtonville, and Elizabeth wrote back inviting her to visit in Selma. Katherine went, somewhat reluctantly, feeling that a preacher's home would not afford the excitement that she was looking for.

Elizabeth felt that another attempt at schooling would be the proper thing for Katherine. "Fill your mind with lofty thoughts," she advised. "We form our destiny from the control that we exercise on our thoughts."

She suggested the Selma Academy, and Katy tried it for a few weeks only. The atmosphere was entirely too proper to suit her, and too far removed from reality. She didn't want to live in a fantasy world of lofty thoughts and poetic phrases. Katy had tasted life and she wanted a steady diet of it from someone who could afford her foibles.

The young men at the school were definitely impressed with her looks, but they were awkward at the game of courting. They were either impetuous or dreadfully shy. None of them seemed to have the maturity and financial standing to guarantee the lifestyle she was seeking.

Abruptly, Katy had a change of heart and informed Elizabeth that she felt that her duty lay back in Fayette County. She might be wise to be nearer the family home, in the event their father needed her. Actually, Katy spent over a week in Tuscaloosa on her way back, sightseeing and browsing through the stores. It was in one of the stores that she ran into a relative of a friend from Fayette. The person informed her that the bank in Fayette had an opening for employment.

Katy drove up for an interview and was immediately hired. Katherine Barkley was bright, good-looking, and just what was needed to brighten the drab interior. She found a nice boardinghouse with facilities for her horse and buggy. She drove down to Newtonville on alternate weekends to look in on the family and enjoy some of Dicey's home cooking.

In time, she met one of the bank's best depositors and the town's most eligible bachelor. The ladies in Fayette were envious of Katherine's strikingly good looks and the ease with which she swept him off his feet. The bachelor owned the local hardware store. He seemed to have established a good reputation in the business community, and she learned that he had ambition for politics as well. His name was Brad Tyner, and they were married within two months of their introduction.

Chapter Forty-Eight

1870

Dicey noticed it first… an occasional vacant look on the old man's face, as if he wasn't aware of his surroundings. "I do believe Massa Thomas be slippin," she commented to Jerry when he brought the morning's milk from the barn. Jerry studied the old man carefully as he rolled him out to the porch.

"Is there anything you want, Sir Thomas?"

The old man shook his head slowly and he stared off into the distance; at lunchtime he wouldn't eat. On other days, he seemed well enough and would become talkative. He would discuss the progress of the crops and wonder how Loretta and little Thomas were doing or when he might expect some grandchildren from his daughters.

"I feel the time has come to make my provisions," he stated on one of the good days as Jerry pushed the wheeled chair down the path to the river. "I've made my peace with the Almighty. It was a struggle, and if you want to know the truth, I never intended to do it. It just seemed to me that God put every kind of obstacle in my path. I never asked Him for a hell of a lot… tried to do most things on my own, but I gave Him credit when credit was due."

Jerry reached the end of the path and pushed the oak stick through the spokes of the wheels, locking them in place. He got the worm can out of his back pocket and baited a hook for Sir Thomas and handed it across. The old man cast the line out over the water, and the cork float lay flat on the surface. He let Sir Thomas continue without interruption.

"Of course, I fell out with God when He allowed Will to die in the war. He'd already taken my Sarah and a stillborn child, and I just felt he had let me down all around. I told Him so in no uncertain terms. I said, 'God, you just hide your face from me; I don't need your kind of help.' He didn't hide worth a damn! He struck me down just like you'd poleaxe a steer. I knew He did it because I cursed at him and He wanted to punish me for my imperfections. I have been an imperfect man, but I was created that way, and so I feel God shares some responsibility."

The logic was crystal clear to Jerry, but he knew that Sir Thomas didn't need his agreement… had never needed anyone to confirm, or deny, one of his opinions.

"You remember the old nigger preacher? The one that came to the Hollimon place? Well, he brought me a message, so to speak, from the Almighty… it was like God said to me, 'Thomas… all your life you have gone around feeling responsible for everything and everybody, and that was the wrong way to feel. You could have saved yourself a whole lot of trouble if you had just left the whole thing up to me to start with… all prescribed and pre-destined.'"

Sir Thomas smiled then, watching the ripples on the water. "When I got that thought, I felt the most peace I've ever known. It was like God had given me a vacation. I know now that I don't have any control over anything—and so I don't worry."

The old man had talked and Jerry listened. Thinking Sir Thomas had finished, he started to check the bait on his hook, but Sir Thomas caught him by the arm with his good right hand. He reached inside his coat and pulled out the letter that he had received from Serina.. It had been folded and re-folded many times and was worn in the creases so that it threatened to tear apart.

"I want you to read this," he said. "Not now. Take it with you and read it in private." He fumbled with a button on his coat pocket and drew out another sheet of paper. It was newer and appeared to have been folded only that day.

"Read this one, too. It's to your interest to know these things. We'll talk about it… another time."

"I don't understand…"

"You will, you will. I have a plan for you, Jeremiah… in a new land away from the Lafe McGills and the Kluxers… a land where you can prosper and have a future."

When Jerry was alone in the field, he opened the old letter along the folds, and it was so thin along the creases that it tore a little, careful as he was. He read it guiltily, feeling that it wasn't quite proper for him to see it, but Sir Thomas had told him to do it. And then he realized the value of the old paper. It was the only link between his mother and his father—in all the years past.

He stared in wonder at the woman's handwriting… his mother's words on paper, a mother that he could not picture in his mind… could barely remember.

She had shared no place in his life and he had not missed her, except a little, at first. The only explanation he had gotten from Sir Thomas was that she had chosen to go away.

He opened the newer paper and recognized Sir Thomas's painful scrawl. He read it in silence, and then he read it again. The paper shook in his hands.

May 14, 1870

Dear Serina,

I am coming now to the end of a long road. I have made some false turns in getting here and I need to say some things while I can. I lost Will in the war. I suffered a stroke after that and have been confined to my bed and chair for a long time now. I thank you for your forgiveness. There is not a thing that I need to forgive you for—the wrong was on my side. You honored me with the child you bore me. He has been my main support. I don't know how I could have made it without him.

I am sending my son to you. I couldn't bear the thought of losing him, so I kept him for myself, and I know that I have been wrong in that also. It is too late now to make amends but I am glad that you wrote to me. I could never forget you.

Yours,
Thomas Barkley

"I am sending my son"… the words swam before his eyes. He had heard the words "my boy," all his life—but never "my son." The enormity of the acknowledgement seized him; he sat down on the terrace row and tears ran down his face.

After a time, he got up and lifted the hoe. He chopped in between the cotton plants, carefully pulling and pushing the blade to remove the grass but not disturb the roots of the cotton plants. He looked with pride at the straightness of the rows. They had been planted and tilled with a precision of spacing that had been Thomas Barkley's trademark. He had followed the exacting requirements of his teacher.

Chapter Forty-Nine

It had been thirty-two years since Thomas Barkley settled on the original homestead in Fayette County, Alabama. He had seen drought and pestilence and war and death, and in his words, "the unexpected events had molded and shaped him."

He no longer attempted to read; his eyes would grow weary, and it was more soothing to just look over the landscape from his position on the porch. His eyes didn't present distinct outlines but rather a blurred sort of formlessness, which was compatible with his train of thought. Many times he was unaware of his surroundings until the slap-slap of the runners on the Sipsey River Bridge announced a traveler on the Byler road. He would, at such times, draw erect in the chair, and if there was anything left in the stoneware jug, he would take a sip, being careful to replace the corncob stopper.

Sometimes he would reach a palsied hand into a can of shelled corn and dribble a few kernels around the porch. The Rhode Island rooster would then approach the chair and give a ritual crow that always amused him.

If he laughed aloud, the rooster would pretend to be offended, dropping a wing low to the floor and circling the chair. The old man was game to the challenge and he would kick feebly with his good right foot. The rooster would then back away until he sensed that the old man was no longer aware of his presence and resume pecking at the corn.

The days came and they went—and in the evening, Jerry would come. Jerry's face was a younger image of the old man, but in a darker shade, and the high bridge of his nose and his long black hair made his appearance slightly exotic.

"Sir Thomas, it's time to go in now."

The old man would nod, and Jerry would unlock the wheels by removing the stick from the spokes. He would roll him back to the bedroom and dress him for the night.

Sometimes, before he drifted off to sleep, the old man would remember how it all began. He would see the covered wagons on the Alabama Road as they crossed the Cherokee Nation. He would see the whiteness of the bottom lands when the cotton was ripe for picking, and the backs of the slaves bent over the rows in the blazing heat of the sun.

Thomas Barkley was the only titled man in Fayette County. He was "Sir Thomas"… had achieved that distinction by siring a half-breed, illegitimate son whose mother had asked how the child should address him. She had been deeply hurt to hear him say that he should call him "Sir" instead of "Father."

And now, in the year of 1870, Thomas Barkley called his mixed blood son to him. On important occasions he referred to him as "Jeremiah," but usually it was just plain Jerry. "I have some business to attend to, Jeremiah."

"Yes, Sir Thomas?"

"I want you to ride into Fayette and get me that lawyer—the one that took old Franklin's place—name's Tom something or other."

"When shall I ask him to come?"

"Today, Jeremiah. Tell him to come today."

"Yes, Sir Thomas, I will tell him."

It was mid-afternoon, and the slap-slap of the runners on the Sipsey Bridge announced their coming. By that time, the old man had peed down the length of his trouser leg. Old Dicey couldn't hear too well any more and didn't know he had called for assistance.

He couldn't maneuver the chair over the threshold to find his pee bucket, and so the fluid spilled off his leg and splattered on the wooden floor of the porch. He saw the buggy come up the drive with Jerry leading on his horse.

"Sir Thomas, I have Mr. Ferguson."

"Damn Mr. Ferguson! Get me in the house and into some dry britches. Damn a condition… when a man can't stand and take a piss when he needs to!"

Jerry smiled apologetically toward the young lawyer. He tilted the chair backward and rolled the old man inside. The lawyer shook his head and found a seat on the steps at some distance from the trickle of liquid on the porch.

Jerry came back, pushing a dryer and more amenable Sir Thomas Barkley. He motioned to the rocking chair opposite the old man, and the lawyer took it.

"I want to do my will, Fergins."

"Uh, that's Ferguson," the young man replied.

"Whatever the hell," the old man said, and the lawyer got out his notebook, and his quill pen, and his ink bottle.

"Now, put down what I say in that legal mumbo jumbo you fellows use," the old man instructed, not unkindly.

Jerry hid his smile behind his hand and excused himself.

The old man remembered his daughters and his grandson for their fair and equal portions of his estate—all but one child, and that exclusion prompted the lawyer to ask, "What about Jeremiah?"

The question just popped out of the lawyer's head, and it shocked him as much as the old man when he heard the question hanging there in the stillness of the afternoon. "I mean —ah..." Young Ferguson shuffled the pages of the notebook and looked uncomfortably at Thomas.

"That's all right, son," Thomas finally answered. "I reckon there ain't anybody in this county who don't know the conditions. I sure as hell never denied the boy was mine."

He looked across the yard in the waning light, and his mind seemed to wander a bit, so that the lawyer thought he had forgotten the question. He came back to it though, looking the lawyer squarely in the eyes. "I couldn't have asked for a better son than Jeremiah," he spoke softly. "My boy, William... didn't have to put up with me the way Jeremiah has done. He died too young... and for too little." He drifted off in thought once more, cursing the war in his mind, a war he had never supported in his heart. "All gone..." he sighed. "All gone."

He twisted in the chair, bracing his spine against the familiar curve of the cane backing. "You don't have to remind me of Jerry," he spoke again. "I am reminded of him when my flour bin is empty, when my cows need milking, when the fireplace needs stoking, or when I need to get off the toilet seat. I'm reminded of him... because he is always there when I need him.

"If I was God Almighty... I'd make him as white as that big old cloud up yonder... but I ain't... and he ain't... and there you have it."

He shifted in the chair now, seeking comfort that eluded him. "His mother was part nigger, but she was also part white and part Cherokee. He's got my features. He walks like I used to walk—talks a lot like me, too... so they say. He don't cuss like me—and nothing, absolutely nothing, keeps him from his rightful place in this world, except for a little bit darker skin." He pondered this contradiction for a time. "Ain't that one goddamned hell-of-a-note though." The old man sat in silence then, and the lawyer waited, not wanting to disturb his thoughts and regretting that he had brought the matter up. "No—you don't have to remind me of Jerry, Mr. Ferguson."

"Please sir—I meant no offense…"

"None taken. When the time comes, Jerry will know what to do—and that's all I have to say about that."

He closed his eyes then and wiped at his forehead, pushing away the silver locks, trying to push away the troubled thought that plagued him.

The lawyer cleared his throat and rose from his chair. "We'll try again tomorrow," he said, but Thomas gave no evidence that he heard, and so the young lawyer got back in his buggy and drove off in the twilight.

Later, Jerry returned and rolled him back in the house. He got him undressed and into his nightshirt and tucked him under his covers.

"Good night, Sir Thomas," he said, but the old man was already asleep.

Katy had felt it her duty to tell her father about the misgivings her new husband had voiced about the possibility of Jerry inheriting any of the plantation. "Brad says it would be awkward to have Jerry listed as an inheritor… that it could also be dangerous for him. Brad is well connected in a political sense to the views of the county."

She said Brad felt very uncomfortable about having a brother-in-law who was a little too dark, in view of his position with the Klan. There had been some whispers, quickly silenced by his capable fists.

"Brad Tyner can kiss my ass in the courthouse square at high noon tomorrow—and the rest of the county after that…" is the way Thomas put it. It didn't matter what Brad Tyner thought, or didn't think, anyway. He had his plan.

"To the son of my deceased son, William Barkley," the lawyer intoned, "Thomas Barkley, that portion of my estate known as the Linebarger Tract, to have and to hold.

"To my daughter, Elizabeth Barkley Day, the sum of eight hundred dollars, drawn on my cash account at the Bank of Fayette, to be used for the upkeep of my servant, Dicey Barkley.

"To my daughter, Katherine Barkley Tyner, one half of the residue of my estate, to have and to hold, for her sole use and benefit, free from the interference and control of her husband.

"To my daughter, Elizabeth Barkley Day, one half of the residue of my estate…"

And so it went. Elizabeth was to take old Dicey home with her and provide for her welfare. She would have done so gladly, in any case, but Thomas made it official. He had wanted his will to be read to the assembled group so that he could "look them in the eye."

Elizabeth and Obadiah came the week before the reading and helped to tidy up the house before the others got there. Loretta and Ashton came from Palmetto with little Thomas. Brad Tyner tore himself away from the hardware store long enough to attend the reading, Katherine nestled closely at all times by his side.

It had been altogether a lively and tiring time for Thomas. The customary solitude of his day had been broken with limitless conversation, but it had all been worthwhile.

And then, they were all leaving. Jerry wheeled Thomas outside onto the porch and everybody came by to shake his hand and wish him well. They said it would be a long time before the will would need to be probated, that he had a lot of good years left, and the old man nodded and thanked them for coming.

Then, they were gone. The slap-slap of the runners on the Sipsey Bridge announced their passage. The old man's back was bothering him again like it always did when he was agitated. The reading and the good wishes and the loud conversation left him tired. He called Jerry over to him and looked all about, but nobody was in sight. Old Dicey was cleaning up in the kitchen, and he could hear the pans rattling in the sink. He pointed over toward the dinner bell post.

"There's a pot of gold buried under that old post," he said, and then he slapped at his head. "You know that anyway. I brought that pot all the way from South Carolina. It's got the money my mother gave me for my share of Barkley Hall—and a bit more. I want you to have it, Jerry."

The boy started to protest, and Thomas stopped him. "You earned it, and, by God, you're going to get it. You run on now—I just want to sit out here awhile."

Thomas looked around and saw there was nothing more to be done, so he retreated once more into the past... to a land of snowy white fields of cotton and the smell of dust and sweat. He remembered the lovely perfumed lady that he had kissed in the Carolina moonlight and taken for his wife. He remembered another woman... with unbelievably dark eyes and long black hair that swung down over a statuesque body.

He reached into the can of shelled corn and scattered a few grains around his chair. The rooster made his ritual crow, and the old man chuckled softly. The rooster waited, head cocked quizzically, but sensed that the old man had tired of the game.

Jerry found him there when it was time to roll inside, his wavy white hair resting on his chest. There was a strange angle to the body, and Jerry suddenly realized that he was not asleep. He ran to his side and shook the old man gently, but the body was rigid.

The world closed in on him, and he dropped to his knees, his arms around the old man's legs and his tears falling on the wooden floor of the porch. He spoke aloud the words that had been in his heart all the days of his life. There were just two words—"Oh Pa."

Chapter Fifty

He stayed for the funeral, stayed until they had all come and paid their respects. He stood in the fresh dirt scattered around the grave and thought about things the old man had taught him and the many ways that he would miss him. He remembered most of all what Sir Thomas had said to him that time long ago when he had felt the first sting of racial slurs.

"What is important is what you call yourself. If you say to yourself, *I am a man,* then you are a man—and nobody can take that away from you." Sir Thomas had said it was Biblical, and he supposed it must be true. He quoted it the way Sir Thomas had said it to him: *"A man is what he thinketh himself to be."*

The Sipsey plantation that had been his cloister was no longer available to him. He was out of his patron's shadow. Sir Thomas, knowing that he was dying, had created a plan for him, and knowing that he could hold him no longer, had finally relinquished him to the other parent.

Elizabeth was the last to go. She walked down the path with him from the cemetery, wordlessly searching his face and finally asking the question. "Will you be all right, Jerry?"

He nodded and reached out to hold her hand. "I'll be fine, Libby."

Elizabeth dabbed at her eyes, and her voice was husky. "Pa told me... promised me... that he had a plan for you. As far as I know Pa never broke a promise."

"No, Sir Thomas never broke a promise, Libby."

"Couldn't you, at last... couldn't you refer to him as Pa?"

Jerry looked away and then with great effort answered her question. "It seems strange to say it out loud. I've wanted to... I said it to him once... the other day, but he was already gone." Suddenly his face contorted, and his shoulders shook. He reached out for her and drew her close to him. It had been a long time since he had sat on Libby's lap and begged her to read to him... a long time since she had tucked him into her bed and watched him fall asleep.

He moved back and wiped at his eyes with a shirt sleeve. "I want to show you something," he said, and he reached into his pocket and opened the letters Sir Thomas had given him. Elizabeth read them, and she was weeping now for the lost love expressed in the scribbled words.

"Dear God, Jerry, what sort of world do we inhabit?"

Jerry swept his arm in a broad circle toward the Barkley acres. "This is the only one I've been privileged to know."

She clutched at his arm, searching his face as he re-folded the letters.

"Is there no other way? Do you have to go?"

He nodded his head in the stubborn manner of his father, the manner that didn't allow for argument. "It was Sir Thomas... Pa wanted it this way."

And now the gray eyes revealed more than the hurt of the father's death. "You can't know, Libby, what it's like to live with people who consider you to be sub-human." His words turned to anger. "You don't know what it's like to have some snaggletoothed, stump-jumping, tenant farmer try to lord it over you just because his skin is white! Sir... Pa... tried his best to protect me from that, but you can't overcome prejudice with your fists.

"Look at the facts, Libby. You're a preacher's wife. Do you think I would ever be welcome in your church? No, I'm not even welcome here—unless there's work to be done, hogs to feed, dirt to till. I live in a place that will patronize me on the one hand or string me up on the other—whatever the mood of the moment. I am the son of Thomas Barkley. If it were not for that fact— I might not be alive today." Jerry saw the agony in his sister's eyes, watched the truth burn into her soul, and he was deeply sorry for her, but he had to go on. "My father made a mistake..."

"No, Jerry, please..."

"Yes, he did. Think back on it now. Before I came along, Thomas Barkley was one of the most respected men in this county. After that, people made jokes, laughed at him, but behind his back, of course."

He shook his head in wonderment. "It didn't have to be that way, you know. He could have just used me like the rest of the slaves, or sold me down the river for a premium price. Isn't that what most of the high-flown planters did with their..." he spat the words, "... yard children?"

Elizabeth shook at his arm, pleading for a respite, but he couldn't stop now.

"Sir Thomas Barkley stood up to everybody and anything that got in his path. He wasn't afraid of anything short of God Almighty. He stood by me... his biggest mistake... always. He acknowledged it in every way. He even had me apprenticed by the court, so my Mama couldn't take me away with her.

He knew I was a mistake—but he didn't love me the less for it."

His voice grew hoarse now, and his eyes strayed up the hill to the cemetery. "That's what brought the ridicule down on him—the fact that he treated me like a son, instead of like a slave. Did the great Thomas Jefferson do as well with his mixed blood children from a fifteen-year-old concubine?

"That old man... we shared more than I can tell anyone. He felt there was a better place for me in Oklahoma. I won't know until I get there, but I've got to find out."

His face brightened again, looking for a moment like the innocent little boy's face she remembered. "He quoted me something. It was from the Bible. You know he was always doing that. Sometimes folks wondered where he found the passage, but I remember this one. It was from Jeremiah, the twenty-ninth chapter and verse eleven. 'I know the plans I have for you—plans to prosper you and not to harm you—plans to give you hope and a future.'

"The way he said it was a little different. 'Jeremiah,' he said, 'I have a plan for you... in a new land... away from the Lafe McGills and the Kluxers. A land where you can prosper and have a future...'" And now he smiled down at her. "Would you rather I stayed here to *sharecrop* for Brad Tyner?"

She shook her head but couldn't force a smile back at him. "No, I wouldn't want that. Please, will you write to me?"

Jerry nodded. "It's the least I can do to repay you for teaching me to read and write in the first place."

She choked up then, remembering the early days and his bright inquisitive mind, the quick way he had of picking up scraps of information and putting them together. "You were my star pupil, Jerry. Oh, you will always be so special!" She reached up for him, and he bent down and kissed her cheek, then turned quickly away so she couldn't feel the sob that caught in his throat.

"Goodbye, Libby," he whispered.

Chapter Fifty-One

He loaded the buggy after a breakfast of slab bacon and two of the fresh farm eggs. He left the rest of the eggs and what foodstuff he couldn't carry in the kitchen pantry. He knew that Brad Tyner and Katherine would be over to pick up anything of value as soon as he was well out of sight.

He put the old Springfield rifle behind the seat and almost reluctantly picked up the shovel and walked over the jasmine-covered dinner bell post. He looked around in all directions, but only the clucking sound of the chickens and an occasional crow from the Rhode Island rooster revealed any other living thing.

The shovel blade hit the lid of the iron pot, and then he hefted it up and sat it on the ground. Carefully he lifted the lid and saw two molded leather shapes. He reached in and pulled the bags from the pot. One represented the exact amount of gold coin Thomas Barkley had brought to Alabama. Its contents had been depleted and replenished many times over the years. The other bag represented the profits over and above expenses that he had hidden away from the banks. It was a sizeable amount, and Jerry hid the bags under the seat of the buggy without counting it.

He walked down to the cotton fields one last time. He wouldn't be around for the harvest. He'd leave that up to Brad Tyner, but he'd have the satisfaction of knowing it had been cultivated the way Sir Thomas wanted it.

The cotton plants looked deeply green in the early morning hour, and the dew still clung to the leaves. He walked down the middles of the rows he had so carefully cleared of grass encroachment.

He noticed a strange thing on the sandy texture of the soil. Every so often a flower bud lay as if someone had plucked it from the stalk and dropped it to the ground. He reached down and picked one up and noticed that the bud had turned yellow. He pulled it apart. A small worm wriggled into his hand. Another and another he pulled apart, and each time a small worm fell from the flower.

Anger swept over him. He snapped one of the green cotton bolls from the

236

stalk. A strange winged beetle clung to the boll. It had a long, needle-like snout that had pierced the skin of the boll, and a dark circle surrounded the hole where the snout had stuck.

Jerry flung the boll to the ground and stamped it with his foot. His first impulse was to report to Sir Thomas and then, he shrugged his shoulders and looked sorrowfully over the field, knowing he couldn't do that any more.

Something bad was happening here… something of calamitous proportion, and he was glad that Sir Thomas was not here to see it happen. It was a plague descending on the Alabama cotton farmer.

Jerry knew that cotton had reigned supreme over the Southland for over two hundred years. He knew it had been the one and only money crop to the large plantation owner and small dirt farmer as well. More than any other crop, cotton had required the meticulous hand labor of the slave, and for that reason, slavery had flourished in the South.

Perhaps it was time for a change. Perhaps this little, loathsome creature with its needle snout would herald a new beginning. He looked again at the rows and the yellowed flower buds dotting the ground. "I'm glad you didn't have to see this, Sir Thomas," he said aloud. He tried it again. "I'm glad you don't have to see this, Pa." It was hard to know which term to use. In his heart he felt like saying "Pa," but when he spoke the words, he had to admit that "Sir Thomas" had the more comfortable ring.

He looked up at the house as he drove away. The furnishings were still in place. Sir Thomas' chair sat on the porch, its pony cart wheels ready and no place to go.

He halted the team when he reached the river bridge and got down and walked the length of it. He rubbed the surface of the hand rails, polished from years of small hands like William's and Jonas's and his own. He looked at the dark water. A scattering of whirligig beetles scurried over the surface. The dank wetness of the Sipsey rose up around him, herbal smells of bay trees and the sour smells of stagnant sloughs.

Now a vision floated to the surface of his mind… a picture of a desperate man, eyes open and staring, his mouth open in a high-pitched scream that died into a muffled, gurgling whisper as the dark muck swallowed him. He wondered if Jed's buggy had settled anywhere near that of the medicine man for whom the sink was named. The thought of the man and his horse and buggy sealed forever in the black depths of Dyer's Sink made him shudder.

But it was a good thought, in a way. No other person in the whole world knew what had happened here. It was a nugget that belonged only to himself and Sir Thomas, and it was something to hold on to.

It was time to leave.

He walked back to the buggy and climbed into the seat. He lifted the reins and clucked softly to the horse and the buggy wheels began to roll over the boards of the Sipsey Bridge.

A long road lay ahead of him. It went past the windowless shacks of the former slaves and the tall chimney sentinels that stood guard over the burnt-out plantation houses. It went ever westward toward a promised land.

Sunlight caught the solid planes of his face and the fleck of red in his long, straight black hair. A firm resolve was mirrored in the twenty-one-year-old gray eyes. He reached in his coat pocket and removed the letter that Sir Thomas had directed him to deliver to Serina. He opened it yet another time. A smile broke across his face as he read what Sir Thomas had written on the paper.

"I am sending my son."

Printed in the United States
18805LVS00003B/214-309

9 781413 715316